T0170152

WOMEN & THE LAW

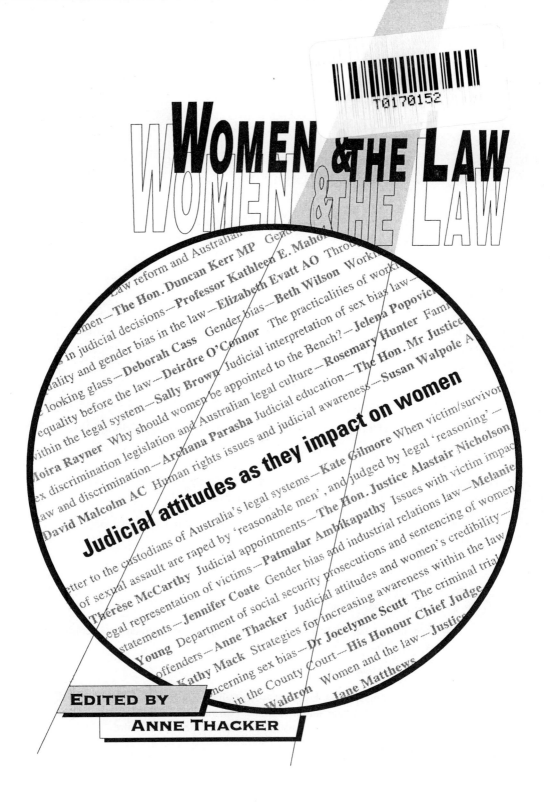

Law reform and Australian women— **The Hon. Duncan Kerr MP** Gender bias in judicial decisions— **Professor Kathleen E. Mahoney** Equality and gender bias in the law— **Elizabeth Evatt AO** Through the looking glass— **Deborah Cass** Gender bias— **Beth Wilson** Working equality before the law— **Deirdre O'Connor** The practicalities of work within the legal system— **Sally Brown** Judicial interpretation of sex bias law— **Moira Rayner** Why should women be appointed to the Bench?— **Jelena Popovic** Sex discrimination legislation and Australian legal culture— **Rosemary Hunter** Family law and discrimination— **Archana Parasha** Judicial education— **The Hon. Mr Justice David Malcolm AC** Human rights issues and judicial awareness— **Susan Walpole** A letter to the custodians of Australia's legal systems— **Kate Gilmore** When victim/survivor of sexual assault are raped by 'reasonable men', and judged by legal 'reasoning'— **Therèse McCarthy** Judicial appointments— **The Hon. Justice Alastair Nicholson** Legal representation of victims— **Patmalar Ambikapathy** Issues with victim impact statements— **Jennifer Coate** Gender bias and industrial relations law— **Melanie Young** Department of social security prosecutions and sentencing of women offenders— **Anne Thacker** Judicial attitudes and women's credibility— **Kathy Mack** Strategies for increasing awareness within the law concerning sex bias— **Dr Jocelynne Scutt** The criminal trial in the County Court— **His Honour Chief Judge Waldron** Women and the law— **Jane Matthews** Justice

Judicial attitudes as they impact on women

EDITED BY

ANNE THACKER

Deakin University Press

Published by Deakin University Press, Deakin University, Geelong, Victoria 3217,
Australia
First published 1998

Compilation © Deakin University Press 1997
Copyright in individual papers remains with the authors.

Produced and printed by Learning Resources Services, Deakin University, Geelong,
Victoria 3217, Australia

National Library of Australia
Cataloguing-in-publication data

       Women and the law: judicial attitudes as they impact on women: proceedings of a
       conference held on 9–10 June at Melbourne.

       ISBN 0 949823 44 9.

       1. Women—Legal status, laws, etc.—Australia—Congresses. 2. Sex
       discrimination in justice administration—Australia—Congresses. I. Thacker,
       Anne. II. Deakin University. Australian Women's Research Centre.

       347.940082

All rights reserved. No part of this publication may be reproduced, stored in a retrieval
system, or transmitted in any form, or by any means, electronic, mechanical,
photocopying, recording or otherwise, without the prior permission of the publisher.

Foreword

WE ARE DELIGHTED to be publishing the collection of these papers which were given at the 1993 conference entitled 'Women and the Law: Judicial Attitudes as they Impact on Women'. This conference came at a crucial time in the public and professional reassessment of the judicial system in Australia. A number of male judges had made statements (mostly in rape cases) which led to a spotlight being focused not just on the processes of the law, but also on the attitudes of those who are its guardians and facilitators.

The conference was organised under the auspices of the Australian Women's Research Centre. It was the first conference undertaken by the new Centre, which was established by Deakin University through a Strategic Development Fund Grant. Apart from research work with both public and private sectors, another commitment of the Centre is to expand educational programs relating to women, and, in particular, to make available to the general public information and informed discussion which has hitherto not been readily accessible.

This conference was part of a process we saw as crucial in increasing the social accountability of institutions like the law and in aiding the development of an informed general public. At the conclusion of the conference, Dr Jocelynne Scutt, heading the Strategy Group at the conference, identified access to the law as the first issue to be addressed on the way to increasing awareness concerning sex bias and the law.

Three hundred people attended the conference, which was reported widely in the media. There was a wide range of people including politicians, members of the judiciary, many women from various parts of the legal profession, as well as men. Legal Aid officers attended and community groups were well represented as were academics and members of the wider community. It was exciting to witness the conference making a mark on current popular discussion.

The papers delivered, and reproduced here, form a unique and valuable contribution to the assessment of the legal processes in Australia and their impact on women. Ranging from professional critiques by members of the judiciary to the personal accounts of women who have experienced injustice from the legal system, they encapsulate an important moment in the history of the relationship between women and the law in Australia.

The conference had three main themes which are reflected in these papers: to identify the content of the law where women may be disadvantaged because of sex bias; to identify what processes within the law hinder equity and justice for women; and to define some strategies for change in the future.

The conference also stimulated government thinking in the area. The Honourable Duncan Kerr MP, Minister for Justice, wrote:

> … this conference was an outstanding success and received significant media coverage and positive responses from members of the legal profession. The conference was also instrumental in the establishment of a committee from the Departments of Justice and Education, Employment and Training to consider gender bias in the law curriculum. The Minister for Higher Education, the Honourable Simon Crean, subsequently made available $300 000 to develop this work. I see this outcome as an excellent example of the kind of collaborative work that should be taking place between the academic and wider community.

Feelings at the conference were powerfully positive regarding the possibilities for change. As Justice Elizabeth Evatt, AO, President, Law Reform Commission of Australia wrote:

> … the standard of presentation and discussion was extremely high and the degree of consensus and positive thinking was very satisfactory. I feel that every speaker made a valuable contribution to our thinking on issues of gender bias and equality.

The conference was made possible by the efforts of a number of people. In particular, we acknowledge and thank the following people—the then current (Labor) Australian Federal Government, specifically the Office of the Status of Women, for their support and sponsorship; Professor Max Charlesworth of the National Institute for Law, Ethics and Public Affairs at Griffith University, who enabled Professor Kathleen Mahoney, who delivered the key note address, to be with us from Calgary University, Canada. Professor Mahoney's contribution to the issue of sex bias in the law was strongly made and her work touched the minds and attitudes of many people who, once challenged, made needed changes. Others include Dr Jocelynne Scutt and Melanie Young who initiated the ideas and discussions which formulated the conference and its content, and Julie Melican, the Conference Organiser, who did a brilliant job in logistics! Thank you to you all.

Note: Some papers have been updated, either in postscripts or in the footnotes, to take account of subsequent developments in the area discussed.

Despite funding problems, this book has been completed with the cooperation of the contributors in allowing their material to be published. Each contribution forms a thread with which to weave together discussions about women and the law within the judicial process and enables us to get a clear and rounded picture of the need for social change compelling us to move forward to an inclusive community.

Finally we want to thank Chris Black, Kerri Erler, Heather Cameron and, above all, Felicity Thyer who spent countless hours getting the conference papers ready for publication.

It is hoped that the publishing of these conference proceedings will provide an invaluable record of the important work being done by women (in the main) for women across the community, ultimately for a better community for all. It is also our hope that publication and distribution of the information, experiences and knowledge gained at the conference means we will continue forward, rather than having to begin again with the task of raising collective consciousness about the position of women. The next generation of women should not have to 'invent' a Women's Movement or the concept of Women's Liberation as the women of the 1920s and then the women of the 1960s had to do.

We also hope to utilise our resources (such as they are) to accelerate the process of change in the community by implementing and supporting mechanisms to resolve the problematic issues that affect women and their access to justice through the law.

Associate Professor Robyn Rowland
Anne Thacker
July 1997

Contents

Day two

Closing addresses

Convocation

Contributors

Patmalar Ambikapathy was born in Malaysia and had her primary school education there. She attended Secondary School and University in England completing a politics/economics and law degree, thereafter reading at the Bar in London. She also completed a Masters at Cambridge. She practised with her father in Malaysia and also in England. She has been more years out of full-time legal practice than in. She raised a family and her children continue to fight for the values of egalitarianism and fair play they were told this country was all about.

Patmalar lives with her husband of 28 years, and works from home. She travels to Melbourne and other parts of Victoria and interstate for her cases. Her practice has been almost exclusively in the area of family crime.

The Honourable Justice Sally Brown was appointed as a magistrate in Victoria in 1985, after practising as a solicitor, barrister and tertiary teacher. In 1990 she was appointed Chief Magistrate, the first woman to head a Victorian court. In 1993 she was appointed a Judge of the Family Court of Australia. Her Honour has maintained a long-standing interest in rape law, domestic violence law reform and juvenile justice issues, and has been at the forefront of judicial education on social context issues, particularly those relating to gender.

Deborah Cass currently teaches constitutional law, international trade law and European Community law at the Australian National University. She has recently completed an LLM at Harvard University and is currently a doctoral candidate at Harvard, examining the relationship between free speech and representative democracy in the context of campaign finance. She is a former recipient of the Lionel Murphy Foundation Scholarship, the Caltex National Woman Graduate of the Year, and the European Community Visitors Award. Deborah is currently co-editing a revised edition of Peter Hanks' book, *Australian Constitutional Law*.

Jennifer Coate was a primary school teacher for several years before completing her Law degree and commencing in private practice as a solicitor. She was appointed as a magistrate in 1992.

In September 1995, she was appointed Senior Magistrate of the Children's Court of Victoria and in September 1996, she was appointed Deputy Chief Magistrate. She is currently still at the Children's Court at Melbourne.

Elizabeth Evatt is a Barrister-at-law in NSW and a member of the Human Rights Committee, a monitoring body established under the International Covenant on Civil and Political Rights. She has been a member of the United Nations Committee on the Elimination of Discrimination against Women, and Chair of the Committee, as well as President of the Australian Law Reform Commission. She recently completed a review of the *Aboriginal and Torres Strait Islander Heritage Protection Act* 1984.

Kate Gilmore is currently the National Director of Amnesty International Australia, the Australian section of the world's largest human rights organisation. She took up this position in July, 1996.

In the previous ten years she worked in the arenas of public hospital administration and violence against women. She was the inaugural coordinator of CASA House (Center Against Sexual Assault). She was also the Victorian representative on the National Committee on Violence against Women. Briefly a part-time commissioner with the Victorian Law Reform Commission, Kate worked in management at the Royal Women's Hospital and Broadmeadows Community Health Services. In each role she was responsible for steering significant organisational change and health service development, particularly for women.

Kate has published on issues related to violence against women, sexual assault, cultural diversity and service provision.

Rosemary Hunter is a senior lecturer in law at the University of Melbourne. She teaches courses in history and philosophy of law, law and discrimination, and rethinking citizenship, rights and gender. She has researched and published in the areas of discrimination law, equal employment and labour law, Aboriginal legal issues and feminist legal theory. She is the author of *Indirect Discrimination in the Workplace* (Federated Press, 1992), and a co-editor and author of *Thinking about Law* (Allen & Unwin, 1995).

Rosemary has participated in many reviews of anti-discrimination legislation. She has also worked with unions, equal opportunity practitioners and community groups on discrimination issues. She is a member of Feminist Lawyers.

Duncan Kerr MHR was appointed Minister for Justice in 1993 and, for a short period, was Attorney General. As Minister for Justice, he coordinated the Access to Justice project leading to the announcement of the Government's 1995 Justice Statement and initiated a number of reforms across his portfolio, including an ongoing update and simplification of the *Copyright Acts*; reforms to the law of evidence and moves towards the establishment of a model Commonwealth Criminal Code and initiation and implementation of the *Crimes (Child Sex Tourism) Amendment Act.*

He is the author of two legal books and numerous articles, and was Contributing Editor of *Reinventing Socialism.*

Thérèse McCarthy is currently the Executive Director of the Victorian Court Information and Welfare Network, a statewide service providing information, support and referral to people going to court across Victoria. She is also a member of the committee of Management of the Centre Against Sexual Assault. Therese was formerly the coordinator of the Project for Legal Action against Sexual Assault, a professional education and training program providing training across Victoria to those supporting victim/survivors of sexual assault going through the legal process. She has also worked as counsellor/advocate with victim/survivors of sexual assault and in women's health services over ten years. She has lectured law and criminology students, the judiciary and other legal personnel on gender bias and sexual assault.

Kathy Mack is an Associate Professor at Flinders University Law School. From 1975–1982, she practised law in California, specialising first in criminal law and later in medical malpractice and products liability. From 1984–1996 she taught law at the University of Adelaide. Subjects taught include the Australian legal system, criminal law, criminal investigation and procedure. Special interests are legal education, dispute resolution, especially mediation, and gender issues and law.

Kathleen Mahoney has been a professor of law at the University of Calgary for 18 years. She has law degrees from the University of British Columbia and Cambridge University and a Diploma from the Institute of Comparative Human Rights Law in Strasbourg, France. She has held many international lectureships and fellowships including the Sir Allan Sewell Visiting Fellowship at the Faculty of Law, Griffith University, Brisbane, the Distinguished Visiting Scholar Fellowship at the University of Adelaide and Visiting Fellowships at the Australian National University, Canberra and the University of Western Australia in Perth. She was a Visiting Professor teaching law at the University of Chicago for the fall quarter of 1994.

The Honourable Justice David K Malcolm AC, was appointed Chief Justice of Western Australia in 1988. In 1990 he was appointed Lieutenant Governor of Western Australia, and in 1992 he received an Order of the Companion of Australia. Positions he has held include Counsel and Deputy General Counsel for the Asian Development Bank, Chairman of the Law Reform Commission of Western Australia, member of the Copyright Tribunal, Queen's Counsel, President of the Western Australian Bar Association, Vice-President of the Australian Bar Association, Vice-President of the Law Society of Western Australia and Chairman of the Town Planning Appeals Tribunal.

The Honourable Justice Jane Matthews is currently a judge of the Federal Court of Australia, President of the Administrative Appeals Tribunal, and Deputy President of the National Native Title Tribunal. She was the first woman to hold the positions of judge in the New South Wales District Court and Crown Prosecutor.

The Honourable Chief Justice Alastair Nicholson was appointed Chief Justice of the Family Court of Australia and a Justice of the Federal Court of Australia in 1988, having spent the previous six years as a Justice of the Supreme Court of Victoria.

His Honour has had an association with the RAAF since university days and was appointed Judge Advocate General of the Australian Defence Force in 1987 and was awarded an Officer of the Order of Australia, Military Division, in January 1992.

His Honour was deputy chairman of the Parole Board from 1982–1985 and chairman from 1985–1988. In 1997 he was elected President of the Association of Family and Conciliation Courts and was appointed the founding President of the Australian Association of Family Lawyers and Conciliators in 1993.

The Honourable Justice Deirdre O'Connor is currently President of the Australian Industrial Relations Commission, a position to which she was appointed in 1994.

In 1990 she was appointed as a judge of the Federal Court of Australia.

She was President of the Administrative Appeals Tribunal from 1990–1994, President of the National Native Title Tribunal from 1993–1994, and President of the Security Appeals Tribunal from 1990–1994.

Archana Parashar is a senior lecturer in law at the Law School, Macquarie University. She teaches family law, and discrimination and the law. Her research interests are feminist legal theory and its relevance for third world women. She is the author of the book: *Women and Family Law Reform in India*, SAGE, 1992.

Jelena Popovic is an Australian born of Serbian and German parents. She was a solicitor in private practice and with legal aid for ten years prior to being appointed a magistrate. Jelena has been a magistrate for eight years and was appointed a Deputy Chief Magistrate in March 1997. She is responsible for State-wide coordination of the Magistrates' Court. She has two children aged eleven and eight, and does not have time for any recreational pursuits!

Moira Rayner is a human rights activist who was the Victorian Commissioner for Equal Opportunity between 1990 and 1994 and a part-time Commissioner of the Commonwealth Human Rights and Equal Opportunity Commission between 1994-1997. She has an honours degree in law and a Master of Arts in Public Policy, and is an Adjunct Professor in the Faculty of Arts at Deakin University. She chairs the Board of Directors of the National Children's and Youth Law Centre, and the independent Council of the Complaints Resolution Scheme of the Financial Planning Association. Her book, *Rooting Democracy: Growing the Society we Want,* was published by Allen and Unwin in April 1997.

Jocelynne A. Scutt is a lawyer, writer and publisher in private practice as a barrister at the Victorian Bar. Her books include *The Incredible Woman—Power and Sexual Politics; The Sexual Gerrymander—Women and the Economics of Power; Even in the Best of Homes—Violence in the Family;* and *For Richer, For Poorer—Money, Marriage and Property Rights.* She is the editor of the Artemis 'Women's Voices, Women's Lives' series.

Anne Thacker has been practising at the Victorian Bar in Melbourne since 1986. She practices in jurisdictions ranging from criminal and civil law to family law, equal opportunity law and administrative law. She has also practised as a Solicitor and Barrister in other states including Queensland, New South Wales and the Northern Territory.

Anne's other involvements with the law have included being a member of the editorial committee of *The Law Handbook*, member of Feminist Lawyers, and writing journal articles on topics including sentencing criminal offenders, human rights and IVF, family law and domestic violence, rape law and community attitudes and the power of judges.

His Honour Chief Judge Glenn Waldron has been Chief Judge in the County Court of Victoria since 1982. Educated at Wesley College and the University of Melbourne, he has acted as a QC in Tasmania, the ACT and Victoria. In 1990 he was appointed Officer of the Order of Australia. Chief Judge Waldron is a former member of the Victorian Bar Council, and a member of the Attorney General's Law Reform Advisory Council and the Judicial Studies Board.

Susan Walpole took up her appointment as Sex Discrimination Commissioner with the Human Rights and Equal Opportunity Commission in February 1993. She began her career in the Industrial Democracy Unit of the South Australian Premier's Department, and spent four years as National Industrial Officer for the Administrative and Clerical Officers' Association, going on to become the Principal Executive Officer for the Women's Bureau in the then Department of Employment and Industrial Relations. She was Deputy Director of the Affirmative Action Agency before joining the ABC in 1988 as a human resources manager, and was appointed Head of Human Resources for ABC TV in 1992.

Beth Wilson was President of the Mental Health Review Board in Victoria until 1 May 1997. She is currently the Health Services Commissioner. Beth has worked on several administrative review boards and has a long-standing interest in medico-legal issues.

Melanie Young is an active member of Feminist Lawyers. She was a solicitor with the labour law firm, Ryan Carlisle Thomas, from 1989–1994. Prior to that she was an Associate to Justice Peter Gray in the Federal Court of Australia. Her areas of practice as a solicitor were industrial, employment and anti-discrimination law as well as crimes compensation and other law in relation to violence against women. In 1994 she became a barrister at the Victorian Bar and continues to practise in the areas of law previously mentioned.

Law reform and Australian women

Courage and conscience

**THE MINISTER FOR JUSTICE
THE HONOURABLE DUNCAN KERR, MP**

Introduction

We are all familiar with the traditional image of Justice as a woman with her eyes covered, holding a set of scales in one outstretched hand and a sword in the other. The blindfold over Justice's eyes symbolises her impartiality; the scales, the weighing of the case before her; and the sword, the penalty to be imposed for breaking the law.

Impartiality is fundamental to our conception of justice. Freedom from bias helps to ensure the equality of all people before the law and that the scales are not weighted unfairly against one or other of the parties.

In recent months there has been much media coverage given to comments made some judges in the course of proceedings involving sexual assault, comments thought by many to be inappropriate. This coverage and accompanying commentary has been interpreted in some quarters as an attack on the independence of the judiciary.

Let me say at the outset that the independence of the judiciary is one of the foundations of our democracy and that it is something I will vigorously defend. I think it is wrong, however, to invoke the constitutional doctrine of the independence of the judiciary to stifle healthy public debate about our laws and the administration of justice in this country.

We have heard the recent comments made by a small number of judges in sexual assault cases. Nevertheless, we should examine the wider question of how the law itself can be discriminatory.

Feminist critique has shown how legal concepts and abstractions which on face value are gender neutral, in fact, are gendered and refer to a male standard which makes women less than equal to men. It has also helped to expose the ways in which all of us, including our judges, are conditioned and socialised and how this affects the way we make decisions. In short, feminist critique has exposed how the scales of Justice are weighted against women.

To be a judge is a difficult job and one which, on the whole, is done admirably and with considerable skill and talent. But like most of us, our judges and their judgments are necessarily and understandably shaped by their gender, their race, their class and a myriad other factors.

In some cases it takes considerable personal effort to acknowledge the extent to which our own experience shapes us, and to work out how to overcome these limitations.

It is crucial that those who administer justice in this country are in touch with changes in community values and are aware of the extent to which their personal experiences affect their ability to apply the law and to judge the actions of those who appear before them.

Gender awareness

The Australian Institute of Judicial Administration is responding to this need and is working to increase gender awareness in the judiciary. Several initiatives were under way prior to the recent community concern over judicial comments in sexual assault cases. The work of the Institute in this area follows on from the work it has undertaken in relation to Aboriginal cultural awareness.[2]

The Government has funded the Institute for a further $100 000 to undertake gender awareness programs which will encourage judges to examine their own preconceptions and values and reassess them in relation to community attitudes. The objective is for judges to become more sensitive to the impact of their comments and decisions on women. A committee headed by the Honourable Justice Deirdre O'Connor is developing these programs. I believe that the vast majority of judges and magistrates already accept the merits of developing their awareness of gender issues and I hope that they will value the opportunity to participate in these programs.[3]

The Government has also agreed to provide funding to the Family Court of Australia to develop programs to enhance the gender awareness of judges and other decision makers. They will examine the cause and effect of violence against women and other gender issues that affect Family Law matters.[4]

It is worth noting that the criticism of the judiciary has been primarily levelled at the comments of State-appointed judges exercising State jurisdiction. The Federal Government is encouraging the States to fully support the Institute's initiatives in gender awareness training programs. The Federal Government has no jurisdiction in this area but recognises its responsibility to lead the national debate on an effective strategy to target violence against women.

The Prime Minister, in his 1993 'Reclaim the night' speech, said:

> Violence against women is intolerable ... all Australian women are
> entitled to be safe, and to feel safe on the streets and in their homes. I
> know that personal safety is a major concern to Australian women ... It
> is the responsibility of democratic governments to fight for freedom from
> fear in the same way we fight poverty, repression or discrimination of
> any kind.[5]

To this end the National Strategy on Violence Against Women has been
developed in cooperation with the States, Territories and the community. My
colleague Senator Crowley has the lead responsibility in this area.[6]

Judicial appointments[7]

Gender issues are being tackled in other ways as well. The Government is
undertaking a review of the process by which judges are appointed to the
Federal Courts.

This was foreshadowed in a speech by the Governor-General at the opening
of Parliament in 1993, when he stated:

> ... achievement of greater cultural, gender and ethnic diversity in the
> judiciary is an important issue and for this purpose the Government will
> be considering the way in which it selects and assesses candidates for
> judicial appointment.

The present make-up of the judiciary is open to the criticism that it does not
reflect the diversity of Australian society. I regret that this imbalance is also
reflected in institutions such as the Parliament and the Ministry of which I am a
member. As nearly 90% of all Federal judicial offices are held by men, there is
an indication that, at least, the process may have failed to identify suitably
qualified female candidates or, at worst, there has been some bias in the
selection process.

As most judges are appointed after practising at the Bar, the lack of
diversity among members of the judiciary reflects the lack of women practising
at the Bar, especially at a senior level. A number of judges have been appointed
after practising as solicitors or working as government lawyers. Such
appointments have, however, tended to be the exception rather than the rule.

I believe that the pool from which candidates for judicial appointment are
selected should include, as a matter of course, suitably qualified academics,
solicitors and government lawyers. It is only by broadening the base from
which judges are appointed that the judiciary will reflect the diversity of the
Australian community.

The selection process for judicial appointments has also led to the equating
of superior advocacy skills with the skills and attributes that are required of a

judge. This assumption tends to exclude other skills and attributes which make a person a suitable candidate for the Bench. I believe that other criteria which may be relevant are interpersonal skills, vision and intellect, administrative skills, capability to uphold the rule of law, and to act in a truly independent manner.

Of course, candidates for judicial appointment will always need to have a sound knowledge of the law and the highest level of personal integrity.

Most appointees to the Bench are selected only after close consultation with Bar Councils, the Law Council of Australia, and the Chief Justice of the court to which an appointment is to be made. There is, however, no formalised process of consultation.

The Attorney-General, Michael Lavarch, proposes in coming months to issue a discussion paper dealing with the selection of persons for judicial appointment which will seek community input on this important issue. These reforms will be made with the intention of increasing the number of women and people of non-English speaking background appointed to the Bench. In doing so, we will have a judiciary that is more representative of Australian society and better able to serve our community. The Government is aware that the selection processes must be monitored within the context of contemporary issues in order to continue to have a judiciary of the highest calibre. To do otherwise would simply pay lip service to concepts of equality.

Violence against women

Violence against women is of critical concern to our community.[8]

The Government set up the National Committee on Violence in 1987 as a result of a joint agreement between the Prime Minister, State Premiers and the Chief Minister of the Northern Territory. A National Conference on Violence was held in 1989 and brought together important research into violence in Australia.

I am particularly concerned by recent statements concerning police and various professionals' limited response to domestic violence. Change is occurring: police in NSW are taking out more than 60% of domestic violence orders, whereas in 1985 they took out less than 10%. In my own State, Tasmania, if a woman takes out an apprehended violence order and travels to Melbourne, that order is still operational. Legislation in each State and Territory will soon provide for the 'portability' of domestic violence restraining orders nationally. It is important to recognise formally that many women legitimately believe that these orders cannot protect them.

Domestic violence orders and restraining orders must only be seen, however, as one tool in a wider system to stop violence against women.

The Government is actively considering the Directions for Action identified in the National Strategy on Violence Against Women.

Prominent feminist author and lawyer Jocelynne Scutt said, 'Until men come out and say no to violence they are all complicit in the violence against women'. As far as I am concerned, it is time for violence to stop.

The Federal Government has led the debate on gun control even though the issue is essentially a matter for individual State jurisdictions. Through the Australian Police Ministers' Council, the Federal Government has actively encouraged State and Territory governments to adopt a common approach to gun control. In the near future, when someone applies for a firearms licence, all police services will have access to national information on domestic violence orders and firearms offences. Suitability to hold a gun licence will be then assessed on the basis of this information. This is an important move to help protect Australian women.

The Commonwealth, State and Territory Governments have also begun work on a National Uniform Criminal Code. This process will include a thorough examination of the laws relating to violence. Any National Criminal Code that the Federal Government is able to negotiate with the States must reflect the seriousness of violent crime against women.

Other initiatives

The Government is taking action over wider concerns about the way women are treated in all areas of law and in administrative decision making.

Our laws and administrative policies must ensure women's equality before the law. The Government has undertaken a number of initiatives to this end.

Law Reform Commission reference[9]

The Australian Law Reform Commission has been asked to examine whether Federal laws, or the ways in which they are applied, operate fairly with respect to women. It has been asked to make recommendations for legislative and non-legislative changes to ensure women's equality before the law. This is an important reference and I look forward to the report.

Family law[10]

The Government will also work toward much needed change in family law. While there now seems to be general acceptance of the principle of no-fault divorce, major issues such as division of property, custody, access, and child maintenance are still the cause of a great deal of controversy.

Changes to legislation will be aimed at achieving the correct balance by protecting the rights of all involved to the greatest extent possible.

The Second Report of the Joint Select Committee on Certain Aspects of the Operation and Interpretation of the Family Law was tabled in Parliament on 24 November 1992. The Committee conducted hearings and considered a broad range of submissions on the operation of the *Family Law Act*. Its Report contains 120 recommendations for change. Since the election, the Report has been under consideration and the Government will respond soon.

The Committee also concluded that there were anomalies in the Child Support Scheme and indicated that the Government should review the Scheme as a matter of urgency to ensure that both parents share an equitable burden of the cost of supporting their children after marriage breakdown. As a result, the Government has already acted to establish a further inquiry into the Scheme.

Protecting the safety of people involved in Family Court proceedings is also a primary consideration for the Government. We will amend the Family Law Act to achieve this purpose. For example, in February 1993 the Standing Committee of Attorneys-General agreed to amend the *Family Law Act* to empower local courts hearing domestic violence proceedings to vary or set aside access orders. The Standing Committee will also consider the Directions for Action identified in the National Strategy on Violence Against Women.

Censorship and child sex tourists[11]

In 1992 the censorship classification guidelines for printed materials were toughened to take a stand against sexual violence and images which denigrate women.

Another issue of particular concern is the exploitation of children in prostitution and pornography. I recently asked the Department to investigate how we could prosecute Australian paedophiles who sexually exploit children overseas. We must also consider options for prosecuting tour operators in Australia who organise child sex tours and suggest ways of strengthening law enforcement cooperation both within Australia and overseas.

Sex Discrimination Act[12]

The Government is also proceeding with the next stage of consideration of the recommendations concerning the *Sex Discrimination Act* made in the 'Half way to equal' report.

Apart from strengthening and improving the operation of existing areas of the Act, one of the important recommendations currently being considered by the Government is the inclusion of a general prohibition of discrimination and an equality before the law provision in the *Sex Discrimination Act*.

Conclusion

This Government is committed to enhancing the position of women in all aspects of daily life. Women's position before the law is an important indicator of the fairness of our judicial system and is of concern to all Australians.

All of us here today are aware of the widespread community concern about the capacity of the judiciary and law enforcement agencies to deal with issues vital to all Australians and particularly women.

In conclusion, I would like to acknowledge that we require a change of attitude motivated both by courage and conscience. The Government, with the help of the States and Territories, will use its law-making power to shape a contemporary society that nurtures and protects the entire community. I believe that the initiatives I have outlined to you today will contribute much to improve the status of women in Australia and remove gender imbalance in the scales of Justice.

2

Gender bias in judicial decisions
The Canadian experience

PROFESSOR KATHLEEN E. MAHONEY

Introduction

In this paper I will address four topics. First, I will attempt to explain why the issue of gender bias is just now emerging from obscurity to prominence among judicial concerns; second, I will describe what gender bias is and why it is a problem; third, I will demonstrate through case examples how gender bias affects legal doctrine; finally, I will describe judicial education programs which have been developed in Canada and some of the methodologies that have been used to deliver these programs in exciting and innovative ways.

The idea that judges may have some trouble being impartial is not new. What is new is the desire on the part of the judiciary and the public to do something about it. Lord MacMillan described the difficulty of achieving judicial impartiality when he said,

> The ordinary human mind is a mass of prepossessions inherited and acquired, often none the less dangerous because unrecognised by their possessor ... every legal mind is apt to have an innate susceptibility to particular classes of arguments[13].

Lord Scrutton made similar comments:

> ... the habits you are trained in, the people with whom you mix, lead to your having a certain class of ideas of such a nature that, when you have to deal with other ideas, you do not give as sound and accurate judgments as you would wish.[14]

Owen Dixon, Chief Justice of the Australian High Court, said that the task of the advocate and the judge is to try and understand the sensibilities of the people coming before the court before looking at or contemplating the substantive issues to be decided. What this group of judges have in common, together with the pool of lawyers from which they are drawn, is that they all share a strikingly homogenous collection of attitudes, beliefs and principles.

The members of this select group are of the view that the beliefs they hold in common represent the public interest. But as the former Chief Justice of British Columbia recently pointed out, to those who hold memberships in labour unions, minority groups and underprivileged classes, such beliefs may not be in the public interest at all. [15] [16] Similarly, women have challenged these same beliefs as being far from their view of the public interest.

This paper is entitled 'Gender bias in judicial decisions—The Canadian experience', meaning equality in the administration of justice—equality before and under the law and equal protection and benefit of the law. Equality has always been a very difficult concept for judges, lawyers, law professors and other students of the law to define or describe. The reason for this difficulty, as Justice Rosalie Abella of the Ontario Court of Appeal puts it, is that equality is evolutionary, in process as well as in substance. It is cumulative, contextual, and it is persistent. At the very least, equality is freedom from adverse discrimination. But what constitutes adverse discrimination changes with time, with information, with experience and with insight. What we tolerated as a society one hundred, fifty or even ten years ago is no longer necessarily tolerable. Equality is thus a process, a process of constant and flexible examination, of vigilant introspection, and of aggressive open-mindedness. If, in this ongoing process, we are not always sure, at any given time, exactly what equality means, most of us have a good understanding of what is fair.[17]

We expect a great deal from our judges; perhaps we expect too much—we expect them to be objective, knowledgeable, independent, discerning, practical, sensitive and above all, we expect them to be fair. [18] We expect this because judges have such an important and crucial role in society. They make decisions which shape and determine people's lives, their livelihood, and their safety. They have the power to decide whether a person's life will be lived with or without their children, whether they will have freedom, employment, self-determination, and whether they will have dignity.

But what we have discovered in Canada, through numerous studies, commissions, task forces, research papers, statistical data and the like, is that despite the good intentions of the judiciary, unconscious and pervasive gender and race biases permeate the judicial system, and this is not fair. In my country this reality is now accepted and recognised at the highest levels of the judiciary, government, the Bar, in the legal academy, [19] and reform efforts have now begun.

Why just now?

What is surprising, is that it has taken this long for gender bias to make its way on to the judicial agenda. Since the 1960s, the modern concept of equality has been on government agendas throughout the Western world. Human Rights Commissions, affirmative action programs, equal opportunity legislation, labour codes, charters of rights and freedoms and other equality tools have been created to identify and remedy international and systemic discrimination. Members of disadvantaged groups have described and documented the nature, extent and consequences of discrimination in almost every social institution and profession. Gender and other forms of bias were found embedded in the business world, in the religious establishment, in higher education, and in government, often operating in multiple ways. But ironically, the judiciary—the very institution which was determining the effectiveness of efforts to achieve equality and which could undermine even the most progressive legal reforms through the exercise of judicial discretion and through courtroom behaviour— was not itself scrutinised by social reformers and analysts. Why? Probably the main reason lies in the unquestioned and commonly held belief that judges are completely objective, disinterested and impartial in all their work.

The pervasive hold of the appealing and powerful idea of judicial neutrality has affected even those whose job it is to criticise and evaluate the judiciary. Lawyers and law professors have historically limited their inquiry and critiques of judgments to the logic and sensibility of the legal analysis they contain and their relationship to precedent. Occasionally, the social, economic or policy implications of judgments are discussed or evaluated—but rarely, if ever, are judgments or groups of judgments ever scrutinised for discriminatory practices and attitudes. Questions are seldom asked about judicial use of societally induced assumptions and untested beliefs—about the use of stereotypes which judge individuals on their group membership rather than on their individual characteristics, abilities and needs. Law review articles are rarely written about judges who view issues solely from the dominant male perspective, who neglect to consider alternative views, who oversimplify or trivialise the problems of women, or who fail to treat children seriously. The importance of variability; of cultural, racial and gender perspectives; of context, contingency and change; are discussed neither in classrooms nor in courtrooms.

Another reason is the courts themselves. Until recently, the judicial arm of government has been loath to accept any culpability with regards to the disadvantaged status of women or other minority groups. The idea that courts could be acting in a manner prejudicial to a specific group in society is generally rejected outright. The failure to entertain this possibility, of course, precludes any attempts to begin to rectify or redress the situation. To further complicate matters, the issue of bias is often personalised and reduced to assertions of individual judges denying prejudice on their part or of their associates. This reaction is inappropriate because it confuses the concepts of overt discrimination with systemic discrimination. While there may still be some incidents of overt prejudice, they are relatively easy to identify and rectify. Systemic discrimination, on the other hand, is far more pervasive and insidious and so much more difficult to eradicate. It often exists without the cognisance of either the individuals or institutions responsible for its practice.

Gender bias—What is it, and why is it important?

Gender bias falls in the systemic category. For the most part, it is a form of subtle but potent discrimination. To begin to deal with it, one must realise that every decision-maker who walks into a courtroom to hear a case is armed not only with the relevant legal texts, but with a set of gender and race-based values, experiences and assumptions that are thoroughly embedded[20], some of which adversely impact and discriminate against women. To the extent that judges labour under certain biased attitudes, myths and misconceptions about women and men, the law itself can be said to be characterised by gender bias.

Gender bias takes many forms. One form is behaviour or decision-making by participants in the justice system which is based on, or reveals reliance on, stereotypical attitudes about the nature and roles of men and women or of their relative worth, rather than being based upon an independent valuation of individual ability, life experience and aspirations. Gender bias can also arise out of myths and misconceptions about the social and economic realities encountered by both sexes. It exists when issues are viewed only from the male perspective, when problems of women are trivialised or over-simplified, when women are not taken seriously or given the same credibility as men. Gender bias is reflected not only in actions of individuals, but also in cultural traditions and in institutional practices.

Gender fairness requires empathy and understanding of the life experiences gender creates. But crossing the gender barrier has always been a formidable task. Can a man really imagine what it is like to be pregnant? To be a victim of sexual assault? To experience sexual harassment or spousal abuse? To be vilified and sexually objectified in pornography? To be a coloured woman or a disabled woman in any or all of the above categories? On the other hand, most men can imagine themselves as a father of a child, as an accused rapist, as a batterer or as a consumer of pornography. When most judges are men, women's experience tends to be objectified. When balancing competing gender-based interests and values, too often insufficient weight or no weight at all is assigned to women's interests. This leaves them less protected or even unprotected by laws which protect men—laws which affect their equality, economic opportunities, independence and personal freedom.

There are many examples of gender bias which I could offer. Gender bias cuts across all areas of the law, its substance, its process, its policy and even in interpersonal relationships in the courtroom.

In tort law you see gender bias in the content of certain courses of action and in the assessment of damages. For example, the *actio per quod*, the most notorious of tort suits, recognised a husband's claims when his wife was injured. The action treated the marital relation as one of master–servant. When a wife was injured, the husband was compensated for the loss of his wife's services including homemaking and sexual relations. At the same time, the action was not available to wives whose husbands were injured. This gender-biased approach laid the foundation for the present day tort law. In personal injury damage assessments, evaluation of the female marital role illustrates that judges do not believe it has any inherent or productive value. It is only very recently that judges in Canada have recognised that impairment of homemaking capacity can be a compensable loss to the homemaker, rather than her spouse. But even where assessments have been granted, they have been pathetically meagre, especially when compared to damages awarded for impairment of working capacity outside the home. On the other hand, where the action for compensation is based on wrongful death of a wife, the damages assessments are much higher.[21] This is because the husband's claim is on a basis similar to the old *actio per quod* and the cost of a market replacement for the wife must be calculated. Judges who are more used to being homemak*ees* rather than homemak*ers*,[22] recognise that a husband whose wife has been killed will have to hire a child care worker, a cook, a chauffeur and a housekeeper and award damages accordingly.

In family law, gender bias exists in underlying assumptions and stereotypes which affect maintenance and custody awards. Researchers have traced the 'feminisation of poverty' phenomenon directly to judicial misinformation and misunderstanding about the economic consequences of divorces.[23] Some of the misinformation includes inaccurate economic assumptions about the costs of raising children and unrealistic expectations about women's ability, especially middle aged and older women's abilities, to earn future income. On the custody issue, the case law indicates that judges are sometimes influenced by traditional sex role stereotypes which disadvantage non-traditional women who work outside the home and men who are the primary parent. They assume children are better off when raised in homes where the mother or mother replacement is a full-time homemaker. The limits this places on the aspirations and goals of women affects their independence, economic security and equality in a way that does not affect men. It also fails to recognise that, more often than not, the mother is the primary parent notwithstanding the fact that she may have responsibilities outside the home,[24] and that removing children from her custody does the children more long-term harm than the lack of an idealised, stereotypical home life.

In criminal law, gender bias is found in many areas, but probably most notoriously in the judicial treatment of sexual assault and wife abuse. Until overturned by statutory amendment, Canadian common law displayed a sweeping, uncritical acceptance of the view that rape complainants were inherently suspect and may well make false accusations.[25] In sentencing practices, gender bias in mitigation principles forgives, partially or fully, male sexual violence through a 'blame the victim' ideology, which limits women's freedom to dress as they like, walk when and where they choose, and drink as much as they want. Victims of wife abuse face serious gender bias due to widespread judicial misunderstanding of the dynamics and seriousness of a battering relationship. This often leads to unjust conclusions being drawn about victims who are reluctant to leave a battering relationship or who do not cooperate in testifying.[26] When a woman is multiply disadvantaged because of her race, disability or other immutable characteristic, the harmful effects are magnified.

These are but a few examples of gender bias. Many more could be offered to illustrate its existence. What must be understood is that the gender bias in the application and interpretation of laws is important not only for individual women before the courts. To the extent that the justice system suffers from gender bias, the system fails in its primary societal responsibility to deliver justice impartially. As a consequence, the administration of justice as a whole suffers. The legitimacy of the entire system is brought into question.

The doctrinal effect of gender bias

The next section looks at gender bias in a little more depth to demonstrate how stereotypes and incorrect assumptions have worked their way into fundamental doctrinal principles in Canadian law and how only a gender based analysis can remove them. I will briefly consider six gender specific cases—two cases dealing with discrimination on the basis of pregnancy; two cases dealing with the concept of 'reasonableness' in the context of wife battery; and two decisions in the same case dealing with the notion of harm in sexual assault.

The meaning of discrimination

The first case is *Bliss v. Attorney General of Canada.* [27] The court was asked to consider whether or not an employment benefit provision was discriminatory when it required pregnant workers to meet more stringent requirements to qualify for unemployment benefits than it required of men and non-pregnant workers. The court held that there was no sex discrimination because, it said, discrimination on the basis of pregnancy does not amount to discrimination on the basis of sex. The court said if the government treats unemployed pregnant women differently from other unemployed persons, be they male or female, it is because they are pregnant and not because they are women. The problem here was that discrimination was viewed solely from the dominant, male perspective. Rather than contextualizing and understanding the effects of gender difference between women and men, the court abstracted an objectified gender. As a result, actual inequities and real life experiences of women were not contemplated. In *Bliss* the judicial scrutiny of sex discrimination completely overlooked the components or consequences of gender in real terms. In other words, the fact that pregnancy is a fundamental component of femaleness went unrecognised. If this approach is correct, it could be argued by analogy that discrimination against the blind or against Sikhs would be illegal, but discrimination against the users of guide dogs or wearers of turbans, quite acceptable.

Another form of gender bias in *Bliss* was in the way the court applied the similarly situated test to the discrimination question. The Aristotelian rule states that discrimination occurs when people who are the same, or similarly situated, are treated differently from one another. If people are different from the standard, it is quite all right to treat them differently. To determine whether Ms Bliss was similarly situated or not, the court used a male comparator. Not surprisingly, compared to men (or non-pregnant women who in that respect are similar to men) pregnant women were found to be different. Consequently, the court concluded that even though pregnant women were treated differently, the differential treatment did not amount to justifiable discrimination. The use of a male standard to determine discrimination is gender biased because it limits women's equality rights to situations where they are the same as men. Under this regime, legal treatment of sexual harassment, prostitution, sexual assault, reproductive choice and pornography could never be characterised or treated as sex equality issues because the male comparators have no comparable disadvantage or need. Women will always be 'different'. Even if governmental action or inaction furthers women's disadvantage in these sex specific areas, it is not discrimination. As Catherine MacKinnon has observed, in practice this approach meant that if men don't need it, women don't get it.[28]

In a landmark case in 1989, the Supreme Court of Canada recognised this flaw. In no uncertain terms, it threw out the similarly situated test saying it could justify Hitler's Nüremburg laws because of the lack of content or principle in either the 'similarity' or 'difference' components.[29] It replaced it with a test which corrects the gender bias problem and has a much greater chance of achieving real equality. The new test determines discrimination in terms of disadvantage. If a person is a member of a persistently disadvantaged group and can show that a law or policy or behaviour continues or worsens that disadvantage, it is discriminatory. No comparator, male or otherwise, is required. The test of 'disadvantage', as opposed to the test of 'similarity and difference', requires judges to look at women in their place in the real world, to confront the reality that the systemic abuse and deprivation of power women experience is because of their place in the sexual hierarchy.[30] Let me show you how the analysis changed when the disadvantage test was applied to a pregnancy discrimination case which arose ten years after the *Bliss* decision.

In the case of *Brooks v. Canada Safeway*[31] the Supreme Court of Canada looked at a fact situation similar to that which arose in *Bliss*. Pregnant women workers had received disfavoured treatment in comparison with males and other non-pregnant women in terms of benefit provisions in the employer's group sickness policy. Although it was a private discrimination case taken under human rights legislation, the issue was whether or not discrimination on the basis of pregnancy amounted to discrimination on the basis of sex. This time around, the court not only found it unnecessary to find a male equivalent to the condition of pregnancy, it specifically held that the disadvantage the pregnant women suffered came about because of their condition—because of their *difference*. In recognising the discrimination the Chief Justice, unlike the court in *Bliss*, looked at pregnant women in their societal context. This is what he said:

> … Combining paid work with motherhood and accommodating the childbearing needs of working women are ever-increasing imperatives. That those who bear children and benefit society as a whole thereby should not be economically or socially disadvantaged seems to bespeak the obvious. It is only women who bear children, no man can become pregnant. As I argued earlier, it is unfair to impose all of the costs of pregnancy upon one-half of the population. It is difficult to conceive that distinctions or discriminations based upon pregnancy could ever be regarded as other than discrimination based upon sex, or that restrictive statutory conditions applicable only to pregnant women did not discriminate against them as women …[32]

Using the disadvantaged approach to determining discrimination makes a profound difference when any sex-specific laws are evaluated contextually in terms of their effect on women. For example, consider reproductive self-determination. If laws which limit women's access to reproductive control were examined in terms of whether or not they increase the persistent disadvantaged status of women, I think they would be found to violate equality guarantees. Similarly, statutory provisions of common law rules requiring women victims to meet evidentiary requirements not demanded of other victims of violent crime; or sentencing patterns which show wife batterers treated more leniently than other assaulters, could be scrutinised under constitutional sex equality guarantees.

Gender bias also arises in the application of seemingly neutral, objective tests which judges use to determine civil liability or criminal culpability. For example, two recent Canadian cases dealing with wife battering raise the issue of 'reasonableness'. The first decision contextualises and makes the concept of reasonableness inclusive. It acknowledges alternate views and it recognises actual inequities and the real-life experience of battered women. The second decision demonstrates how sex-discriminatory stereotypes can skew results in a gender-biased way such that violent treatment of women by men is totally or partially legitimised.

The first case, *Lavallee v. R.,*[33] was a criminal case involving a woman who was charged with second degree murder after she shot her partner in the back of the head with a rifle. The shooting occurred after an altercation in which the woman had been physically abused. The court found she was fearful for her life, as she was taunted with the threat by her common law husband that if she did not kill him first, he would kill her. The accused was a frequent victim of her partner's physical abuse, requiring medical treatment for various fractures and other injuries. At trial, Ms Lavallee was acquitted by a jury of second degree murder on the basis of self-defence. The Appeal Court set aside her acquittal because they said the facts of the case failed to establish the essential ingredients of the defence. The Trial Court's decision was subsequently restored by the Supreme Court of Canada where the substantive meaning of self-defence was fundamentally altered as a result of a gender-based inquiry and analysis.

The essential ingredients the Appeal Court found lacking were evidence of imminent attack and reasonable apprehension of death or grievous bodily harm. The Appeal Court concluded this because the fatal shot was fired as the man was walking out of the room. In other words, there was no assault in progress. Thus the reaction of shooting him was not in response to reasonable apprehension of bodily harm. The Supreme Court of Canada, however, said that while the imminence of death or grievous bodily harm is an essential ingredient of the defence, common law interpretation comprehends only a male concept of reasonableness in a combative situation. The Supreme Court concluded that battered women who kill their partners do not fit into the law's traditional concept of self-defence. The Supreme Court said the requirements of the defence evolved out of a 'bar-room brawl' model—eyeball to eyeball, fist to fist—a male concept envisioning combatants of relatively equal size and strength. When applied to battered women who fight back, the model doesn't work. The court explained it this way:

> If it strains credulity to imagine what the 'ordinary man' would do in the position of a battered spouse, it is probably because men do not typically find themselves in that situation. Some women do, however. The definition of what is reasonable must be adapted to circumstances which are, by and large, foreign to the world inhabited by the hypothetical 'reasonable man'.

In other words, the court found that gender was germane to the question of reasonableness and decided that in order to be fair to women, it was necessary to reconsider the defence by taking evidence of the situation of the battered woman into consideration. The court concluded that the method of defending against the threat of death may be different for a woman than it is for a man. It said that the objective standard of reasonableness was not to be viewed as it had been historically in Canada, solely from the male perspective. Changing the configuration of the self-defence doctrine this way corrected gender bias in the law. By making gender relevant to the concept of reasonableness in *Lavallee*, the court arguably opened the door to the reconstruction of many other legal doctrines based on reasonableness such as the defences of provocation, duress and necessity.

In contrast to *Lavallee*, consider the case of *A.L. v. The Crimes Compensation Board (Saskatchewan)*[34] which also raised the issue of the legal content of the reasonableness concept. The facts of the case were that, after a history of abuse during the marriage, A.L. was severely assaulted by her husband. The assault occurred after an argument during which the husband threatened to leave her and the children without financial support. The wife then said she would pack his suitcase and went to the bedroom to do so. He followed her there and assaulted her. She sustained serious physical injuries, including a broken back. The husband subsequently pleaded guilty to the assault, was convicted, and jailed.

At the time of the event, the victim was 45 years of age, had been married 25 years and had 9 children, 4 of whom were dependent on her.

Following her husband's conviction for the assault, A.L. applied to the Crimes Compensation Board for compensation for her injuries because the back injury prevented her from continuing her employment. The Board denied her application on the grounds that she 'knowingly put herself into circumstances that caused injury to herself', a situation which was found to fall within an exemption under the *Criminal Injuries Compensation Act*.[35] Furthermore, the Board found that her actions in going to the bedroom to pack his suitcase amounted to provocation stating 'the applicant should have been aware that her actions on the date in question would aggravate him and lead to his violent behaviour'.[36]

The Act, like the common law of self-defence, relies on the concept of 'reasonableness'. Here it was used in two ways; first, to determine whether the injury was a reasonably foreseeable consequence of the complainant's behaviour that should have been avoided; and second, to determine whether the ordinary reasonable man would be deprived of self-control in the circumstances of the case.

If the Board was correct in the way it applied the reasonableness standard to foreseeability in *A.L.*, a woman's mere presence in a place where violence is foreseeable could disentitle her to compensation benefits. Would this mean that if a woman goes to a bar alone or goes for a walk alone at night and is assaulted, she is contributing to her own assault? What about hitchhiking alone or inviting a male to her apartment? In Canadian society, violence against women is a reality and it is foreseeable in such places, but should women be blamed for it? In addition to blaming victims, this approach penalises women for doing things that men freely do without any penalty or restriction. It is gender biased because it gives credence to the stereotype that women who are beaten are partially or wholly responsible for the violence directed against them. Moreover, the Board's decision implies that the solution to the foreseeability problem for women is to leave the abusive setting in which they live if they wish to be compensated for their injuries. If this is correct, one could argue by analogy that victims of sexual harassment at their place of work, or victims of crime in high crime neighbourhoods, must be partially to blame for their victimisation unless they quit their employment or move away.

The Board's assumption that women like *A.L.* can leave their abusive husbands but unreasonably refuse to do so, is also gender-biased because it makes the assessment from the male perspective and fails to take into account the dynamics of wife abuse and the general context of inequality within which women live. First hand accounts by many battered women demonstrate that they are often trapped in their relationships. A decision to stay with an abusive husband is perfectly reasonable if, from the wife's point of view, there is no other place to go. Financial and emotional dependence on their husbands; concern for the welfare and custody of their children; lack of emergency housing and day care; lack of support from law enforcement agencies; the fear of public exposure; inadequate social support networks; the fear of greater injury and the tendency of society to blame women rather than their assailants are some of the reasons battered women cite for staying in violent relationships.[37] All are related to the unequal social position of women which the Board failed to take into account when interpreting the 'reasonably prudent person' test.

On the provocation issue, the reasonableness test once again tilts against women's interests. The Board in the *A.L.* case found that the wife contributed to the injuries by packing her husband's suitcase after he announced he would leave. The Board saw this conduct as a provocative act which precipitated the husband's act of violence.

The defence of provocation has a reasonableness requirement. In order to exculpate an accused from responsibility for an offence or reduce his culpability, the provocation must be such that it deprives an ordinary reasonable person of self-control. In concluding that packing the husband's suitcase in response to his threat to leave amounted to provocation, the Board must have concluded that his rage in response to such an act was reasonable and that breaking his wife's back was an act which should be partially forgiven. Legitimising these attitudes and reactions is clearly gender-biased in the most damaging of ways. If the law accommodates the violent enforcement of male dominance and female subordination, it permits more powerful members of society to prey with impunity upon more vulnerable members. The decision effectively says a battered wife cannot protest her husband's actions or do something that may cause him to become angry and beat her again, such as challenging authority or control over her. Thus, this case perpetuates women's disadvantage, justifies male dominance and denies women equal benefit and equal protection of the law. Even if the woman's conduct is not exemplary in the Judge's eyes, it is surely not legal justification for her to be assaulted and battered—'the author of her own misfortune'.

The nature of 'harm'

The final case I want to use to illustrate gender bias is one called *R. v. McCraw*.[38] The accused was charged with three counts of threatening to cause serious bodily harm contrary to the Criminal Code. He had written anonymous letters to three women graphically detailing various sexual acts which he wished to perform upon them and concluded each with a threat that he would have sexual intercourse with them even if he had to rape them. The court was required to address two issues; whether or not the letters constituted a threat, and whether the letters threatened serious bodily harm. The trial judge acquitted the accused. He did so on the reasoning that the letters were not really threats, but if they were, they were not threats of serious bodily harm. On the threat issue, the judge found that in the accused's mind, the letters were more 'adoring fantasies' than threats. On the harm issue, he decided that rape does not necessarily result in serious harm or even *any* harm to the victim because the threat to rape is no more than a threat to have nonconsensual sexual intercourse, not a threat to cause serious bodily harm.

This is a good case to analyse for gender bias on a number of grounds. As I have mentioned previously, one of the requirements of judicial decision making is an ability to empathise with parties before the court. Detachment must be the posture from which judges render their final decisions, but it should only be assumed after the judge has exercised his/her ability to empathise with the parties to the lawsuit.[39] Here, as far as the threat issue was concerned, no empathy with the victims of the threats is apparent, notwithstanding their evidence that the letters frightened them to the extent that they no longer felt safe when they were alone. Had the victims' perception of the letters been considered by the judge, it is highly unlikely he would have characterised them as 'adoring fantasies'. Not only was the judge's empathy limited to the imagined mental state of the accused, his choice of the words 'adoring fantasy' is inappropriate. Both the words 'adoring' and 'fantasy' connote love, caring and pleasure and completely disguise and misrepresent the ugly reality of sexual violence. Moreover, the idea that a threatened sexual assault could simultaneously be an adoring fantasy, I would say, trivialises violence against women and blurs the distinction between voluntary, normal sexual relations and hostile, coerced violations of bodily integrity. More than condemning and deterring sexual violence, which one would think is an appropriate thing for a judge to do, the tone of the judgment legitimises sexual domination of women by men, eroding the most basic of all rights, that of inviolability of the person. This approach carries over into the analysis of the harm issues.

In the judge's opinion, the requirements of threatening 'serious bodily harm' were not met in the case. In fact he went further, suggesting that sexual assault generally does not itself necessarily involve any kind of physical harm to the victim. To a non-legal person, this view would be absurd. The question must be asked—why would a judge hold such a view? I would submit that the reason is because his views are grounded in the legally created, gender-biased stereotype that women lie about sexual assault. It goes back to the days when a woman victim's evidence of rape was not believed unless it was corroborated, either by other witnesses or by indicia of wounding which would corroborate non-consent. As a result, the harm of sexual assault came to be associated with the corroborative evidence; the evidence of wounding, kicking, stabbing, strangling and so on, rather than the act of unconsented-to intercourse. By saying that forced sexual intercourse is not necessarily harmful, the judge failed to consider the victim's perspective. The judge obviously viewed rape as a sexual act.

To view it as such empathises with the rapist. As the rapist sees it, rape is an expression of sexual desire, a source of sexual pleasure, albeit forced. Harm to the victim occurs only if she resists. In other words, she is in control of the harm. The trial judge's analysis gives the accused the benefit of assuming no resistance and in effect renders the threatening section almost meaningless for women. In order to meet the requirements of the section he would have to threaten more than rape.

When this case reached the Supreme Court of Canada, a contextual analysis was adopted which resulted in a more just conclusion. Addressing the harm issue, the Supreme Court of Canada recognised that gender bias occurs when issues are viewed only from a male perspective. The court said, 'to argue that a woman who has been forced to have sexual intercourse has not necessarily suffered grave and serious violence is to ignore the perspective of women. For women, rape under any circumstance must constitute a profound interference with their physical integrity'.[40] The court stressed that the threat issue must be determined on the basis of what a reasonable person would think, then added, 'bearing in mind that at least 50% of ordinary reasonable people in our society are women'.[41] The court said that rape is a crime committed against women which has a dramatic, traumatic effect and to ignore the fact that rape frequently results in serious psychological harm to the victim would be a retrograde step, contrary to any concept of sensitivity in the application of the law.[42]

The effect of this decision was not only to bring a woman's perspective into the law of sexual assault and threats of serious bodily harm, it changed the notion of serious bodily harm doctrinally. Until this decision, psychological harm, particularly in sexual assault cases, was not a factor in deciding what charges would be laid or in the sentencing of the accused. Where there was no evidence of wounding, prosecutors would charge rapists with simple sexual assault—the least serious of all the sexual crimes. Now that psychological harm is recognised as serious bodily harm rapists can be, and are being, charged under the more serious sexual assault provisions of sexual assault causing bodily harm.

The foregoing is intended to provide some insights into the nature and effects of gender bias in judicial decisions and to stimulate discussion on this important matter. Once the conversation begins, it inevitably leads to discussions about solutions. In Canada, judicial education programs on gender and race issues have been developed in a number of provincial jurisdictions as well as at the federal level as a means of dealing with pervasive gender and race bias in the law. The following section describes the content and methodology of some judicial education initiatives.

Judicial education programs

One of the most active participants in judicial education in Canada is the Western Judicial Education Centre (WJEC), a project of the Canadian Association of Provincial Court Judges. It organises continuing education programs for Provincial and Territorial Court Judges from Western and Northwestern Canada.

The WJEC is built on a cooperative model. It works in very close cooperation with the Chairpersons of provincial and territorial education programs to ensure that provincial court judges receive a full range of continuing education programs. Since 1988, by internal agreement, the members of this cooperative group have focused on developing programs dealing with delivery of justice to Aboriginal people, gender equality in judicial decision making and racial, ethnic and cultural equity. In addition, a 'participatory' model of program delivery has been adopted, which is capable of implementation in any part of the country at any level of court. This model includes a close association with law schools and continuing legal education societies in Western Canada as well as non-legal professionals and private citizens. Advice and direct resource commitment of these organisations and individuals is obtained, often at no charge. As a result, a strong community support base as well as a high quality product has been created.

One of the key elements of judicial education programs is peer leadership. Judges are trained by other judges and 'outsiders' to instruct and lead other judges. This method of delivery challenges judges to participate and to take responsibility for their own continuing education while respecting the fundamental principle of judicial independence. At the same time, members of the broader community interested in and concerned with improving the quality of justice delivery, participate in the workshops and other sessions. Women, Aboriginal people, children, racial, cultural and ethnic minority group members, and other people very unlike judges, supply knowledge judges require, but seldom receive. They describe and discuss the problems they experience in their daily lives as well as in the courts. They lead discussions, present papers, participate in social events and sometimes provide entertainment to educate judges about their cultural and social reality.

The WJEC workshop held in June 1991 in Yellowknife, Northwest Territories, is a good example of the pedagogy and philosophy of the program. The theme for the workshop was 'Equality and Fairness: Accepting the Challenge'. It dealt exclusively with Aboriginal justice and gender equality, assigning equal time to the two topics.

The Aboriginal program included police, Crown counsel, defence counsel, native court workers and correction officials as speakers and contributors. They addressed issues on two major topics; the identification of systemic discrimination against Aboriginal people and the values that Aboriginal people hold, and an examination of the ways in which the justice system can more adequately respond to Aboriginal offenders.[43] An important aspect of the Yellowknife program was the inclusion of Elders and translators from members of native communities including the Dene, Metis and Inuit. Their importance to the proceedings was programmatically acknowledged in both the substantive sessions as well as in the ceremonial aspects of the sessions. For example, each day an Elder from one of the communities offered a prayer at both the opening and closing sessions.

The gender equality portion of the workshop was of two days duration and was designed around three thematically linked analytical approaches. The first was an exploration of the principles of equality in the substantive law; the second, an investigation of the systemic social and economic consequences of sex discrimination, particularly in terms of violence and poverty; and third, an exposé of the consequences individuals experience because of gender inequality and gender bias in the courts.

Survivors of sexual assault as well as crisis centre workers provided the judges with first hand information about the consequences of poverty and violence against women. Other topics on the program looked at the issues of sexist language and the credibility of men as a group compared to women as a group.

Throughout the seven day workshop, a variety of teaching techniques were used, including lectures, dramatisations, panels, and question and answer sessions. In the small groups, other techniques such as discussions, brain storming, buzz groups, videos and video commentary were used. Previously prepared papers on gender equality issues were distributed in the workshop materials which also contained two videotapes on the topic 'A Judicial Approach to Gender Bias'. A written guide to the video material was provided, setting out questions for discussion and other explanatory material. Each judge was provided with a full set of materials in advance of the workshop.

It is noteworthy that a three day 'Training the Trainer' workshop on 'Gender Neutrality in Decision Making' was held three months prior to the Yellowknife meeting for the judge facilitators. The purpose was to give them a deeper understanding and awareness of gender issues as well as to provide some pedagogical training in delivery formats, and facilitation skills.

Evaluations were done by the judges on a daily basis. This enabled the administrators to collect highly specific data on their reactions to the content, presentation skills, teaching methods, stated objectives and new knowledge they felt they had gained.

Conclusion

The Canadian experience in identifying and correcting gender and race bias in the courts is in its formative years. The acknowledgment that unequal and unfair treatment of women and racial minorities occurs within the judicial system was the important and crucial first step. The second step was the recognition that in order to remove these biases the judges need to better understand the impact of poverty, race, illiteracy, disabilities, discrimination, alcohol and drug abuse, sexual and physical abuse on social behaviour. This led to the further recognition that legal principles must be linked to the social context in order to achieve complete justice and fairness within the legal system. This last, in my view, is the most crucial step in rooting out gender biased principles.

By virtue of the fact that judges have taken a leadership role in opening up the channels of communication, they have not only removed artificial barriers to the acquisition of important knowledge required to address issues previously unaddressed; they have set an important example to other actors in the legal system about self-examination and improvement. What is innovative and exciting about the new judicial education initiatives in Canada is the idea that the community as well as judges have a direct connection to, and investment in, the work that judges do.

In the gender program, the views of minority as well as white, able-bodied women must be heard. Although gender issues affect all women, the interrelationships between gender equality, disability, diverse cultural values and practices must be understood in order to achieve a full and complete understanding of women's experience.[44]

In June of 1992, the WJEC co-sponsored the fourth of the Western Workshops and addressed many of these concerns. By building on the success of the 1991 Workshop, the organisers were able to focus on issues of racial and ethnic discrimination and their compounding effects on gender discrimination. Special attention was given to the problem of spousal assault within the multicultural context, urban natives and the justice system, and views of Aboriginal women. In addition to the teaching techniques described above, one day of the workshop was held at an Indian Reserve where, hosted by the native people, the judges learned about Aboriginal cultural beliefs and values and perceptions about the delivery of justice. Other optional trips included a Metis settlement visit to learn about Metis history, culture and present concerns and visits to various social service agencies and community resources which support the poor, the disadvantaged, victims of violence and young offenders.

While all of the problems and challenges of gender and race bias education have yet to be entirely resolved, the process of judicial reform has definitely begun. It is important to understand that this is an internal voluntary reform movement rather than an imposed one. One can only hope that this development will continue and flourish within the Canadian judiciary and spread to other jurisdictions outside my country, so that the ultimate objective, equal justice for all, will be achieved.

3

Equality and gender bias in the law
The Australian scene

JUSTICE ELIZABETH EVATT, AO

THE CURRENT AIM is to identify areas of the law where awareness of sex-bias and the rights and changing social roles of women is needed; to identify processes within the law that hinder equity; and to define strategies for dealing with these problems for presentation to bodies concerned with programs for community and judicial awareness on these issues.

These aims overlap the project of the Australian Law Reform Commission on Equality Before the Law for Women. The Commission has been asked to consider what should be done to remove any unjustifiable discriminatory effects for women of the law or of the application of the law to women, with a view to ensuring their full equality before the law.

The Commission is asked to consider whether there is a need to amend existing laws, to introduce new laws, to change the way laws are applied in courts and tribunals, or to change the way laws are made. We are also asked to consider non-legislative approaches to reform.[45] This law reform exercise is separate from that which the Australian Institute of Judicial Administration (AIJA) is undertaking in relation to judicial education, though there are overlapping areas of interest. [46]

The background of the Commission's reference includes press reports of, and the community reaction to, several rape cases which occurred over the last 18 months. First there was the *Hakopian* case, which caught public attention because of the judge's suggestion that the rape of a prostitute might be less serious, and therefore carry a lesser sentence, than the rape of a 'virtuous woman'.[47] The Victorian Law Reform Commission later pointed out that while the actual impact on a particular victim is a relevant consideration, there is no evidence that a victim's occupational status or sexual experience is a good guide to the psychological impact which a rape may have.[48] The Commission recommended that, in taking into account the impact of the offence on a complainant in the course of sentencing an offender for a sexual offence, a court must not make any assumption about that impact that is based on the fact that the complainant was, or had been, a prostitute.

The second case was that of a judge who is said to have instructed a jury that the law did not prevent a husband from using 'rougher than usual handling' of his wife in an attempt to persuade her to agree to sexual intercourse. This comment was disapproved of by the Court of Appeal.[49]

These cases, and others reported by the media since, have led to strong criticisms of the judges concerned and to demands for judicial education. This in turn has led to an inquiry by the (Federal) Senate Standing Committee on Legal and Constitutional Affairs into the question '(a) whether recent publicity surrounding judicial comment in sexual offence cases is a proper reflection of a failure to understand gender issues by the judiciary; and (b) the appropriate response to any such failure'.[50]

It would, however, be a mistake to see the reference to the Law Reform Commission and the work of the AIJA as simply a response to the well-reported judicial comments. It would also be a mistake to see these exercises as being solely concerned with the correction of individual error by a few members of the judiciary.[51] The *underlying* problem, which those comments illustrate, is that of the 'deeply entrenched and insidious gender bias of the law, which is hard to identify and even harder to eradicate'.[52] That bias is the main cause of discrimination against women in the legal system and it is the subject of the Commission's inquiry. The law and the legal system as a whole, rather than individual judges, are the issue.

I want to give a brief outline of our project.

In what ways does Australian law reflect gender bias?

What is gender bias?

One of the matters the Commission is asked to report on is community attitudes associated with gender bias as it relates to women.

The link between the Law Reform Commission's project and the subject of this conference is that *gender bias* is a form of systemic discrimination, a failure of the law to accord fair and equal treatment to women in its substance, in its application, or in its procedure. Gender bias is due, in part, to the attitudes brought to bear by courts on issues affecting women. Regrettably, these attitudes have too often been based on stereotyped roles for men and women and on assumptions about their status and capacities. Because of the role of judges in developing the law, these judicial attitudes, prejudices and biases affect not only individual cases but also the substance of the law.

In a system *free* of gender bias, women who come into contact with the law would be treated as individuals and not according to stereotyped views based on gender, or on assumptions as to the proper roles of men and women. Decisions of courts and other agencies would be made without bias arising from the conscious or unconscious resort to such assumptions.

Gender bias, on the other hand, makes the law *less effective* in preventing harm to women or in providing them with an appropriate remedy if harm occurs. As a result, women do not enjoy equality before the law or the equal protection of the law. Thus, fair and equal treatment of women requires that gender bias be overcome wherever it exists.

How gender bias affects the law

How do we go about identifying gender bias in Australian law? I note first, that we share a common legal heritage with Canada and the United States. Historically, the laws were made and applied by men; women were excluded from participation, and lacked legal status and capacity in many respects. The subject matter of the law was, in many instances, built upon patriarchal attitudes, for example in family law and in regard to violence against women.

Studies of the legal system carried out in North America by judicially appointed task forces show that male judges tend to adhere to traditional values and beliefs about the natures of men and women and their proper roles in society.[53] They found overwhelming evidence that gender-based myths, biases and stereotypes are deeply embedded in the attitudes of many male judges as well as in the law itself and that gender difference has been a significant factor in judicial decision making. It was shown that:

> ... the theoretical underpinning of the law was in many instances biased in favour of men. This was demonstrated in the specific application of legal rules and results across all legal subjects, such as tort, contract, criminal law and property law. It was shown that judges unintentionally or unwittingly or unknowingly reflected a gender bias in their judgments.[54]

Australian feminist lawyers have written convincingly that gender bias is as much a part of the Australian legal system as it is in North America. There are comparable examples to back up their arguments. These show that much of the law is based on outdated assumptions about gender roles and fails to take proper regard of women's experience.

The results can be seen:
- in the exclusion of women from participation in the law;
- in the law's long standing failure to recognise and deal adequately with violence against women and sexual harassment;
- in rape laws which focus on the male offender's belief about consent rather than on the protection of the victim's right to personal integrity in all circumstances;

- in assumptions made by courts about the nature of women and women's sexuality that have been described as 'little short of ludicrous';[55]
- in the failure of the legal system to give proper value to women's unpaid work, in compensation law and matrimonial property law;
- in assumptions about the dependency of women, which permeate several fields of law, including social security;
- in the failure of the law to recognise and then to fully enforce the principles of pay equity;
- in terms and conditions of employment which assume, despite the facts, that a worker is a male breadwinner in full-time employment, and which fail to have regard to the needs of workers with family responsibilities;
- in the failure of the law to deal adequately with the portrayal of women in media and advertising;
- in the law's failure to give proper weight to the evidence of women; and
- in the failure of courts to recognise the effect of indirect discrimination against women.

This conference will, I hope, produce valuable further information to show how the effects of the attitudes I have mentioned have reached into and infected many parts of the legal system.

What can be done to remove gender bias from the law?

Options for reform

As I said earlier, gender bias affects the substance of the law, the application of the law and legal procedures. The strategies needed to overcome gender bias must deal with all of these aspects as well as with attitudes. The Commission will put forward in its consultation documents a range of issues and proposals including: legislative reform to remove bias from the substance of law; more effective protection of equality and the equal enjoyment by women of rights and freedoms; removal of barriers which impede access to justice, such as a lack of awareness, disempowerment and cost; programs to increase judicial sensitivity to issues of gender bias; increased participation of women in the legal profession, in the legislature and in the judiciary.

I will mention a few of the ideas that are emerging. Before doing so, I make the comment that the Commission is a Federal agency. It has been the State judiciary which has been involved in the recent publicity and which largely deals with the criminal law but there is a Federal concern in these matters. All judges exercise federal jurisdiction to some extent. Standards of justice and fairness are human rights obligations which are a Commonwealth responsibility.

Individual instances of bias

While much of our attention will be given to the way in which gender bias has entered into the substance of the law, it is also important to consider individual cases in which bias has been shown. Judges value their independence and impartiality highly, though they are more willing these days to accept that they are affected by many inbuilt attitudes and values—so much so that only the other day I heard a colleague say 'the only judge who can be truly impartial is one who cannot understand submissions of *either* party!' When biased attitudes are displayed, which go beyond an interpretation or application of established law, the rights of the individual can be adversely affected. Equally, there may be a concern that the attitudes displayed in one case could affect the judge or magistrate in his or her approach to other cases. If a judge is wrong in law, a correction can be made in an appeal and there is, of course, a legal rule against bias. If a judge has a personal interest or a predisposition in favour of or against a party, this is a disqualifying factor which should be revealed and may be relied on in an appeal.

The Commission will ask whether this rule should be extended to deal with the expression of gender bias. For example, when a judge displays a prejudicial attitude towards women, including the expression of stereotyped attitudes or disrespect of any kind, should that disqualify the judge from dealing with other cases where those attitudes may affect the interests of women?

A judge is unlikely to hear company laws involving his or her company shares because of the possibility of bias. Should a judge or magistrate who, in previous cases, has made observations which reveal an attitudinal bias about domestic violence, be able to hear cases involving domestic assault?

Another option is to regard gender bias as an occasion for judicial discipline in those jurisdictions which have established mechanisms for this purpose. In Canada, Judicial Commissions are disciplining judges for gender bias behaviour such as sexist remarks to women lawyers and litigants and inappropriate comments in rape cases.[56] Both these suggestions depend on a thorough understanding of gender issues by both lawyers and judges.

More effective protection of equality

The Commission's terms of reference refer to equality before the law. We do not interpret this narrowly to mean that men and women should be given identical treatment. Our approach is that women are equally entitled to the enjoyment of rights and freedoms and to fair treatment by the law. This means that the content of rights must be equally meaningful for women as for men and that may require revision of the substance of rights. On whatever basis we approach the issue, equality before the law and fairness cannot be achieved if there is bias in the substance of the law, in legal procedures or in judicial attitudes.

One possible response to bias is a comprehensive guarantee of equality to protect women (and possibly others) from discrimination by Federal or State governments or public agencies. Australia is one of the few Western nations without guarantees[57] such as the 'equal protection' provision in the United States Constitution[58], or similar provisions in the Canadian Charter of Rights and Freedoms[59] and the New Zealand Bill of Rights[60].

In 1988 the Legal and Constitutional Commission recommended that the right to equality be entrenched in the Constitution and put forward a model provision for this purpose: S. 124G

- (1) Everyone has the right to freedom from discrimination on the ground of race, colour, ethnic or national origin, sex, marital status, or political, religious or ethical belief.

- (1) is not infringed by measures taken to overcome disadvantages arising from race, colour, ethnic or national origin, sex, marital status, or political, religious or ethical belief.

Equality protection could also be provided in an ordinary Act of Parliament or Bill of Rights. While this could be removed by a subsequent Act of Parliament, it has the advantage that it would allow the concepts included in the legislation to be tested in practice before they were included in a binding constitutional document. That was what happened in Canada and is now happening in New Zealand. [61]

An equal rights and anti-discrimination provision should be broad enough in its scope to allow legal challenges to take full account of women's disadvantaged position. (Of course it is not expected that equality provisions would be restricted in their application to gender issues.) Canada provides a good precedent for entrenched equality provisions. Such provisions mean that any law inconsistent with the equality principle are invalid to the extent of the inconsistency. Women would be able to challenge all law, policies and programs—Commonwealth, State and local—which result in unequal outcomes for women and which perpetuate women's disadvantage. A general prohibition of discrimination, with legal sanctions, would give legitimacy to women's equality and thus give women some power. It would make a clear statement about the value and dignity of women. On the other hand, the interpretation of a Bill of Rights is left to the courts, which may be ill equipped to resolve equality issues. Their tendency to take a narrow and legalistic approach is well known. The results may be disappointing if the courts do not have a clear understanding of the meaning of discrimination and its effects on women. Overseas experience suggests that women need to work very hard, and need considerable back-up resources, to put persuasive arguments to courts on some of these issues. Unless we act in other ways as well, gender bias could frustrate equality laws.

Removing bias in the substantive legal profession

In dealing with the substantive law the Commission will examine laws relating to relationships, to employment, to aspects of economics, for example discriminatory aspects of the *Social Security Act* and sexually transmitted debt, and discriminatory aspects of company law and insurance law. These and many other aspects of civil and criminal law, and the law relating to nationality, immigration and refugees, will be looked at to see whether they perpetuate discrimination against women.

Greater participation by women in the legal profession

Another way to change the legal culture, the values, attitudes and gender bias of the law would be to increase, considerably, the participation of women in the legal profession, especially in key judicial and other influential roles.

Women are well represented among students in Australian law schools, and have been for some time. However, this has not led to an equivalent number of women moving into the higher levels of the profession. The lack of numbers creates many problems for those women lawyers who sometimes feel that they are up against a legal system which is permeated with the attitudes and prejudices of male hierarchies. Women who seek to participate in the law may have to behave and operate in the same way as men in order to succeed.[62] They have to pursue personal goals of equality on male terms rather than to seek to integrate other values and attitudes to the system.

> Women had (and still have) to show that they too could be like the atomistic, individualistic man of law. To show any other face was to show weakness, to admit defeat, to show that they were not really as good as the boys.[63]

If the system is gender biased and discriminatory towards women, participation in the system could mean that women participate in their own oppression. The absence from legal practice of women who do not want to be forced to adopt the style and outlook of the male hierarchy can only serve to reinforce the effects of gender bias.

Similar problems arise in relation to the judiciary. It is fairly widely accepted that the judiciary is drawn from a narrow class of people, of similar background and outlook.[64] One view is that the small number of women in the judiciary is partly the result of the attitudes already described. Should we try to ensure that more women are appointed to the judiciary and would it make a difference? The Commission will be seeking information about the obstacles to the participation of women in the legal profession, to identify how far these result from gender bias and discrimination. The study will cover the teaching of law; obstacles to employment and promotion in the law, the segregation of women lawyers into defined fields; hostility to women lawyers in courts and tribunals; issues such as sexual harassment of women lawyers.

Could women judges influence change?

Justice Bertha Wilson of the Canadian Supreme Court asked the question whether women judges would make a difference. She drew on the opinions of feminist writers who believe that women *would* make a difference because of their different perspective, and because they can introduce a new standard of judicial neutrality and impartiality into the justice system.[65] This would, she thought, be most beneficial where the law has an inbuilt gender bias. Practical ways in which women on the bench could make a difference are that they help to break down stereotypes about the role of women in society; they increase public confidence in the courts as being able to respond to the legal problems of all classes of citizens; they make it easier for women lawyers to appear as counsel before a woman judge; and reduce the risk of sexist comments (on questions of dress and other matters).

We will be inviting suggestions as to how to overcome these problems.

Selection of the judiciary

The Commission will call for views on the methods of selection and appointment of the judiciary, and ask whether there is any discrimination against women in that regard. Proposals to broaden the base of appointments are often met with opposition, on the basis that this would in some way be inconsistent with merit.[66] [67] If the goal *is* that of merit, it is important to be clear what standard is set, and how to ascertain who is capable of meeting that standard. The results of the Commission's work will, I hope, be of value in the government review of judicial membership mentioned by the Minister for Justice (see the paper 'Law reform and Australian women').

Proposals for judicial education

In my view the case for the inclusion of gender bias and gender awareness in continuing judicial education programs has been well established. When programs of this kind were introduced in North America in the 1980s they were supported by a substantial number of leading (male) judges and educators.

Similar proposals have been made in Australia in reports to government over the last few years, well before the recent incidents. Some examples follow.

In 1990 the National Committee on Violence Against Women recommended that the AIJA provide for the continuing education of judicial officers in matters relating to victims of violence generally and victims of domestic violence, sexual assault and child abuse in particular.[68] The National Strategy on Violence Against Women recommended that the training of lawyers, judges, magistrates and police include programs to promote attitudinal changes in relation to violence.[69]

The Victorian Law Reform Commission, in its report on rape, suggested that one process for change should be education of the judges by the Judicial Studies board.

The Commonwealth Parliamentary Joint Select Committee on the Operation and Interpretation of the Family Law Act recommended that the Family Court develop a more systematic and intensive program of judicial education in relevant non-legal matters, and particularly in factors, such as domestic violence and child abuse, which can influence the welfare of children.[70]

All these recommended that judicial education programs should deal with issues such as violence and rape, other reports have proposed that cultural and racial awareness be included.

Judicial education programs of these kinds have been supported internationally in the UN system, and they have been supported by Chief Justice Malcolm of Western Australia in 1991. Now the issue has been taken up by the AIJA. Other reports to government have recommended that cultural and racial awareness be included in judicial education. This conference could have a significant input to the process.

One of the sources which the Law Reform Commission is drawing on in its work is the Convention on the Elimination of all Forms of Discrimination against Women. That Convention calls on nation states to change social and cultural patterns of conduct and to eliminate prejudices and practices based on the idea of the inferiority or the superiority of either of the sexes or on stereotyped roles for men and women. The Commission will consider the contribution that continuing legal education for the judiciary and for the profession can make towards promoting these goals and helping to reduce gender bias in the law.

Conclusions

Judges shape the law, and they can, within limits, choose to be responsive to the needs of the times, or slavish followers of outdated concepts. It is clear that judges have prejudices and biases, of which they, (and, dare I add, the public) should be aware, if judicial neutrality and impartiality is to have real meaning. In a sense then, the reference to the Law Reform Commission is a challenge to the accumulated prejudices of lawyers and judges of the past rather than an attack on the individual. The goal is a simple one—namely that women receive fair and equal treatment from the law.

The consultation process

The Commission expects to publish a consultation document and thereafter we shall carry out an extensive consultation process around Australia. We will in due course visit each State and Territory, capital cities and some regional centre. We hope to involve women of all walks of life, and especially women who have particular difficulties in their access to the law.

Postscript

In 1994 the Australian Law Reform Commission published its Discussion Paper and report on Equality Before the Law. The publications are as follows:

ALRC Discussion Paper 54, *Equality Before the Law*, 1993
ALRC 67, Interim: *Equality Before the Law: Women's Access to the Legal System*, 1994
ALRC 69 Part I *Equality Before the Law: Justice for Women*, 1994
ALRC 69 Part II *Equality Before The Law: Women's Equality*, 1994

4

Through the looking glass
The High Court and the right to political speech

DEBORAH CASS

THE FOLLOWING DISCUSSION is about a case that is not about women, or specifically about judicial attitudes to women. It is not about how the law deals with rape, or sexual assault or violence in the home. It is about the Constitution and free speech; what sort of speech is protected, and why. And I want to suggest to you that although this case is not about women, it has ramifications which are important for women, both as women and as members of a democratic system of government.

Free speech, like motherhood, is often taken for granted. And yet it is also rarely questioned. Judges often cite the right to speak freely as *the* critical factor separating democracies from non-democratic systems. But the slogan alone does not ensure the freedom. Courts decide which speech is free and for what reason. Australian law has to date been largely removed from this debate because it was always assumed that the common law, not the Constitution, protected free speech. That immunity may soon evaporate. In 1992 the High Court found that the Australian Constitution includes an implied right to free speech, at least in relation to political matters (the so-called Political Ad Ban case).[71] As a result, legislation prohibiting political advertising during election periods was struck down as unconstitutional.

I want to use the case as a starting point to discuss issues of free speech related to women, and to look at the way feminist legal theory might analyse the judicial attitudes in this case. I will suggest that the court has taken a very limited and potentially gender-blind approach to free speech, basing this argument on three grounds. First, the court has accepted the notion that free speech will necessarily lead to the discovery of truth. Second, it has accepted the idea that speech in the private sphere cannot be regulated. And third, it has ignored problems of access to speech, and problems of who is doing all the speaking. All three present problems for women.

But first, a brief summary of what the decision was all about. The court found that the Constitution encapsulates an essential feature of the Australian political system, namely representative democracy. Representative democracy requires elected representatives to be directly chosen by the people. Direct choice includes the right to communicate and receive information necessary for the making of that choice.

The right, the court found, is not absolute. It can be restricted, but only on two grounds. First, there must be compelling justification for the limitation. Second, the measures adopted to achieve that objective must be proportionate to the problem to be addressed. To be compelling, the reasons for restriction of free speech must be reasonably necessary in a democratic society. So legislation which prohibited broadcasting of political advertisements during election periods, subject to limited exceptions, was *prima facie* an interference with the implied constitutional guarantee.

What I want to do now is to discuss some problems with this approach and to indicate why I think they have a particular relevance for women.

First, let us consider the relationship between free speech and truth. A major justification for free speech is that it will lead to the discovery of truth. Truth and falsehood will compete in the marketplace of ideas, and truth will eventually prevail. So it is argued, in this case, that political advertising, for all its shortcomings, should not be prohibited because it furthers the pursuit of truth. Presumably true political ideas, and false, will compete in the marketplace and people will thereby be able to discern the truth; that is, which party is presenting the best program.

Is the marketplace theory adequate in relation to political advertising? Does truth always overcome falsehood in the marketplace? The Senate Select Committee which recommended the legislation thought not. It heard evidence that neither the content of advertisements nor the manner of presentation of policies and viewpoints of candidates were aimed at accuracy. Phillip Adams referred to advertisements as 'image equations [which] precluded rational political dialogue'.[72] Political ideas are often presented in disconnected and abbreviated fashion. Advertising relies largely on emotional techniques. John F. Kennedy's father, Jack Kennedy, apparently said he was going to sell John Kennedy like soap flakes, and so he did. The majority of the court however, held that the risks of trivialisation were outweighed by the greater risk to the pursuit of truth in banning all political advertisements. Only one judge found that it was:

> ... open to the Parliament to make a low assessment of the contribution made by electronic advertising to the formation of political judgments.[73]

In the light of the experience of women, one might be sceptical of the court's faith in truth's ability to outweigh falsehood, particularly in relation to representation of women. If the marketplace theory were correct and truth had won over falsehood, would women be represented the way they currently are? For example, would images of women thrilled at having chosen the right kind of margarine prevail over the reality of most women's lives— that they are just pleased they had time to buy the margarine? Would we be constantly bombarded with degrading images of women? Does the abundance of sexually explicit degrading imagery, and sexually violent imagery indicate a truer representation of women? Does the freedom to represent women in dog collars on magazine covers, or with knives pointed at their crotches in videos, facilitate the discovery of truth about women?

I am not suggesting that the High Court dealt with any of these issues, or that it would necessarily find this way in any future case. But the uncritical acceptance of the equation that 'more speech equals truth' does open up these questions.

This raises a related problem: feminists have long been concerned with the very notion that the law claims to encapsulate truth. Law claims to be based on values which are universal, which are equally true for both men and women. But over forty years ago, in *The Second Sex* (1949), Simone de Beauvoir noted that 'representation of the world ... is the work of men. They describe it from their point of view which they confuse with the absolute truth.' Law is a representation of the world which must not be confused with absolute truth. Otherwise we would forever be stuck with the law which said men who force their wives to have sex are immune from prosecution for rape. Obviously, law represents a gendered truth, rather than absolute truth. Similarly, law that says all speech must be free represents a gendered version of truth.

A feminist analysis of free speech also demonstrates that not only does the market fail to recognise some forms of speech but that it actively suppresses them. Speech is not simply a question of competition for airtime. In the view of leading feminist legal theorist, Catherine MacKinnon, women are 'silenced socially' by pornographic speech. One judge in the Political Ad Ban case maintains that it is necessary, however, to prove that some speech silences others. But as MacKinnon argues, regarding pornography, the limitation pornography places on women's right to speech is difficult to demonstrate because 'silence is not eloquent.' Likewise, here, the harm caused to the political process by muzzling those other viewpoints is virtually impossible to demonstrate empirically to the satisfaction of the policy makers and the judiciary. How can we ever know whether, for example, other groups such as farmers, women, migrants, Aborigines, are currently being silenced? The damaging effect of suppressing marginal viewpoints is hard to quantify.

My second argument is related to the court's reliance on a distinction between the public and private sphere. The court says that government cannot regulate how political messages are received because this is a private choice, outside government control. Feminists have argued that the distinction between the so-called public and private spheres is an artificial creation. And the private is also a 'sphere of social power.' If the court were to continue to adopt this distinction, relied on in the Political Ad Ban case, it may have negative consequences for women concerned with the harm caused by, for example, pornography in the so-called private sphere.

The last point I want to make relates to access to free speech. Free speech claims to be based on tolerance of all viewpoints. But this assumes that everyone has equal access to avenues of speaking. The reality is quite different. In Australia, diversity or pluralism is not a feature of our media market. Media ownership is highly concentrated. The costs of obtaining access to broadcasting are high. Justice Brennan (as he then was), quoting from the Senate Select Committee Report, notes that a lack of financial resources is an enormous factor in the amount of 'free' speech a political group is able to buy. The Australian Conservation Foundation spent just over $136 000 in its 1990 election campaign; the Forest Industry Companies Association over $1 million. Major parties spent almost half of their campaign expenditure, totalling $15 million, on television advertising in 1992. Although access is possible in theory, it is often not available in practice.

Women, as a group or as individuals, do not have the same access to speech as men. Women are under-represented in all aspects of media production and control. Women are under-represented in institutions of government, and in business—two spheres likely to be reported by the press. The only places where women are well represented, the home or community sector, are not usually seen as worthy of report. So the access women have to opportunities to speak is limited.

To sum up, then, the High Court's decision, although important for freedom of speech generally, may not benefit women. If the judicial attitude to speech continues to be followed, it could lend support to the fallacy that all speech must be tolerated because all speakers have equal access to the market to express their view. It could perpetuate the spurious justification that truth will necessarily overwhelm falsehood in the marketplace. And it could inhibit moves to regulate harmful pornography or other forms of discriminatory speech.

The slogan 'free speech', without interpretation, signifies little; and this is why judicial attitudes to the interpretation of the Constitution, even indirectly, are important to women.

5

Gender bias

Guano and administrative review

BETH WILSON

THE LEGAL SYSTEM in Australia reminds me of the steel spire which was stuck on top of the Arts Centre in Melbourne. The spire, like the law, is hierarchical and derivative, having been copied from overseas. The design of the spire has had some unintended consequences. It has an extraordinary capacity to attract seagulls, especially at night. Round and round the poor little creatures fly, mesmerised by the laser beams, pelting unwary tourists with deposits of guano.

I work in an area of the law which is at the bottom of the hierarchy—the Mental Health Review Board. All lawyers know that the law is intended to be hierarchical. This is supposed to be a good thing. We are indoctrinated into this way of thinking during our training. The High Court is at the top of the spire (where the Privy Council used to be until we came to our senses and got rid of it); we then descend a level to the State Supreme Courts, and further down we encounter the lesser County or District Courts and finally the Magistrates' Courts. But if we continue our descent even lower, to the very base of the spire, we come upon another group of players in the legal system, the Administrative Review bodies, which in turn have their own hierarchies.

At the bottom of the lower hierarchy, at street level, are the 'first tier' Administrative Boards where I have worked now for almost a decade. It is not difficult for me to recognise that I am at the lower level because there are many women working there as decision makers, and appearing as aggrieved parties seeking justice and redress for their grievances.

Now, because we are at the base of the spire, we look up to those at the top, hoping for guidance, leadership and wisdom. If our superiors do not provide us with those things, then a bad example will filter down through the system. Recent publicity about sexist comments from senior judicial figures has made very clear to the general public what we women working in the law have known for a long time. Good old-fashioned misogyny exists throughout our legal system. And for women at the base of the spire, sexist remarks make us feel just like unwary tourists receiving the unwelcome deposits of guano from those who fly high above us. Comments which are contemptuous of women place a very heavy load on us.

I do not intend to criticise only the judiciary. After all, I recognise that we have tried to make judges out of men, and that has not always been a good idea so far as women are concerned.

The law exposes women, especially women litigants, to a range of professionals who also like to indulge in guano dropping. Let me give you some real life examples of what I mean. At the Social Security Appeals Tribunal a solicitor submitted:

> My client has never worked, she just stays home and looks after her husband and seven children.

A medical expert's written report to the WorkCare Appeals Board stated:

> She is a plain unhappy looking girl of thirty eight (years) who might have been quite attractive once when young, in a slim sort of a way.

In a two-page report to an Administrative Board, a psychiatrist wrote:

> His daughter was a nice sort of a girl who appeared to be psycho-sexually suggestive.

That report dealt with an examination of a man who had injured his shoulder. His daughter had accompanied him to the examination to act as interpreter. The psychiatrist mentioned her appearance four times in the report, which was supposed to be dealing with her father's mental state.

I can never understand why medical experts in legal proceedings frequently insist on describing women in terms of their attractiveness or otherwise, their age and their weight. Many times I have received reports stating something along these lines:

> She is a plain looking middle aged woman of thirty eight (years) who is grossly obese.

The woman who appears before me usually turns out to be half my size and much better looking!

The medicos tell us that they include these comments for the purposes of identification, to ensure that they have examined the same person who is actually appearing before the Board. However, their descriptions of women do not match the way in which I would describe them.

The most important consideration, though, is just how these women must feel when they read that kind of insulting description. Remember that these medical examinations are imposed upon them by the legal system. They do not have the privilege of choosing their own doctor and must submit to an examination by a specialist chosen by another party to the proceedings, usually an insurer. Insensitive or downright offensive reporting does not assist in the therapeutic process.

Gender bias and guano dropping is generated from many sources. Some members of the Bar are particularly culpable. One has only to recall the now infamous remarks of counsel in the case of *R v. Hakopian,* where the rape of a sex industry worker was likened to 'a woman wandering through a Housing Commission car park wearing make up, mascara and a seductive mini-skirt'. According to that barrister, the community expectation in those circumstances would be 'what did she expect?'.[74] Unfortunately, similar examples of barristers being out of touch with community attitudes are all too frequent and it comes as no surprise to hear women who have been subjected to violent attacks say that the violence against them continued in the courtroom.

Justice Evatt has discussed the ways in which we might go about recognising gender bias. However, let me assure you, in my area of work, I do not have much difficulty in recognising the guano. I beg to differ from Professor Marcia Neave here, because my experience has been that gender bias is not subtle. It is all too obvious and very prolific. My fear is not that our judges are out of touch with community attitudes, but that they *reflect* them. I believe it is not unreasonable to expect that our judges will be better, not worse, nor the same, as the 'run of the mill'. After all, the positions that they hold at the top of the legal hierarchy involve responsibility as well as privilege.

We all know the problem of gender bias exists. The question is, what are we going to do about it? There is much work to be done. Teaching better and more appropriate ways of communicating to legal system professionals is, I believe, the key to solving the problem. Getting the offenders to recognise and admit that they have a problem is the hard part.

I do not want to conclude on too negative a note so I will acknowledge that there have been some significant improvements in the way that professionals speak about women.

When I first started working on Boards and Tribunals, it was common to read remarks like 'she doesn't work'. It has now become more usual to read 'she does not work in the paid work force'. There have also been some exemplary examples of senior members of the legal profession recognising that gender bias exists and being prepared to tackle it. Chief Justice Malcolm of the Western Australian Supreme Court has been quoted in a newspaper article as admitting that when he was first confronted with the notion of gender bias, he was defensive. He is now a leader in this country in confronting the problem and doing something positive about it.

There are many women, and men, working in the legal system who are distressed by gender bias. The workload in remedying the situation must be shared by men.

Those of us who work at the base of the spire, plead with those above us to set a shining example, like that of Justice Malcolm, because we would rather be bathed in enlightenment than drowned in the guano.

Postscript

It has been discovered since this paper was written that the spire of the Arts Centre in Melbourne has begun to crumble. The word is that the struts are no longer supporting the edifice and unless it is to crash to the ground the spire will have to be taken down completely and rebuilt. While I do not wish to force the metaphor too far, it is tempting to speculate about the possibilities which might arise if we subjected our legal system to a complete overhaul.

6

Working on equality before the law
The Australian Institute of Judicial Administration

JUSTICE DEIRDRE O'CONNOR

I HAVE COME TO AN understanding of the theory of sexism fairly late in my life. But, I have long been interested in what I think this conference is about; that is, human rights, and the guarantee of equality before the law. I actually believed, and still do believe, that this is provided in the Australian judicial system. It is provided by all decision makers. There are many more decision makers who may be affected by the issues raised in this conference besides judges.

I want to impart some information about the Australian Institute of Judicial Administration (AIJA) project that I am often associated with. I am part of a committee, I am its Chair and that is because, as you would expect from a legal organisation, I am the senior legal person. I was not the first person on the AIJA that has an interest in this. We are, in fact, a fairly homogenous group and we are all working together to get our project up and running, and we hope, successfully completed.

You may be aware that the AIJA has become interested, and of course involved, in two aspects of equality before the law. One of those aspects involves racial issues. Although I have no involvement in that with the AIJA, I mention it because I think that it is relevant to a consideration of matters that I want to raise later.

The other area is the area of gender. Here it is called gender bias but the AIJA probably prefers to call it gender awareness.

The Australian Institute of Judicial Administration has an important role in providing support systems for judicial administration and the judges and other members of its organisation. It is an independent organisation, made up of people in the law who get together for mutual self help. It undertakes projects involving research into sentencing practices; it looks at all the different aspects of the administration of justice; it looks at the cost; it looks at any topic relevant to the running of courts, the judges' functions and the functions of all those who are part of the judicial system. And it has seen that the question of potential bias on account of race, or potential bias because of gender, are fundamental issues in making the system operate effectively. So it was quite prepared to do what it has done in these other areas—prepare or develop programs which may be of interest to the various courts, tribunals and agencies that are members of the AIJA.

So, that is how it all started. The matter of gender was brought to us after a response to the National Strategy to deal with the question of violence against women where, as anyone who has read that report will realise, there was a great deal of criticism of the way these issues were dealt with in the judicial system. The courts were criticised by those who attended the inquiry, and the strategies which came at the end of the inquiry suggested that we ought to look at whether this was, in fact, a major problem and if so, whether we should respond to it.

It was the AIJA's response that led it to establish a committee to identify the problem and prepare materials that may be of assistance to courts and tribunals in carrying out their work and eliminating bias from their systems, if such bias existed.

I might say that this report of violence suggested that the problem of gender bias or inequality for women in the legal system was systemic. It was not just a couple of isolated incidents; it was at all levels and in all areas of the law. It was not just rape victims or a certain class of woman, and it was not just evidenced occasionally.

It should be noted that no evidence was provided apart from the anecdotal evidence of that report. But Professor Mahoney makes it quite clear that the beginning of such an uncovering in Australia through this particular report has its counterparts in all parts of the world. We are not unique in identifying this kind of problem in our society.

The AIJA's role in this project involves working with judges and decision makers to address this issue. Our first initiative was to run a seminar with Professor Mahoney; but we propose, now, with the support of a court, to develop a committee to bring in information and then develop an Australian package of materials that can be used by courts and tribunals in making their members aware, and responsive to, the issue. We have developed a strategy, and over the next half year the planned initiatives will begin to unfold.

It is not a short-term project and it is very important, when developing materials of this kind, that those people for whom they are intended, participate absolutely in the preparation. That is to say, the courts must 'own' the process. They must see that it is relevant to what they are doing. It cannot be (and of course the question of judicial independence is involved, if this were to happen) imposed by any political system. It must emanate from the courts themselves and, frankly, it could not be imposed by the AIJA, even though it is an independent organisation.

We feel that the courts themselves must examine the evidence for and the incidence of, this problem to see what ways and strategies and techniques can be developed. We can, of course, rely very heavily on Canadian experience to develop these. What is available for the judges to look at, and how the materials marshalled in sessions can be presented to judges, can be determined by a variety of means. It may be that the same kind of approach used in Canada will be suitable for some of the courts and tribunals in Australia.

We are embarking on a long journey. Our committee's job is to set it up, monitor it, and, we hope, successfully conclude it over a period of time. We will keep Australia informed. Many seem to be interested in the various steps that we are taking along the way. But I must stress that the Institute does not see this as an issue that you can produce one paper on, or have one eminent expert speak to people about and then say well, that is that then; this is not the solution to the problem. It is not a problem that can be addressed in that manner.

The members of our committee on the AIJA, the faceless people who stand behind me, include a variety of decision makers and people involved with this problem on a day-to-day basis. There is myself, Sally Brown, the Chief Magistrate of Victoria; Justice Neil Buckley of the Family Court; Steven Skihill from the Attorney-General's Department, and also the Director of Public Prosecutions in Victoria, Mr Bongiorno. I am sure we will work hard to make sure that what we present to the judiciary is relevant to them and helpful in addressing this issue.

When one is looking at the issue of gender, one must approach it in somewhat the same way as the committee I was on in New South Wales in the late 70s, looking at the reform of rape law in that State, approached their task. That is, when dealing with one issue that seems to be a problem in the system, you must be careful that you do not damage the system while you are eradicating one of its problems. I do not wish to appear to be an apologist for anything that might mitigate against equality before the law, but I do say that it does not seem to me to be sensible that one should be involved in a process of attack on institutions in circumstances where the damage to those institutions could create greater injustice in society. It is a delicate process and, I might say, it is one that needs a high level of leadership. It must come from within those very institutions. I would like to say publicly that it seems to me that the approach that has been taken both to the issue of race and gender in Western Australia, led by Chief Justice Malcolm, commends itself well to other parts of this country and to the Federal system.

It is not enough for people who do not have the role of heading an organisation or recognised body to call for things to be done and people to talk about education for judges. The leadership for addressing any problems within the judiciary or within tribunals or any other decision making bodies in the country must come from within those bodies themselves.

So I hope the AIJA courses sensitise the institutions to that and that the bodies see the wisdom of responding to criticism and challenge, as opposed to creating divisiveness which may damage the institutions in our society. I speak with some concern about that because I have recently been to the Commonwealth Law Conference in Cyprus, where I attended the Human Rights sessions and listened to other nations talking amongst themselves about human rights issues. I speak particularly of black Africa, where, when one hears the basic human rights problems and compares them with the issues that we are addressing in Australia, one has to repeat the cliché once again, that we are certainly in a 'lucky country'. Ours is a country with magnificent institutions that, whatever their deficiencies, are solid and accepted by our population, and it is a stable society. I think that whatever we are doing should be directed towards improving and developing them as opposed to weakening them and thus making them less able to respond.

7

The practicalities of working within the legal system
A magistrate's view

CHIEF MAGISTRATE SALLY BROWN

I HAVE READ THAT, when Lord Hailsham was Lord Chancellor he was asked why he was so opposed to allowing judges the freedom to make their views known publicly, through the media. He replied that they would make bloody fools of themselves. Some of you will think us perfectly able to make ourselves look like idiots by what we say on the bench without recourse to public platforms. But today I speak in this public forum as a woman, a lawyer and a magistrate.[75]

Only over the first did I have no control, and I am well aware that my voluntary assumption of the last two roles renders me suspect in many of your eyes—a situation exacerbated by the fact that, prior to becoming a magistrate, I was a barrister, and am still a member of the Victorian Bar. You will say that I am part of the system and am an apologist for it; to some extent you are right.

Lawyers and judges do not enjoy a good press. In twenty years of practice I have heard most of the jokes which rely for their punch line on the humiliation of lawyers; I know that we all call our dogs Loophole and double-cross every bridge we come to. So, at the risk of fulfilling some of your worst expectations, I will say this: you have heard how stereotypes can limit and damage women, and of the important distinction between damaging myths and stereotypes, and useful generalisations. To reach that cardinal judicial but homely virtue of fairness, the judiciary must learn to engage in a continuing process of vigilant self-examination, and in relation to issues such as gender and race, must firmly draw the distinction between destructive stereotypes and handy generalisations. But, as Fay Weldon advised her fictional niece in *Letters to Alice*, we must reform ourselves as well as the world. And we will further neither our objectives nor our credit if we impose on all judges and lawyers stereotypes of behaviour, motive or thought, which can be as ill-considered, unfair and damaging as those imposed on women.

I will put 'a magistrate's view' into context first. Most people who come before a court in Victoria will have their case heard by a magistrate. Most people sentenced to imprisonment in Victoria are sentenced by a magistrate. In 1992 the Supreme Court dealt with 49 criminal cases and the County Court, known as the major trial court, heard 275 criminal jury trials and 904 pleas of guilty. Almost every one of those 1228 cases had first been through the Magistrates' Court as committals. In that year more than 90 000 other people had their criminal cases heard and decided in the Magistrates' Court. Bear in mind that in that year, too, 396,000 cases were dealt with by the PERIN Court; that is, the largely administrative system which enables more minor offences such as traffic and speeding offences, parking infringements, and breaches of local government by-laws to be dealt with out of the courtroom unless a person elects to have a court hearing.

Out of the criminal field we dealt with the 7626 applications for orders under the *Crimes (Family Violence) Act* and the *Family Law Act*; access, custody, maintenance and property cases; over 6000 applications for criminal injuries compensation, and the 122 619 civil complaints filed in the court. I am confident that the people whose lives we affect, whether by sentences of imprisonment or other penalties, or by making or refusing to make other orders sought, think that we are members of the judiciary. So do some barristers, judges and politicians. But many do not. On Saturday night I went to the Bar Dinner and heard numerous people explain that there had been no judicial appointments since the Bar Dinner last June (1992). Apparently the eight magistrates appointed since then do not count. A number of politicians have publicly stated that the government thinks there should be more female judicial appointments, but since assuming office the present government has appointed seven magistrates, all excellent, all men.

So it is from this rather ambivalent position that I speak. A 'judge's view' might be different. Paradoxically, the very denial of the significance of the Magistrates' Court has perhaps given the Court and me the freedom to act in ways which some of our judicial brothers might think novel or radical, and may have made the transition to a court composed of men and women easier. The scrutiny is less intense. Importantly, if no less paradoxically, some of the greatest support and encouragement the court and I have received has come from those big brothers in the superior courts, and in particular from the Chief Justice and the Chief Judge.

To stereotypes. Is it true that the players in the system—lawyers, police, those already on the bench—do not want women judges or magistrates, and that the wider community does? My experience suggests that the answer is that both groups are happy for women to be appointed to the judiciary, that some people in each category take longer to get used to the idea and that sometimes we construe surprise at a novelty as criticism of a principle or rejection of change. When I was appointed Chief Magistrate I received the following letter, signed 'An Irate Citizen':

> Dear Madam,
>
> Did you know that in the Thirteenth Century they were cleverer than our politicians, saying that women, serfs, those under the age of 21, open lepers, idiots, attorneys, lunatics, deaf mutes, those ex-communicated by a Bishop and criminal persons were ineligible for the bench. That's from a book called 'The Mirror of Justice', and it is a pity the Attorney-General hasn't read it.
>
> No wonder law and order is on the decline when the biggest court in the State is headed by a radical, feminist, separatist, lesbian, man-hating shrew. You should do the decent thing and resign but people like you never do.

The 'Irate Citizen' made it clear that he or she does not want women judges. But the old lag who calls me love rather than Your Worship isn't making a political statement, nor is the lawyer who says to a witness 'Tell His Worship what happened then' either blind to my gender or being linguistically derisory. When I speak to people out of court in my position as Chief Magistrate more surprise is expressed at my height, or the fact that I am not Catholic (an in-joke) than at my sex.

In 1985 Margaret Rizkalla became the first woman magistrate in Victoria. I began a few weeks later, Linda Dessau and Jacinta Heffey the following year—and now we are fifteen. None of us would be so naive as to deny that outside the courtroom, litigants and practitioners may have blamed an unsatisfactory outcome on their bad luck in 'striking a sheila'. But in the many letters of complaint I receive from disgruntled defendants, witnesses, litigants, lawyers—and irate citizens—it is rare to find the sex of the magistrate cited as a contributing factor to the perceived injustice, and I doubt I will ever again experience the palpable frisson that ran through the Mildura Court the first day I walked on to its Bench in 1986. Only later did I learn that a previous incumbent had imposed an esoteric dress-code on women lawyers, proscribing trousers, coloured stockings and dangling earrings, and I was sporting all three.

Early on I think it was more difficult for the police to get used to the idea of female magistrates than for the lawyers. Uppity barristers and solicitors could console themselves with the notion that we weren't actually real judges, just trumped-up JPs, and the majority of lawyers who practice regularly in the Magistrates' Court aren't uppity and took it in their stride. But the police culture is still a very masculine one and many older members had been brought up with the system under which Clerks of Courts were promoted to magistrates on seniority. As no female clerk had ever been so promoted, the first woman to sit the Clerk of Courts exams only doing so in the 1970s, it was a substantial cultural change for clerks and police.

The response from at least some police was apparent in a case where a member of the force was himself charged with a criminal offence. The barrister briefed to appear for him is married to a Victorian magistrate. The case was called before another female magistrate. Shortly before lunch the barrister made a submission about his client's innocence which was knocked back. He and his client left the court for lunch, and the police client's first remark to him was 'God, what do you do with these women magistrates?'. 'You marry them', said his barrister.

As for the Clerks of Courts, they may well have had legitimate cause for concern that outsiders were taking the jobs which once would have been theirs, but I rarely felt that any of their concerns were sex-based. The very few who sneered derided our backgrounds, and with exemplary impartiality, disapproved of male and female outsiders.

What about acceptance by other magistrates? My initial concerns were ill-founded. From the outset, some of the oldest magistrates, those with carefully honed reputations as curmudgeons, opened their doors to us. Jack Caven once said to me, 'If anyone ever says to you I was against girl magistrates, it is not true', a sort of pre-emptive prior inconsistent statement objection, but once there the practical help was extraordinary. There were not and there are not tensions of that sort. But there are others.

Obviously, some magistrates, male and female, would not agree with my views on domestic violence or rape victims, or accept that unquestioned notions of gender and race can interfere with legal analysis and outcomes. Some welcome conference sessions on these things and themselves seek out speakers; others are wary of an agenda clearly labelled feminist. If a number of consecutive appointments are female there may be a rumble that women are getting the plum jobs. You will know what I mean if you have overheard the remark 'do you have to have a sex change operation to get a job around here?'. However, I have never worried too much about that since the day I overheard a response from another barrister which was 'In your case, X, I think a brain transplant might be necessary'. The fact remains that fifteen of the seventy people appointed as magistrates since 1985 are women; that is, about 21%. But around the traps I think there is a perception that it is much higher.

In summary, there has been very little resistance, in my experience, to the female magistrates as individuals. There is a resistance to the ideas which some of those magistrates express on issues such as domestic violence and the systemic nature of discrimination against women. But some men express those views too, and I can think of a number who would willingly acknowledge that their views have changed, and that part of that change is due to a change in the culture of the court, to working with women and listening to the many speakers who have attended Magistrates' Court Conferences to talk about issues such as family violence, sexual assault victims and child witnesses.

That said, I must add that workplace cultures are fragile, and can revert to old habits if leadership falters. I think that for some years female lawyers may have encountered more equality, and less discrimination, when practising as barristers or solicitors. Not for nothing have judges traditionally referred to each other, on and off the bench, as 'brothers'; they know that in that brotherhood is strength. It is important that women continue to be appointed to the court, that their skills and experience are used to best advantage and that it continues to be considered normal to have 'sisters' on the bench. If this is not done it is not only individual women who will suffer, but the system and the respect in which it is held.

A generalisation which I will quickly address here is that magistrates resist education. It is not true. The effect of discussions and seminars will vary; as with any group some will be open-minded and some defensive. There are a number of people who have spoken to groups of magistrates about their own work and the problems people experience within the court system, including women from refuges, those working with the Domestic Violence and Incest Resource Centre, Centres Against Sexual Assault, psychologists counselling rape and incest victims, workers from the Children's Hospital Sexual Assault Unit, Community Policing Squad police, interpreters and various community groups. We have budgetary constraints; my budget for this year includes $5000 for all education needs of the State's 91 magistrates, and that includes hiring a venue for our annual three-day conference in July. To bring only half the magistrates in Victoria to this conference would cost $9450. To run the five full days of continuing legal education which we undertake through the year the magistrates now voluntarily match that government contribution, paying a conference fee to raise another $5000. If governments are serious in their concerns about these important issues, they must be prepared to fund them, as developing local programs to raise awareness and produce meaningful attitudinal changes requires money.

A quick foray into another stereotype: only practising barristers should become judges. Of the seventy magistrates appointed since 1985, thirty one have come from the Bar, ten were former Clerks of Courts, ten were lawyers from offices such as the Legal Aid Commission, the Director of Public Prosecutions' Office and the Victorian Government Solicitors' Office, nine were from full- or part-time positions as magistrates in other States or members of various Tribunals and eleven were practising solicitors. Across the board,

43% of those appointments have been from the Bar, but of the women only 33%. Similarly, 15% of all appointments have been from the ranks of practising solicitors, but in the case of women the figure is 27%. The numbers are small enough for statistics to be dangerous, but it is fair to say that post-1985, magistrates, and particularly female magistrates, have come from a wide variety of backgrounds; a number had other jobs and careers before studying law; some have worked as permanent prosecutors here and overseas; some have taught everywhere from primary school to university. And western civilisation as we know it has not stopped!

A checklist of necessary judicial qualities might include: a sound knowledge of the law; a good analytical mind; common sense; personal confidence; diligence; a willingness to learn; and, very importantly, an ability to make decisions. These qualities are not found only among barristers. What is found is trial experience, which is certainly a huge help, and if people without it are appointed to trial courts, strategies will need to be developed to assist them as they acquire it.

The last generalisations I want to look at are that the judiciary should express the community view, and that the media does express it. Public opinion is often fragmentary, contradictory, volatile, based as much on myth as reality, and difficult to interpret with any degree of certainty. Most of you would say 'the community disapproves of drink-driving', but more than 12 000 members of the Victorian community were convicted of drink-driving offences last year, and they are only the ones caught. Some of those 12 000 people would assert that people who kill others should be locked up forever, but every one of them took the chance they would do just that when they turned on the ignition.

'The community wants a stop to family violence', the media asserts, but it is members of that community who perpetrate the violence, cover it up and make excuses for it. 'The community demands that no means no', but the rapists are members of the community and so are the thousands of people who believe that women who talk or drink alone, or wear anything more provocative than a hooded, ground-length mackintosh, ask for it or, if it comes to the crunch, that women are essentially duplicitous. You have heard how a way of thinking about women has become part of our culture, is institutionalised in the societal infrastructure and played out in individual acts and attitudes. These attitudes are one of the things lawyers have not monopolised; it may be tragic and infuriating, but these attitudes comprise the dominant community view. Courts must be responsive to broad social change, but people who say we must follow public opinion and the community view usually mean their opinion and their view.

Even the more responsible press expresses this ambivalence. The *Age* [in 1993] ran a series titled 'The war on women'. On Saturday's front page men confessed that their view had been that men run the world and make the decisions, and if their wives or children did not accept that—thump! The editorial denounced domestic violence. But it also deliberately distanced itself from wider considerations and expressly denied any systemic base for male violence.

> Treating violence against women as simply part of the broader issues of male oppression of women misses the point, and will therefore fail to save any women from violence.[76]

How does that fit with the actual quoted experience or the male perpetrators interviewed? And hands up anyone who agrees that wiping out all male oppression against women would not save a single woman from violence.

I have been a magistrate for eight years, and my views about many aspects of the system have changed. I am much slower to defend its institutions but still determined to work within it. Conferences like this focus attention on inequities, systemic discrimination and the need for reform. We cannot afford to be like the English judge, asked to join a law reform committee, who said: 'Reform? Good God, no. Things are bad enough as they are'.

Recently researching a paper to present to commerce graduates, I came across a poem by Carol Duffy called 'A businessman's love poem'. Its refrain was:

> A face like yours could sell a million floppy
> disks, change hardened ad men into optimists.
> You were as beautiful as low inflation,
> as tax evasion.

So let me say of this conference:

> A conference like this could launch a dozen judgeships,
> turn nostalgic lawyers into pragmatists.
> It is as natural as a witchetty-grub
> or the Melbourne Club.

Postscript

Sally Brown was appointed a Justice of the Family Court of Australia in 1994.

8

Judicial interpretation
of sex bias law

MOIRA RAYNER

T HIS IS A PAPER about change. It is about what happens when parliament decides to recognise *individual* rights because a person is a member of a disadvantaged *class*, when our laws and courts develop through remedies for individual wrongs; about providing domestic remedies for wrongs which grew from international human rights treaties; and about resolving disputes without making decisions. I am really talking about the power of a dominant culture.

I am not going to discuss the position of women in the law or sex discrimination law specifically because people with better knowledge than mine have recently written books about it, and you should read Margaret Thornton, Regina Graycar, Jenny Morgan, Rosemary Hunter and Jocelynne Scutt instead of listening to me regurgitate their opinions or research.[77] I will, instead, talk about what I know best: what it is like to administer an Act whose meaning and scope is constantly under legal challenge.

Of all the complaints I can receive, the greatest number concern sex discrimination. This is not going to go away: this financial year complaints of sex and pregnancy discrimination and of sexual harassment have increased between 27% and 52% on last year.[78] Not all of these are made by women: about one third of all sex discrimination complaints and 5% of sexual harassment complaints are made by men, but women make relatively few complaints about other kinds of discrimination.

The Federal and State anti-discrimination laws I administer provide 'informal' means of resolving complaints about discrimination. They were developed because of the recognition that some groups are relatively disadvantaged in our community. The right not to be treated less favourably because of sex, race, religion, disability and other reasons is an international human rights obligation undertaken by Australia. Such obligations are not, *per se*, enforceable in Australia. From time to time we enact domestic laws to implement them, such as the Commonwealth *Sex Discrimination Act 1984*.[79] All the mainland Australian States and Territories have also enacted anti-discrimination laws as the Victorian Government did in 1977, enacting the *Equal Opportunity Act* and creating my statutory Office.[80]

These laws are all different but share common features, such as creating a statutory Commissioner to receive and resolve complaints as well as to promote equal opportunity generally; and exemptions selected for policy reasons, such as freedom of religion (such as exempting the appointment of priests from sex discrimination laws) or allowing 'special programs' to remedy disadvantage which might otherwise be discriminatory (e.g. health programs for migrants).

These laws do not provide ordinary remedies, such as the right to sue for damages, or to prosecute for an offence. We know that people who feel themselves marginalised do not easily use traditional dispute resolution processes, such as courts and lawyers. The parliamentary drafters of anti-discrimination law meant to establish soft, informal and accessible processes. What has happened is the formalisation of the processes, legal challenges to jurisdiction and complaint handling procedures, and Supreme, Federal and High Court reviews and appeals. These are now significant features of anti-discrimination law. Lawyers are involved in most public hearings and increasingly in the conciliation phase of complaint handling.

The first step is unfamiliar to our common law courts because a complaint must be made to the Commissioner so that he or she can try to resolve it by conciliation.

This model requires:
* impartiality—the Commissioner does not have the function to apportion blame or determine guilt; and
* confidentiality—every effort can be made in good faith during conciliation to explore resolution by consent and without risk that it will be used to the detriment of a party if the case goes to a hearing.

It also requires informality, but within a structure which provides a 'real' remedy if the soft processes should fail. This is a tribunal with determinative power, which is available once the Commissioner, at the request of the complainant, has decided to stop trying.

The whole complaint handling process was meant to be informal, non-adversarial and low key. This is not how Australian litigation generally works. Typically, anti-discrimination laws require only that a complaint be 'in writing' (no form required). The specialist tribunals have lay members, the rules of evidence do not generally apply to them (for example, the Victorian Equal Opportunity Board must only act 'fairly and according to the substantial merits of the case') and, typically, permission is required if someone wants to be legally represented.

But these laws have been shaped by the adversarial system they work within, and by the training, values and assumptions of those who make them work. Once, Commissioners for Equal Opportunity and their equivalents were often social workers; today, they are nearly all lawyers. Lawyers have been involved in the tribunals, the conciliation of complaints, and in advising parties from the beginning. They have changed the law by their presence.

I will demonstrate how courts, lawyers and the tradition of the common law have contributed to the mutation of the complaints process by looking at their approach to conciliation, 'special programs', the philosophy of the Victorian *Equal Opportunity Act*, and to my administration of the Act.

Procedural formality

The courts have tended to characterise a conciliator's role in natural justice terms—that is, having a duty to give parties an opportunity to know what is alleged against them and to reply and to be 'judged' by a disinterested person.[81] In one Federal Court case, *Koppen v. The Commissioner for Community Relations,* Spender J said the rules of 'natural justice' applied to a conciliator who had convened a compulsory conference.[82]

I do not think this is necessary or appropriate. Under most Australian anti-discrimination laws conciliation is confidential, consensual, cannot result in findings of guilt or innocence, and conciliators have no powers other than to require that parties attend in some circumstances. I agree that conciliators must be 'impartial', but for quite a different reason: genuine conciliation depends on the participants' trust and the perception of neutrality.

The reception, investigation and conciliation of complaints has become formal in many important respects. In my own jurisdiction this has been particularly so since a decision of the Victorian Supreme Court in 1990, in the *Nestlés* case.[83]

In this case, Vincent J was asked to find that the Equal Opportunity Board did not have jurisdiction to hear an unresolved complaint referred to it by the Commissioner because the complainant's letter to the Commissioner did not disclose unlawful discrimination. The complainant had given detailed particulars of the complaint to the Board after 'the complaint' had been dealt with by the Commissioner, but the judge decided that the Board's right to proceed with a hearing depended entirely on that first letter, the document referred by the Commissioner to the Board as 'the complaint' on which conciliation efforts began. Though he agreed that such documents should not be treated as if they were a formal pleading, he felt that it was a matter of 'essential fairness' that no person should be subject to the processes and coercive powers of a statutorily created authority unless there was, at the outset, a sufficient basis for initial intervention.

The coercive authority of the Commissioner is basically just the power to call for information and to call meetings of the affected parties with the Commissioner and with each other.

Once this decision was published it caused the Commissioner immediately to consider the quality of decisions at the point of receiving a complaint. All that the Act requires is a 'written complaint'. If that document is technically deficient it might be successfully challenged before the Board or on appeal, or even when the Commissioner gives notice of the complaint to the Respondent. In either case, if the judge was right, a legally significant decision has to be made. If the Commissioner is to remain impartial, he or she cannot draft the complaint, or drum up evidence to support it. Nonetheless, the Commissioner must be sure that on its face the complaint alleges unlawful discrimination. It might be that new information comes about through the investigation process. Proper scrutiny of each complaint necessarily delays conciliation and could be counter-productive to a quick and informal and effective response to a complaint.

I have a duty to try every reasonable effort to resolve complaints by conciliation. I have an unreviewable discretion not to continue to deal with a complaint which is 'frivolous, vexatious, misconceived or lacking in substance'—unreviewable, because rejection on these grounds entitles a complainant to require a public hearing—and a reviewable discretion to extend the time for making a complaint beyond the twelve-month limitation period.

The *Nestlé* case was alleged to justify the imposition of 'natural justice' and other duties to constrain the whole of my complaint handling in an application to the Supreme Court in 1991/92: in *Mercedes-Benz (Australia) Pty Ltd v. The Commissioner for Equal Opportunity*[84] (September 1992) the respondent employer obtained an interim injunction to prevent my conciliator calling even a voluntary conference. A woman who had already applied for relief against 'unjust dismissal' in the Victorian Industrial Relations Commission (IRC) complained to my office about sexual harassment at work more than 12 months earlier. Time was extended for lodging the complaint beyond the twelve-month period, observing the rules of procedural fairness, for 'good cause', giving written reasons.

The employer promptly sought to review not only this decision but also the 'decision' that the complaint was capable of being resolved by conciliation, evidenced by the appointment of a conciliator, in part because it was claimed that the subject matter and remedies in the IRC and under my Act were virtually identical. It was also claimed that I was under a duty to act fairly, which the Supreme Court could review, from the moment of reception of a written complaint. The appeal failed, Haynes J finding that the relevant facts and remedies were essentially different, that there appeared to be no risk of conflicting decisions from the Equal Opportunity Board and the IRC; but the ground that the court should review the Commissioner's decision to try to conciliate the complaint was not argued on appeal.

There have been other recent efforts to review a range of my duties and discretions and the possibility of such challenges is a constant intrusion in the conciliation process.[85] One of the last, a review of reasons for extending time for lodging a complaint by one day, was soundly rejected last month, Ormiston J saying that the hearing should proceed without a multitude of interim challenges, which, hopefully, is a signal that these approaches will merely be expensive, not desirable.[86]

The defeat of special programs

In Victoria there has been some lack of success in applying the statutory exemptions to benefit women as a disadvantaged group. In one case, McDonald J decided that the closure of a Council pool on one night out of seven for a 'women only' night, which the Council had done for six years, discriminated against the recreational use of the pool by men[87] (since the pool was not being used for 'sport' the Council could not rely on the specific exemption for sex-segregated 'sport' in the Act).

In another, the Equal Opportunity Board itself found that the University of Melbourne's closure of the gymnasium 'light weights' room to men for a few hours of women-only time during the week, to promote women's health, was not a 'program designed to remedy disadvantage' contemplated by Section 39(f) of the Act.[88] The University, it would seem, led considerable expert evidence in relation to women's health needs, but did not demonstrate that it had devised a 'program' other than closing the light weights room. Most recently, in *City of Brunswick: Re Application for Exemption from provisions of Equal Opportunity Act 1984*[89] the Board declined to grant a highly contentious application for an exemption for 'women only' time at the Brunswick Council's pool.[90] The outcome of these cases is that, to obtain the benefit of an exemption or exception is not, therefore, a matter of good intentions, but one which requires strategic legal planning.

Philosophical approaches to anti-discrimination law

These, and other judicial or quasi-judicial decisions raise squarely the issue of the philosophy behind the Act, and whether the philosophy underpinning the legal system prevents its realisation. Take, for example, the Victorian Supreme Court decision in *Arumugam*.[91]

Fullagar J dismissed a complaint of race discrimination by a selection panel in spite of finding that the panel was racially biased, because he believed it was necessary to prove intention to discriminate. Most discriminators have no awareness or intent, and indirect discrimination, of course, is measured by its impact, not by intention or motive. Fortunately, though the *Arumugam* decision stood for five years, every other judge has managed to distinguish or avoid it, which is surely a triumph of common sense.

Judges have significant discretion in interpreting anti-discrimination law. Discrimination concerns 'unfairness' or 'unreasonableness' or 'detriment' relative to others in similar circumstances. Judges can only exercise discretion according to established legal principle and also their own understanding not only of the law, but of what it is meant to achieve. This turns on their opinions and experience of what is proper and how people ought to relate to one another.

In a 1991 decision of the Victorian Supreme Court, Marks J described his view of the purpose and scope of the Act with remarkable clarity, even some feeling. The Act was

> … a piece of well-intentioned legislation having the purpose of reducing tensions in the community, promoting fairness and reducing the operation of prejudice …',

which was not meant, though the Act was far from clear, to prevent someone dismissing an employee

> … where his or her activities (even if political) were directed against the interests of his or her employer even to the point of wreaking its, his or her destruction … the law [he said] is careful to ensure that wide and unrealistic latitude is not given to such language so as to sanction the exercise of power in a way which upsets the balance intended by the legislature to be kept. It must be obvious that unless the law is strictly observed by those entrusted under the Act to apply its provisions and its language afforded a meaning consonant with the fair disposition of justice between accuser and accused, the community is in danger of being visited by a fearful engine of oppression.[92]

Speaking as either the engine-driver or, according to some, the stoker, I perceive that it is not easy to determine the 'balance intended by the legislature to be kept', and in doing so a court is exercising a virtually unfettered discretionary judgment. I do not have to make those decisions, and 93% of all complaints are resolved without a public hearing through alternative dispute resolution processes. For the 7% proceeding to a hearing, however, someone will make an assessment of the facts and the law, and where there is a discretion to be exercised it is shaped by the belief system and experiences of the decision maker on a case-by-case basis.

The High Court has, since the cases I have mentioned were decided, redirected the Victorian Supreme Court as to how it should approach the interpretation of the Act in light of the purpose of the legislation in the 'scratch tickets' case, *Waters v. Public Transport Corporation*.[93]

In that case the then Government had successfully argued in the Supreme Court that the Public Transport Corporation could lawfully discriminate against people with disabilities if directed to do so by the Minister, and raised a number of highly technical legal arguments on the interpretation of the *Equal Opportunity Act*, including an argument that even indirect discrimination had to be intentional. Mason and Gaudron JJ pointed out that:

> ... the principle that requires the particular provision of the Act must be read in the light of its statutory objects is of particular significance in the case of legislation which protects or enforces human rights. In construing such legislation the courts have a special responsibility to take account of and give effect to the statutory purpose ... In the present case, the statutory objects ... include, among other things, 'to render unlawful certain kinds of discrimination and to promote equality of opportunity between persons of different status.' It would, in our view, significantly impede or hinder the attainment of the objects of the Act if s. 17 (1) were to be interpreted as requiring an intention or motive on the part of the alleged discriminator that is related to the status or private life of the person less favourably treated. It is enough that the material difference in treatment is based on the status or private life of that person.

The Commissioner's role in promoting an appropriate interpretation of the Act[94]

The legislation intended to protect human rights is constantly redefined by legal challenges in courts and tribunals accustomed to different codes that are not necessarily familiar with or comfortable with its form and purpose. The result has not only been increased formalism, but increased legal involvement in the conciliation process as well as in tribunals and courts, which was not originally intended.

The Commissioner may not have, as I do not have, a statutory right to be heard in cases concerning the interpretation of the Act which is any greater than a member of the public, though he or she is responsible for its administration.

Recently I obtained leave from the Equal Opportunity Board to be heard on the interpretation of my 'victimisation' provisions in *Commissioner for Equal Opportunity v. Equal Opportunity Board & Ors.*[95] If the respondent's argument succeeded it would exclude complaints of 'victimisation' by employees or officers of a corporation, or behaviour which was not in itself being sex, race or other prohibited discrimination. In the interests of facilitating the apparent purpose of the provision, I argued for a broader interpretation, which did not persuade the Board. As I had no right to a remedy, since I was not a party to the complaint, my application for judicial review in the Supreme Court failed (with, of course, costs).

There is a public interest in the Commissioner, rather than a particular party, promoting a proper interpretation of the Act which benefits all Victorians. The issue was particularly important to the Commissioner because the *Nestlé* case suggests the possibility of jurisdictional challenges to the complaint at any point, and increased formalism in my processes.

Ormiston J reminded me, however, that the decisions of the Board are of no binding effect and that I may, until the Supreme Court rules otherwise, ignore them. Such is not, of course, my practice. He pointed out that:

> The decision of that Board on that occasion does not constitute a precedent in the sense properly understood in the law. For it to be binding in any way, a decision must be the judgment of a superior court of record. It is unfortunate that various publishers have chosen to publish 'reports' (as they purport to call them) of decisions of tribunals in circumstances where those decisions can have no binding effect, not merely upon courts of law obliged to consider the same provisions, but upon boards or tribunals in the same jurisdiction. They may be interesting to those who appear frequently before the Board, and of course I would not deny the interest of the Commissioner, in the general sense of the term, in knowing what is done from time to time by that Board, but if she is of the opinion that the Board was wrong then she should act accordingly, and the Board, and ultimately this court, will say whether she was right or wrong in holding that opinion—but only if the matter comes before the court in a manner which should be determined by the court as a proper dispute between parties who have a right to be heard.

Naturally, as a lawyer, I understand this no doubt technically correct statement of the law, but it does not address the reality of the situation, and the fact that both the Commissioner and the public would prefer that anti-discrimination law was not uncertain, and to avoid frequent Supreme Court challenges, which no one can afford. It is particularly inappropriate that individual complainants risk considerable legal costs to clarify poorly drafted law or errors of law made by tribunals, at their own expense.[96]

Margaret Thornton devotes a chapter in her 1990 book, *The Liberal Promise*, to 'The legal culture and the reproduction of inequality'.[97] Her thesis is that equal opportunity laws and tribunals around Australia have been captured by the formality, ritualism and hierarchical authority of the traditional legal system. In terms of legal procedures there is little visible difference between the proceedings of the Equal Opportunity Board and any other court. They are adversarial, and there is little use of the inquisitorial powers anticipated by the Act. It seems most likely, as she says, that employing legal practitioners has shaped the tribunals' procedure, to the confusion of the unrepresented complainant:

> While the legislation constitutes a fertile field for respondents and their lawyers, the casuistry of lawyers is likely to leave an unrepresented complainant totally bemused when that person knows that he or she has a substantive complaint of discrimination but is defeated by formalism at the threshold. [98]

That view has certainly been expressed to me.

For much the same reason, the considerable number of jurisdictional challenges which choke the unauthorised reports that plague Ormiston J in this area of law have changed the quality of the conciliation process.

These remarks do not mean that I believe that there is no place for lawyers, the common law tradition, or the traditional courts in the administration of anti-discrimination law, nor am I an uncritical supporter of informal court procedures. There is a very sound argument to be made for adopting clear and established procedures in tribunal settings. Clarity and formality about who stands where and speaks when, *provided that it is equally obvious to and useable by lay people and lawyers, and does not become an end in itself,* offers a structure for making sense of the extraordinary activity called judicial decision making, which has such important legal consequences for ordinary people. Informality easily slips into unspoken conventions which are equally exclusive and forbidding. In many respects the concept of informality seems attractive to those who are already secure in the belief that discretions will be exercised beneficially: the reasonably well-educated, employed and respected.[99] People who are marginalised for reasons of class, colour, language or minority culture do not share this confidence. It is more important for them to know that the law prohibits discrimination; that the rules prohibiting discrimination are clear, that their rights and responsibilities are clearly identifiable, and that they can be enforced.

I am, however, committed to informal, conciliatory and free dispute resolution by the people, for the people, outside the courts. This is achieved by a workable, informal, prompt and accessible conciliation process, free from the harrying of jurisdictional and procedural challenge, and adequately resourced to be prompt, informal, and palpably fair. In the 1990s these ideals are imperfectly realised.

The nature of the Australian legal tradition has diminished the informality and effectiveness of the complaints process adopted by anti-discrimination law. There are three things that will make it work:

The *first* is legislation which is drafted in plain English and explicitly based on a community commitment to protect human rights, which will direct judicial officers who might be required to interpret it, how to do so, to give effect to their purpose;

The *second* is the establishment of accessible, affordable, informal, efficient and effective mediation, conciliation or alternative dispute resolution services with clear responsibilities and the capacity to achieve the ends of anti-discrimination law; the protection of human rights, the promotion of equal opportunity and to eliminate the kinds of discrimination which we know to be so destructive. This means clear legislation and proper resourcing and

The *third* is appointing judges, or informing or educating existing judges, who interpret anti-discrimination law, so that these women and men are:

- conscious that the exercise of their considerable discretions is shaped by their own experiences and upbringing;
- able to distinguish between their own world views, opinions and prejudices and the cold equations of the law, or at least able to question their own assumptions; and
- personally sensitive to the experience of discrimination, the effect it has on the individual, and on the community.

It is not unachievable, if the community wills.

Postscript
Changes to the Victorian *Equal Opportunity Act*

Since this paper was delivered in 1993 the Victorian *Equal Opportunity Act*, and its interpretation, has undergone, and is about to undergo further, significant amendments and development.

1   On 1 March, 1994 amendments to the Victorian *Equal Opportunity Act* abolished the position of the Commissioner for Equal Opportunity. It was replaced with a five person Commission, including a Chief Conciliator responsible for the day to day administration of the Office of the Commission but accountable to the Commission for the performance of her functions, and subject to the provision of the Public Sector under the *Management Act 1992* (the Commissioner was an independent statutory officer and not so subject).

2   Among the significant changes to the way in which complaints must be handled are:
   - the imposition of time limits within which complaints must be conciliated, failing which they can be referred without conciliation to a public hearing before the Equal Opportunity Board;
   - respondents acquiring the powers in certain circumstances to bypass conciliation entirely and engage in adversarial proceedings before the Equal Opportunity Board;
   - requirements that the Commission consider applications to strike out the complaints on the basis of their lacking substance or for other reasons, applications to extend the time within which complaints can be made, and that the Commission consider any complaint about the way in which conciliation has been handled, by the Chief Conciliator;

- empowering the Attorney-General to direct the Commission not to conciliate any complaint, on the grounds of its public significance, and to refer it directly to the Equal Opportunity Board for a public hearing; and
- enabling a party to legal proceedings before the Equal Opportunity Board to seek an order for costs against an unsuccessful party. These costs are to include the costs of being involved in the proceedings, which appears to amount to an indemnity rather than the usual 'costs following the event' requirement of civil courts. (No other equal opportunity tribunal has such a clause.)

3   In 1995 there were other changes in the grounds upon which complaints may be made. The *Equal Opportunity Act* was repealed and re-enacted to include age, lawful sexual activity and physical appearance as grounds for complaints of discrimination as a result of the Victorian Government's third review of the *Equal Opportunity Act* in as many years (by the Victorian Law Reform Commission in 1991 [the Commission was abolished in 1992], by the Scrutiny of Acts and Regulations Committee of the Victorian Parliament (October 1993) and a Government appointed committee).[100]

4   A decision of the Victorian Supreme Court in August 1994 has demonstrated the effect of the decision of the High Court in *Waters v. Public Transport Corporation* (1991). Two Aboriginal students complained under the Victorian Equal Opportunity Act that the effect of closing the Northland Secondary College, a school with a significantly disadvantaged student population of whom between fifty five and sixty two students were Aboriginal, had been to deprive them of all opportunity of an education because of their unique cultural disadvantages as Aboriginals and was in breach of the indirect discrimination provisions of the Act. They claimed that they could not meet the conditions of accessing education on the changed terms on which education was now offered to them, without a Northland College in the State education system. This they said was indirect racial discrimination.

The Victorian Supreme Court found that the *Equal Opportunity Act* must be interpreted in accordance with its purposes, as described by the High Court in Waters, to protect and promote the human rights of those who had been identified by the legislation as likely to be disadvantaged. The *Equal Opportunity Act* had, in effect, given the Equal Opportunity Board, though it lacked any fiscal accountability, the right to adjudicate between the 'competing' claims of financial concerns of the Government, and individual claims and aspirations. In other words, in some circumstances those individual claims might be found to be more important than the Government's financial responsibilities, under the indirect discrimination provisions of the Act.

The Supreme Court also said that s. 17(5) of the Act, which defines indirect discrimination, could properly be interpreted, as the Board had done, to allow an individual who was no longer able to access services which had at one time been available to him or her, but had been reduced because of government cut-backs, to make a claim for direct discrimination. If the services had been accessible to that person prior to the alteration and no longer were accessible, because of the person's membership of one of the disadvantaged groups targeted by the Act, that change in the delivery of those services would trigger the operation of s. 17(5). If the Board did not decide the government's concerns were reasonable, in some circumstances delivery of services at a current particular (accessible) level could amount to a guaranteed minimum of services.

5   I am no longer Victoria's Commissioner of Equal Opportunity, but became a consultant in discrimination law to national law firm Dunhill Madden Butler, and a part-time Human Rights and Equal Opportunity Commissioner in 1994.

9

Why should women be appointed to the Bench?

MAGISTRATE JELENA POPOVICH

IN THIS PAPER, I want to use my experience as a magistrate—picking up on issues, making *ex tempore* judgments, basically flying by the seat of my pants—to discuss some of the issues raised by others in this conference.

Firstly, I would like to pick up on a comment by Marcia Neave (at this Conference) about this being the first time issues relating to women and the law have been addressed. I remember that Monash University hosted a Women and Law Conference in 1977 which, as far as I was concerned, shaped me. It helped develop some of my then embryonic ideas and it also made me realise that I was not alone in the Law School—that there were other like-minded women who later became my good friends. It is gratifying that the issues covered in that Women and Law conference back in 1977, which then seemed to be tainted with the epithet of being a bit ratbaggish, are those same issues now not only recognised, but given prominence for the importance they hold. It is wonderful that they are all being addressed in this conference, albeit at a much more sophisticated level.

I have decided to address the question 'why should women be appointed to the Bench?' We all seem to have been accepting that it is a truism that women should be appointed to the Bench. Well, why is this so? Sally Brown gave the statistics about the number of women on the Magistrates' Bench in Victoria. There are no women on any other judicial Bench in Victoria. We actually have about fourteen women magistrates now. I could be corrected about this, but I believe that is the greatest percentage of women on any Bench in Australia. I feel very privileged to be part of that group of women and I also feel privileged to be part of that group of magistrates.

One of the great things about being one of the larger group of women on the Bench is that, apart from our own interpersonal relationships, we are actually able to play a very direct educative role with our brothers on the

Bench. One of the things that occurs is that we are able to discuss matters of importance with our brother magistrates on a fairly open basis. Many matters engender heated, but stimulating, discussions between the female and the male magistrates. I think we women have been performing an ongoing educative role. My point is, I do not think it is sufficient to appoint one or two token women to the Bench. I think if we are going to do it, it has to be done in numbers, so the women together can pursue that educative function. There has been some research undertaken by Kathy Laster and Roger Douglas, which I endorse. They have written an article entitled 'Women magistrates—And now for something completely different'.[101] In it they state:

> It appears that at least one reason female appointees have been accepted is not that they have been willing to become more like men, but because over time the males on the bench have become less stereotypically male.

Their conclusion is that the appointment of women is now regarded as positively beneficial to the Magistrates' Court jurisdiction.[102] My final quote from that article, which I commend to you all, is that

> … the increasing number of women on the bench demonstrates the capacity of the law to adapt and change to meet new social conditions.[103]

The relatively successful integration of women into the lower courts is a concrete rebuttal of those who would keep women out on the grounds that they cannot do the job, or on the more subtle basis that they simply would not be accepted yet.

I come from a working class, migrant family. One of the things that I remember vividly as I was growing up was my mother saying to me, 'whenever you need a professional, go and see a woman. If you have got to go to the doctor or a specialist, go and see a woman. They have got to be ten times better than the men to get the job'. My mother's humble advice certainly reflects what I think is a fairly accurate statement, and it is something I have always adopted myself. Another reason I think it is important to have women on the Bench, is that it gives us prominence. It means people have to deal with women who are in a position of power and see that we can do the job capably and competently. This means that we can break down some of the remaining male bastions.

This year, I am the Coordinating Magistrate at Prahran Magistrates' Court and I have had to deal with many different members of the public and representatives of organisations, and they are all surprised to see a woman in that position. I have had some difficulty dealing with the police, because the police still have preconceived ideas about what women are like, and they get a real shock when they realise I can get things done. I think it is important that more women are appointed to positions where they can put on a public face and show what they are capable of doing.

This is may sound really banal, and a bit embarrassing too, but I think it is important for us to be role models for other women in the profession, and in the community. I can remember, when Sally Brown and Margaret Rizkalla were appointed to the Bench, the sheer elation that my friends and I experienced at those events. I get that sense when young women appear before me. They have something to strive for, and they know it is achievable. That is incredibly important for the upcoming generations of young women.

I think that the public has accepted women in the judiciary very readily, but there just seems to be a little bit of resistance to us by those who make the appointments. I don't particularly understand why. Perhaps I should ask, what are those people who make the appointments afraid of? Are they afraid that they will become feminised like the magistracy has? Are they afraid that we will show them up by being more capable than they are—in the way of the example given by my mother? Or are they worried about the shift of power? I am somewhat concerned about why it is so difficult to have women appointed to the Bench. I think there is an enormous amount of talent out there that can be drawn on.

My concluding remark is that I am a little bit of a spokesperson for non-English speaking people too, and the comments that I have made about the importance of having women on the Bench, in my view, similarly apply to having people from non-English speaking backgrounds and indigenous people on the Bench as well. We have got to be a representative Bench.

Postscript

Since the conference in 1993, a number of women have been appointed to the Bench in Victoria. Currently there are three sitting on the Family Court Bench, one on the Supreme Court Bench, three on the County Court Bench, one on the Court of Appeal Bench and there are fifteen magistrates.

10

Sex discrimination legislation and Australian legal culture

ROSEMARY HUNTER

T HIS PAPER PICKS UP from Moira Rayner's remarks on the judicial interpretation of sex bias law. She discusses the ways in which dominant cultures affect interpretation of legislation and she gave a number of examples of that particular process from the Victorian Supreme Court.

I want to identify two aspects of the dominant legal culture that affect interpretation of sex discrimination legislation. First of all there is the context, or the lack of a context, for the legislation. In Australia we have no, or extremely limited, constitutional guarantees of equality. By comparison, in the United States and Canada, the existence of constitutional equality guarantees provides the context for the interpretation of sex discrimination legislation, and in fact the two areas, the Constitutional equality guarantees and the legislative equality guarantees, tend to be mutually reinforcing.

Australia, on the other hand, is like the United Kingdom, without constitutional guarantees of equality and so without that kind of interpretative context. However, even in the United Kingdom they are now feeling the influence of the European Court of Justice's human rights jurisprudence, and that is having a very beneficial effect on the interpretation of sex discrimination law there. We remain without that kind of interpretative context for our sex discrimination legislation. Secondly, there is no common law tradition of protection against discrimination. Instead, what we have are common law traditions of protection of freedom of contract, and protection of managerial prerogatives. Those two common law traditions in fact militate against the kinds of things that sex discrimination legislation is trying to do.

The second aspect of the dominant legal culture which affects the interpretation of sex discrimination legislation is the personnel who do the authoritative interpreting; that is, at superior court level. The judicial standpoint is generally characterised by a lack of experience, either of discrimination or of practising in the jurisdiction. The discrimination jurisdiction is a relatively new one and people on the bench are unlikely to have had any experience even of practising in the jurisdiction. Though there are now numbers of lawyers who have practised in that jurisdiction they are relatively junior. And so we end up with a judiciary to whom the law often appears to make no sense.

There are a number of effects of these aspects of the interpretive climate. First of all, as Moira Rayner (in this Conference) pointed out very well, there is hostility towards, or lack of sympathy for, the legislation, and that is manifested in restrictive interpretations of particular provisions; in the judicial tendency to treat discrimination as if it were a criminal offence, requiring a higher standard of proof; the making of dismissive comments about the legislation encouraging people to take technical jurisdictional points; and a monotonous succession of appeals by respondents upheld at Supreme Court level. All of that has an impact on what happens at the tribunal level.

Beth Wilson (in this Conference) also made some extremely pertinent points about the court hierarchy. Equal opportunity tribunals are also living in fear, in many ways, of being 'slapped down' by the higher courts, thereby making the complainant worse off. A complainant who wins at tribunal level is in an awful position if the unsuccessful respondent then appeals to the Supreme Court and the appeal is upheld. The complainant is left with enormous legal costs and is certainly traumatised by the experience as well. This leads to highly defensive decision making at the tribunal level, increased formality, and so on. The net effect is that we lose many of the benefits of having a specialist tribunal in the first place. The legislation is set up on the sound basis that there is a need for a specialist tribunal to interpret it, but if that specialist tribunal is then being 'terrorised' by its superior court, it has little scope for manoeuvre, little scope for constructive interpretation of the legislation. In her book, *The Liberal Promise: Anti-Discrimination Legislation in Australia,* Margaret Thornton notes that the maintenance of a right of appeal through the traditional court structure acts as a powerful means of ensuring that tribunals act in conformity with accepted judicial norms.[104]

The second effect of the dominant interpretive culture is the interpretation of standards such as reasonableness. Professor Kathleen Mahoney (at this Conference) raised the issue of reasonableness in a criminal law context. It also comes up in the discrimination context. For example, in deciding whether practices that have an adverse impact on women are reasonable in indirect discrimination and in determining many of the defences to discrimination, the concept of reasonableness is employed. That standard tends to be interpreted from a dominant perspective; for example, if you have to weigh up the comparative importance of eliminating discriminatory practices and the profitability of a business, how do you decide? It is a similar issue to land rights. If you have to weigh up the importance of the economic benefits versus the importance of redressing past discrimination, producing justice for a particular group, how do you decide? There has certainly been enough critical and feminist scholarship on standards such as reasonableness to convince us that there is no self-evident, common sense, consensus view about what is 'reasonable'.[105] Obviously, the judgment is going to depend upon the position from which the question is viewed.

Feminist scholars have made the further point that standards such as reasonableness are themselves gendered. In Western Enlightenment consciousness, reason and rationality are highly valued characteristics whose gender associations are male. By contrast, discrimination is often characterised as an emotive issue; that is, female-associated and less highly valued. So within that linguistic hierarchy it is clear that rational managerial decision making will always take priority over the elimination of emotional discrimination.

If we combine that analysis of language with an analysis of power relations, we arrive at the notion of a hierarchy of credibility. The social tendency for definitions of reality projected by people in positions of authority to be accepted in preference to those of their subordinates means, for example, that an argument presented by an employer who speaks from an institutional viewpoint is more believable and credible than an argument presented by one disaffected, grudge-bearing employee. A good reported example of that particular process is given, I think, in the *Styles* case, which was decided by the full court of the Federal Court.[106] That case contains a decision on the reasonableness element of indirect discrimination.

The full Federal Court placed a great deal of weight on the reasons given for the appointment of a male to the position that was in question because he had a particular substantive grading. The court chose to ignore the evidence that had been presented about past discrimination in the particular government department, about the overt and covert barriers to the advancement of women in that department, and stated instead that the grading enjoyed by this man arose from 'the meritorious use of merit and ability'. The way in which things had always been done and the way the workplace had to be organised prevailed. The court made barely a reference to the discriminatory effect of the particular condition that was in question.

The third effect of the dominant interpretive culture is manifested in the interpretation of special measures or affirmative action provisions in sex discrimination legislation. I think we have reached the point where it is something of a lottery as to whether any given program or arrangement that has been designed to benefit women by excluding men will be found to be covered by the legislative exceptions or not.[107] That is not a very certain or comfortable position for women's organisations or special programs to be in.

There are situations where the Australian Industrial Relations Commission, for example, has had to deal with sex discrimination arguments in National Wage Cases,[108] in submissions that have been put by women about pay equity,[109] in arguments about the need for affirmative action measures to be included in union rules,[110] in areas where there are exceptions in the discrimination legislation and an issue has been litigated through the Industrial Relations Commission.[111] There has been considerable ignorance displayed about concepts of sex discrimination and equality, and that leaves some doubt about the fate of the recently enacted amendments to the *Sex Discrimination Act* (Cwlth) and *Industrial Relations Act* (Cwlth), which give the Federal industrial bodies much greater responsibility for preventing discrimination, for example in dealing with complaints that awards are discriminatory, in reviewing awards, approving certified agreements and enterprise flexibility agreements, ensuring equal remuneration for work of equal value, adjudicating on alleged unfair dismissals, and in performing functions generally.[112] On its past record, the Industrial Relations Commission is not well equipped to make decisions on these issues without some rapid judicial education. One hopeful sign is the appointment of Deirdre O'Connor, a judge who has some experience with judicial education, as President of the Industrial Relations Commission.

The English feminist legal theorist Nicola Lacey has noted:

> The male domination of the legal forum in terms of its personnel; the male domination of the legal system in terms of the composition of the legislature and powerful interest groups; and the construction of disputes in individual terms and their resolution through a closed system of reasoning.

In this context, she argues,

> ... doubts must arise as to whether the legal forum really represents a useful place in which to attempt to ... seek concrete improvements in the treatment of women in our society.[113]

It draws a fairly grim conclusion from the evidence of what has happened in the actual procedures by which sex discrimination legislation has been litigated.

So what strategies may be adopted to deal with these problems? It is clear that we need to create a climate for the constructive interpretation of the legislation:

- *Judicial education, including education of Industrial Relations Commissioners.* Issues dealing with sex discrimination and equality should be an item in any program, both as to what the legislation is about and as to increased self consciousness in determining matters such as reasonableness.

- *Broaden the range of experience represented on the Bench.* In this context it is worth noting Justice Mary Gaudron's important contribution to discrimination jurisprudence from her position on the High Court.
- *In Victoria we could allow appeals from the Equal Opportunity Board directly to the Appeal Division rather than to a single judge of the Supreme Court.* That reduces the possibility of hitting a thoroughly unsympathetic judge. It has been the experience in New South Wales, where appeals are taken directly to the Court of Appeal, that after a period of time the Equal Opportunity Tribunal's decisions have begun to be treated with greater respect in fact by that court, although it is arguable that the personnel there are also important, noting that Justice Michael Kirby is the President of the New South Wales Court of Appeal.[114]
- *Use of legislative or regulatory guidelines.* For example, use objects clauses in legislation (there is none in the *Victorian Equal Opportunity Act*), or specify factors to be considered in calculating matters such as reasonableness.[115]
- *Enable feminist third party amicus interventions in litigation.* There has been some discussion about the practices of LEAF in Canada, and also the Women's Legal Defence Fund in the United States. They have a great deal more scope than we have here because courts there will accept *amicus* briefs and written factums, so written intervention from a feminist perspective is possible. It is not currently possible in Australia and perhaps one of the things we should be considering is enabling or empowering courts to be open to have put before them those kinds of arguments.

But finally, I think what we need most of all is for a sophisticated understanding of equality to become an accepted, normal, natural and important part of legal discourse in Australia.

11

Family law and discrimination

ARCHANA PARASHA

THE ISSUES IN family law are similar to the discrimination area. In the family law area, as in discrimination, there has been recognition that family law disputes need special personnel. We have in place a special court, the Family Court, which has been created because the mainstream courts were considered not entirely capable of dealing with family disputes.

The *Family Law Act 1975* for this purpose has actually provided that judges who are expected to be appointed as Family Court judges should not only be good and efficient lawyers as all other judges must be, but 'by reason of training, experience and personality the person must also be a suitable person to deal with matters of family law'.[116]

The Act also provides that the retirement age for Family Court judges is 65 years, the ideal being that people dealing with family disputes should not be too old. The Family Court has had a chequered history. There have been incidences of violence directed against the court. There are speculations about the reasons why the Family Court has invited such a reaction, but without going into those reasons, a few responses have been that formality is being brought back into the court system and the Family Court judges are now given jurisdiction not only over Family Court disputes but over other certain specified areas—the idea being that the kind of work Family Court judges do should be interesting for them. I will let you interpret that.

The existence of the Family Court has met with a fair amount of resistance. A lot of men are not happy that they seem to be denied their rights under the law. A lot of women, as we know, rapidly descend into poverty after divorce. Obviously there are a lot of other problems and questions surrounding this issue which need to be answered. However, a question I want to look at is whether judges are incompetent, uninformed, simply patriarchal, or should we be looking deeper and focus on the principles of law, rules of interpretation and concepts of law incorporated in family law itself? These issues are important because they are partly related to the current discussion in the community about judicial attitudes and the need to educate the judges. What I want to argue is that we need to spread our attention a bit more broadly than that. We should also look at the content of law the judges are applying; how the law allows judicial discretion to be exercised and what kind of training is given our law students who are going to be prospective judges.

So, it is not only a question of a few individuals who are the problem. What I am arguing is that we need to look at the system as a whole. I will focus briefly on the *Family Law Act* and its reliance on the discretion of judges to decide cases. The two dominant areas in which discretion plays an important part are property division and child custody disputes.

Property division

The *Family Law Act* is considered (by some) to be heartbreaking in that it almost allows the Family Court judges to override 'ordinary' principles of property ownership and recognise that the home maker might have a right to property at the end of her marriage. The Act gives the judge authority to take into account the contributions made by both parties. These contributions can be grouped under three headings: direct and indirect financial contribution, direct and indirect non-financial contribution, and the contribution made as a home maker.

Now this, in itself, is a progressive step, but the Act does not tell us what relative weight is to be given the different kinds of contributions. It is somewhat impractical to expect the judges to give a lot of weight to a home maker's contribution when the rest of our society does not do so. When judges have to weigh up the contributions, what invariably happens is that when the decision is about the matrimonial home, every judge feels quite comfortable saying the contribution of the home maker and the wage earner or income earner is on a par. But when we are looking at assets which are not the matrimonial home, such as a business, legal practice, medical practice or whatever, judge after judge feels comfortable in saying that the contribution of the woman in running that business, in having that practice, was either not there or was negligible.

The consequence is that when property division takes place, judges give the woman a part in what is seen as the joint property of the matrimonial home, but everything else remains the man's property. Often women are given some share, but it is hardly ever 50% or more. This follows the High Court, which went to great lengths to emphasise that there is nothing in family law which justifies the presumption that men and women usually make equal contributions (*Mallett v. Mallett*).

The next step in making a property division is that the future needs of partners can be taken into account. If the amount that a party gets on the strength of contribution is not enough, their future needs will be taken into account and adjustment made.

On the other hand, there is no legal presumption that an adjustment will be made if the property division at the first stage is enough to look after a party's standard of living. What constitutes a reasonable standard of living? Judges once again feel as comfortable as the rest of society in expecting that women can have a lower standard of living than men.

What I am trying to say is that, yes, these attitudes are there, but these attitudes are not specifically those of judges. Judges are not given enough direction, especially in family law, regarding how to interpret the provisions of the *Family Law Act*.

Child custody disputes

The same problem arises with regard to child custody disputes. When the Family Court is directed to decide child-related disputes by keeping the best welfare of the child as the paramount consideration, what constitutes the best welfare of the child is left to be determined by the judges. Now the Act tells the judges that the court must weight a number of factors which have a bearing on the welfare of the child. In any particular case, which of the factors are relevant and their relative importance, is also decided by the judge.

The Family Court is specifically debarred from relying on presumptions like status quo, or the 'mother role'. I want to focus briefly on the role of mother in child custody cases. The law says there is no legal presumption that the mother should get custody of children as a priority. Here, the law is reflecting another change of community attitude to the view that there is nothing 'natural' about women having to be the primary caretakers. At the same time, the social reality remains that most children are looked after by their mothers, or by other women. In that context, when the judges are given direction by the *Family Law Act* not to rely on the presumption of 'mother role' in child rearing, what is happening is the judges are left relatively without direction beyond their own interpretation of what the community expects or what they expect of the community.

Legal education

Last, I want to focus on the role that legal curricula in law schools play in helping students understand the nature of law. The attitudes that judges bring to decision making are partly a consequence of the very narrow legal education in most of our law schools and faculties.

Australia, as a common law country, has inherited the tradition of viewing legal education as training for a profession rather than as a broadly-based intellectual activity. Things are beginning to change, but rather slowly. In most law schools, the primary emphasis is on training students in 'black-letter' law (which does not include family law as a core subject). There is not adequate recognition of the wider nature and relevance of law, as more than a self-contained body of rules.

The conventional understanding of law is as a neutral, universal principle body of rules. This is now being challenged by many analysts using, for example, feminist or critical legal perspectives. However, most law school curricula have no place for such analysis. As a consequence, there is no serious effort made at integrating the study of law with history, sociology or philosophy of law. It follows that the interconnections between law, state and society remain unarticulated. For example, the study of family law as a set of legal rules, contained in specific legislations, will not equip us with adequate tools of analysis to understand the function of family law. If it is common knowledge that the consequence of divorce is poverty for most women, how do our judges deal with the problem?

One common response is that judges simply apply the legislative rules, another response is that judges determine individual disputes and it is not part of their job to correct the wider imbalance in the financial status of women and men. Both responses are technically correct, but extremely narrow. It should be possible for judges to be responsive to social reality. But that will happen only if legal discourse is open to the study of issues beyond rules and precedents. For example, in determining the prospective element in property division, judges could be less complacent about the inevitability of a lower standard of living for most women. Such responses are possible, but they involve something more than goodwill on the part of the judges only.

For any meaningful legal change, the educational institutions are the first port of call. We can and should ensure that students understand the power of law in maintaining patriarchal structures; that formal equality is a myth and that power imbalances because of gender, race, or ethnicity, for example, are real and oppressive. The possibilities for change can only be realised, if as a first step, we acknowledge that there are serious problems with the law. Feminist analysis of the law is highly sophisticated, but most law school curricula marginalise it by including it only as an optional course. Furthermore, most students are never exposed to a critique of law. It is this insular nature of law which needs to be challenged, if law is to be responsive to changing perceptions of social justice.

Postscript

The *Family Law Act 1975* was amended in 1996 and it no longer uses the terms 'custody' and 'access'. It now relies on the concepts of 'parenting plans' and 'residence parent'.

12

Judicial education

CHIEF JUSTICE DAVID MALCOLM, AC

I AM VERY CONSCIOUS of the fact that, if I indulge in any self-examination, I find that I fit the stereotype, at least on the face of it. I am, of course, white, middle-aged, Protestant. Looking for matter in mitigation, I would have to seize on the fact that I am Celtic, but apologise that I am Scottish rather than Irish, strongly Anglican, not Catholic or Presbyterian, and therefore suspect, because some of my Scottish ancestors must have adopted the motto, 'If you can't beat them, join them'.

These unfortunate characteristics are compounded by the fact that I am a descendent of early settlers, South Australia, 1836, Western Australia, 1839. There are other difficulties as well. I suppose I am a product of education at a boys' single sex boarding school which is one of a particular reputation. I spent six years in single-sex men's colleges at University in Perth, and in Oxford. To compound my accumulating felonies, I spent many years in practice as a barrister and was not only appointed a Queen's Counsel in Western Australia, but in New South Wales as well.

So, all of these difficulties stand in my way. Regrettably, in the eyes of some, I suppose, I am also a member of Perth's equivalent of the Melbourne Club. And so, it seems to me that it is almost time that I should be retiring before I have to retire hurt. However it is not impossible, from those difficult beginnings, to emerge as somebody who does have a belief in fundamental human rights, equality, and indeed the advancement of women.

My great aunt, Edith Cowan, was the leader of the women's movement in Western Australia in the latter part of the 19th century. She was the president of the National Council of Women in Western Australia, the movement which attained the right of women to vote. They voted for the first time at the 1900 constitutional referendum in Western Australia.

She was one of those people who founded women's maternity hospitals, women's refuges, she was a leader in the foundation of the Children's Court, and in the movement to remove the disqualification of women as members of parliament which resulted in legislation in 1920. She was the first woman in Australia to be elected to a parliament in Australia and only the second woman to be elected to a parliament in what was then the British Empire. In 1923, by dint of persuasion, argument and a rational approach to her colleagues in the parliament, she procured the Western Australian parliament to enact the *Legal Status of Women Act* of 1923, which had only one provision, namely 'No person shall be disqualified by reason of sex, from holding any public office, practising any profession, or engaging in any employment, and in particular, being a legal practitioner under the *Legal Practitioners Act* of 1893'.

That ended a most extraordinary saga. This year is the centenary year of the *Legal Practitioners Act* of 1893 in Western Australia, which, in gender-neutral language, provided that no person should be disqualified, and any person who met the relevant qualifications under the Act should be entitled to be admitted as a legal practitioner. In the Supreme Court in 1904, the Full Court solemnly held that the word 'person' in the *Legal Practitioners Act* could never have been intended to extend to the female of the species! Well that has changed, and the profile of the legal profession in Western Australia has also changed greatly.

I want to take just a brief opportunity to tell you something about steps which have been taken in Western Australia in relation to judicial education and the establishment of a task force on gender bias.

In August 1990 I attended a conference in Edinburgh on the subject of Equality and the Administration of Justice: Race, Gender and Class. The conference chairperson was Dr Diane Acha-Morfaw, an Advocate in the Republic of Cameroon and the Head of the Department of English Law at the University of Yaounde, Cameroon. In the context of women and the law, one of the seminars I attended dealt with education and changing attitudes. The first speaker on the subject of education and changing attitudes was Professor Kathleen Mahoney of the University of Calgary and co-editor of *Judges and Equality* (1987). This book canvassed a number of issues relating to equality. It showed that the theoretical underpinning of the law was in many instances biased in favour of men. This was demonstrated in the specific application of legal rules and results across all legal subjects, such as tort, contract, criminal law and property law. It was shown that judges unintentionally, unwittingly or unknowingly reflected a gender bias in their judgments. Upon my return to Australia I immediately ordered a copy of the book.

One result of the publication of Professor Mahoney's book was that a number of Chief Justices of the Provincial Courts in Western Canada decided that it was necessary to introduce an educational program to make judges aware of this gender bias.[117]

In the meantime The Honourable Madame Justice Bertha Wilson of the Supreme Court of Canada addressed the question will women judges really make a difference? [118] In her lecture, Justice Wilson canvassed the need for judicial impartiality and reviewed the literature on the subject of hidden gender bias among the judiciary. Research in the United States had found that unarticulated or unintentional sexism was apparent. Professors John Johnston and Charles Knapp of New York University, in 'Sex discrimination by law: A study in judicial perspective' (1976)[119] found that judges were guilty of sexism, which they described as follows:

> Sexism—the making of unjustified (or at least unsupported) assumptions about individual capabilities, interests, goals and social roles solely on the basis of sex differences—is as easily discernible in contemporary judicial opinions as racism ever was.

In the United States, legislative reform enhancing legal representation of women litigants and increased numbers of women lawyers and judges, accompanied by intensive judicial education programs across the country have combined to expose and combat the problem of gender bias in that country. Naturally, the educational program proposals were highly controversial. They would have failed but for the support of a substantial number of leading male judges and educators. Gender bias is now a subject which judges and educators think about, talk about and care about. This process has clearly been followed in Canada. The Canadian Judicial Council and the Canadian Judicial Centre both recognised the need for judicial education in this area and included these issues in their 1990 and 1991 Summer Seminars for Judges.

On my return to Australia, after the Edinburgh Conference, I decided to pursue this matter with a view to developing a judicial education program in Western Australia. I obtained some information and materials from Canada in relation to educational programs which had been developed there for the judiciary. I appreciated that it was a delicate matter because any suggestion of compulsion would conflict with notions of judicial independence. Great care needs to be taken in this area to ensure that such independence is not compromised. My approach was to endeavour to demonstrate that there was a problem. Before I went to Edinburgh I was convinced in my own mind that I was not at all biased. While I remain convinced that I am (like the vast majority of Australian judges) innocent of any intentional or overt bias against women in the law, what I have heard and what I have read has convinced me that there is a need for judges, myself included, to be made aware of the possibility of unconscious bias in decision making and of bias in the substantive law in its application to women. Our comfortable self-image of neutrality and impartiality suppresses the very sensitivity which is necessary to achieve equality.

It was against this background that I formed the view that similar judicial education programs to those developed in Canada and the United States should be introduced in Australia. Preferably, this would be done under the auspices of the Australian Institute of Judicial Administration (AIJA) but, if necessary, it should be done in individual courts.[120]

The issue of hidden gender bias in the law, legal institutions and among male lawyers and judges in Australia has been subjected to a detailed examination by Regina Graycar and Jenny Morgan in *The Hidden Gender of Law* (1990). In her foreword to the book, Justice Elizabeth Evatt says:

> Australian lawyers can thank Reg Graycar and Jenny Morgan for exploring these hidden areas of gender bias in the law and exposing them for our attention. Sometimes no more is needed than to expose what judges have actually said about women. For example:
>
> 'Many a married woman seeks work. She does so when the children grow up and leave the house. She does it, not solely to earn money, helpful as it is, but to fill her time with useful occupation, rather than sit idly at home waiting for her husband to return. The devil tempts those who have nothing to do.'
>
> They also introduce us to the writings of feminist jurists who have thrown new light on old concepts and revealed clearly the failure of the legal system to acknowledge, let alone accept, that there should be another way to see things.
>
> This analysis brings to light a society permeated by gender bias, a society in which women's role, women's work, and women's contributions are not given their full value, and which has failed to protect women from male violence and oppression. The message is that the legal system incorporates this bias and helps to perpetuate it.

In mid-1992 I learned that Professor Kathleen Mahoney was visiting the University of Adelaide. I immediately arranged for her to visit Perth and, among other things, speak at a seminar on Gender Bias in the Administration of Justice.[121] The immediate result of the seminar was that I received a number of concrete offers to assist in the development of the education program. This work has since been coordinated, under my direction, by the Office of Women's Interests of the State Government.

The Office of Women's Interests subsequently agreed to fund the appointment of a consultant. Ms Elizabeth Handsley of Murdoch University Law School was engaged in January 1993 as a consultant to prepare the education program.

Following the example set by a number of States in the USA and in the Canadian Provinces, I have proposed the appointment of a task force on women and the law to investigate the extent to which gender bias exists in the law and the administration of justice in Western Australia, and make recommendations for its elimination. The task force would examine this matter in relation to the substantiative law, the judiciary, the procedures of the courts and the organisation and work of the legal profession. It is proposed that administrative support for it would be provided by the Office of Women's Interests. I have been assured of full support and cooperation in relation to this proposal by the Law Society of Western Australia, the Western Australian Bar Association and the State Attorney General, as well as a range of women's groups and organisations. What I am concerned about is to ensure that we facilitate equality of women before the law and in the administration of justice, as well as equality of participation in the practice of the law and the administration of justice.

Conclusion

There are obstacles to be removed. The judiciary, the profession and all who work in the courts need to be aware of and understand the hidden or unconscious gender bias in the law and the administration of justice so that it can be consciously and conscientiously eliminated and avoided.

13

Human rights issues and judicial awareness

SUSAN WALPOLE

E LSEWHERE IN THIS VOLUME, Her Honour Justice Elizabeth Evatt (1996) has presented a very useful scheme to gather our thoughts on the issue of women and the law. She talked of law as a form of systemic discrimination that needed examination in three areas: its substance, its application and its procedures. Law in Australia is a peculiar mixture of statutory and common law, application and interpretation of those laws, and administrative procedures. Each of these categories, in fact, overlap.

Australia substantially lacks an interpretive context, such as a written Bill of Rights, within which to consider human rights generally. This gap is a very interesting one to contemplate when considering issues of substance. One part of the *Human Rights and Equal Opportunity Act*, for example, and the Federal *Sex Discrimination Act* attempts to fill a void by addressing the issue of sexual harassment as a form of discrimination. But we should ask why it was necessary to have statute law in this area at all.

The common law seemed unable to deal with gender-based harm such as sexual harassment or pregnancy discrimination, and it is not unreasonable, in my opinion, to think that things could have been different. The law of tort could have been developed to accommodate complaints of sexual harassment through judicial understanding of sex discrimination issues. The conceptual link between the tort of assault and trespass and that of sexual harassment was never made. This is in stark contrast to the revolution in the law of torts which saw major developments in the tort of negligence. Atkinson's 'neighbour test' and development of the 'duty of care' led to the variation of the tort of negligence and the development of that huge, personal injury jurisdiction with its extension into areas such as professional negligence and other aspects of modern consumer protection. Had the legal system recognised the damaging consequences of gendered harms the 'duty of care' could have been adapted to include issues such as sexual harassment and a new tort of sexual harassment could have emerged.

The lack of a remedy in the common law for a harm such as sexual harassment was overcome by its inclusion in the *Sex Discrimination Act* and in the various State legislations which prohibited this as a form of sex-based harm.

This discussion will concentrate on sexual harassment, because it is the largest single category of complaints received under all the sex discrimination and anti-discrimination Acts in as far as they protect women. The prevalence of this category of discrimination shows the growing community awareness of its unlawfulness. It also denotes its ordinariness in the working lives of many women. The profile of women who complain about sexual harassment at work highlights their powerlessness. Most are young, commonly between 15 and 24 years of age, most work in low pay, low status 'dead end' jobs. Many complaints come from very small businesses, usually with less than 5 employees. The complainants, generally, by the time they get to use the law to complain, have either been forced out of their job because of the impossibility of continuing to work there, or they have been sacked because they would not cooperate with the harasser.

It is frightening to note the number of cases coming to the Human Rights and Equal Opportunity Commission's (HREOC) attention which involve serious sexual assault. Civil law proceedings (such as are available through the human rights, equal opportunity and anti-discrimination legislation) are seen by complainants as offering great advantages over the criminal justice system, for the latter requires a very much stronger test of proof. It is often difficult to establish work-related assault in the small business sector, and of course, there is the question of perception, as has been demonstrated time and time again— many women who are victims of crime perceive the criminal justice system as adding to their harm, not as a form of redress, so they do not use it.

This last perception should, in itself, be a cause for serious concern to law makers, law enforcers and the judiciary. If one half of the population holds an entire section of the law under suspicion, if not contempt, then surely this must undermine the entire legal system. In any event, failure of the ordinary legal processes to grapple with human rights and discrimination and develop even a modicum of intelligence indicates a deeply entrenched problem, perhaps too deep for an educative program alone to overcome.

Certainly in 1984, when the *Sex Discrimination Act* was passed, it was clear that neither the common law nor the various elements of the criminal law, such as assault, were able to deal with concepts of sex discrimination. In fact we should never forget the public debate that was generated by the passage of the Act. Sex discrimination laws were going to end the world as we knew it, and even to breathe the word 'discrimination' would undermine our entire legal system, allowing us 'harpies' to usurp matters properly dealt with by the neutral, objective and fair tradition of law. And this is only nine years ago! Neither the destruction of the world as we know it, nor the usurping of the system by us 'harpies' has eventuated.

As Moira Rayner has pointed out (in this Conference), there is still plenty of room for the legal world to move. What we got, to fill the substantive void that the law did not care to fill in its ordinary process of development, was a statute and an administrative system to implement that Act's objectives. Moira has described some of the problems attached to this model. It would be silly not to admit that, even at the level of philosophy, there is not likely to be some conflict between the traditional and the new view. The concept of natural justice has at its roots the valiant individual fighting against the might of the State, in all its forms. The newly legislated set of rights starts from the premise that some groups in society need the support of that State to be able to exercise their rights either individually or as a part of a group. This is what anti-discrimination laws specifically recognise and attempt to address. In thinking through this contradiction it is useful to remind ourselves of what the classic textbook by Smith states about administrative law:

> The administrative process is not and cannot be a succession of justiciable controversies. Public authorities are set up to govern and administer. If their every act or decision were however to be reviewable on unrestricted grounds by an independent judicial body, the business of administration would be brought to a standstill.

We are in some danger, at least at the level of perception, of this happening in the area of discrimination law. Apart from issues of substantive philosophy, part of the reason for this clash lies in the issue of how laws are applied and what procedures are used. In ordinary matters of criminal and civil litigation, matters are resolved through advocacy and reference to rules of interpretation. In discrimination law, the process is one which adopts quite different methodology. It is a process of inquisitorial method, where rules of interpretation necessarily shift as society changes. To give an example (and it is an interesting one, which unfortunately I do not have time to develop here): It has been the experience at HREOC that claims of direct discrimination like, '... he said to me I couldn't have the job because I was a woman ...' are falling away because people are learning the right words to use. What is happening, however, is that we have an increase in indirect discrimination, which poses a whole different set of problems in terms of interpretation and, in turn, reflects a shift in social reality.

To return to the methodology. An important aspect of the inquisitorial method is that it can take account of facts which are revealed over time. All the evidence does not have to be argued from the beginning, in front of a non-participating judge. Enquiries can be made and further questions of fact pursued. I argue that this process is one likely to be more friendly to women than the advocacy system, particularly in cases where the dreaded word 'sex' arises. It is the common experience of HREOC that, particularly in cases of sexual harassment, the element of time and the ability of women to add to their initial complaint is crucial.

I have been disturbed by the lack of knowledge and understanding of the HREOC complaint handling processes. This can lead to overt hostility towards the legislation itself. It is a particular problem with lawyers acting for either complainants or respondents, since their entire training is based on a contrary model.

There is another important group who have problems grappling with the complaints process under discrimination legislation (for similar reasons as the lawyers): unions.

I mention unions specifically because, under the *Sex Discrimination Act* (SDA), unions are the only group entitled to bring complaints on behalf of others. There is some irony in this situation, as recent amendments to both the *Sex Discrimination Act* and the *Industrial Relations Act* now give me the right to appear on behalf of an individual complainant in the Industrial Relations Commission. This is a singular power, not held by any other person or body. The interplay between my office and the Industrial Relations Commission is going to be a very interesting one. The amendments allow me to hear and determine a complaint that an Award or an Enterprise Agreement is discriminatory and to seek an appropriate change in the Industrial Relations Commission. I have the right of appearance, although I can be refused the change on the basis of the Industrial Relations Commission's public interest test.

There is obviously a lot of room for judicial imagination to be exercised here, especially on questions of substance. However, it is not only the judiciary which will have to deal with these issues of substance; so will the Industrial Relations Commission itself. As has been pointed out in other papers, for example, despite the Industrial Relations Commission's rulings on equal pay, we still have a long way to go before we achieve that particular outcome. The reasons for this are many, but part of the answer lies in the Industrial Relations Commission's own body of substantive decision making, and in judicial law-making that affects its operations.

Many legal people have been involved in the processes that go to make a National Wage Case, or a test case decision by the Industrial Relations Commission. (I will just add, by way of parenthesis, that the language here is very interesting since the courts have held that the Industrial Relations

Commission is not a judicial body but rather an administrative one. Nevertheless, they still run test cases.) For those who have no experience in this area, it is useful to look at one of the most important Industrial Relations Commission decisions concerning equal pay—the 1985 Comparable Worth test—case because I think it reveals some things about the processes that are adopted.

At the time of the Comparable Worth test case, I was working in the Women's Bureau in what was then the Department of Employment and Industrial Relations in Canberra. The Bureau had considerable input into the Federal Government's case, partly because it had been very influential in having nursing—the vehicle for the case—professionalised through the conferring of university degree status rather than on the job training. And that is not an irrelevant issue.

The following are in fact my notes from the case which were written specifically for the *Industrial Relations Digest*, which is a government publication.

The Comparable Worth test case was based around a claim by the Royal Australian Nurses Federation, and the Hospital Employees Federation in relation to rates of pay for nurses. The proposal by the ACTU to run a test case on the issue of comparable worth was first announced in 1985 with the release of the ACTU's equal pay manual. The matter was referred to a full Bench of the Industrial Relations Commission and hearings were conducted late in that year. There were three key issues before the Industrial Relations Commission. First was that the Commission reaffirm its 1972 'equal pay for equal value' decision. Second was that the Commission would process this particular claim and others that may flow from it through existing National Wage Case mechanisms, and third, that the Commission endorse the 'comparable worth' concept as a concept integral to the construction of the 1972 'equal pay' decision.

As is usual in a major test case in the Industrial Relations Commission, many parties appeared: the ACTU, the Australian Nurses Federation, the Hospital Employees Federation, the Commonwealth and Victorian Governments and the Confederation of Australian Industry. The National Council of Women and the Campaign of Action for Equal Pay had also intervened in the case. (It is interesting to note, in terms of procedures, that this is extremely common in the Industrial Relations Commission when major test cases are run. The commission exercises its discretion in terms of appearances very wisely.)

The Commonwealth Government argued (and this is a very interesting argument, given the small number of Awards likely to be affected by the decision, and taking into account the question of flow-on) that claims should be processed under the anomalies provision of the *Industrial Relations Act*

(Principle 6(a)). The Confederation of Australian Industry, however, put the view that the appropriate procedural mechanism was the inequities provision (principle 6 (b)). The Industrial Relations Commission held that the claim should be processed under the anomalies provision, reasoning that, as the claims likely to come before it as a result of the test case 'carry great potential for undermining the current centralised wage fixing system', the anomalies procedure provided protection for that system. In this context, the Commission would still allow claims to be heard.

Much argument was put to the Commission on what exactly constituted 'comparable worth'. All submissions referred to the 1972 equal pay decision and in particular, to the last sentence of principle 5(b), that 'in some cases comparisons with male classifications in other Awards, may be necessary'. In referring to the various submissions, the Commission also noted the possible impact such elements as difference in hours worked, over-Award payments and promotional structures could have on the aggregate differential between male and female pay. It stated that many of these areas were not readily amenable to Award wage prescription.

In any event, the Commission rejected the term 'comparable worth' as inappropriate and confusing. This decision was based on the varied nature of the overseas experience and on its reaffirmation of the 1972 principle. Specifically, the Commission rejected the United States doctrine of 'comparable worth' involving the value of work in terms of its worth to the employer as contrary to the 1972 decision.

'Comparable worth', in the Commission's view, was also capable of being applied to work which was essentially or usually performed by males, as work essentially or usually performed by females. The Commission stated that such an approach would strike at the heart of long accepted methods of wage fixation in this country and would be particularly destructive to the present wage fixing principles.

Finally, the Commission noted that, 'from the material that was put to us, it appears that all parties acknowledge that a number of special factors may be relevant to the review of nurses salaries, and they referred the case on to an anomalies conference'.

That is a fairly brief outline of what the arguments were in that case, although we no longer operate under a centralised wage fixing system (which may or may not be cause for a different sort of debate). Those brief quotes illustrate that, in a very important area of judicial, or at least administrative, decision making, the sorts of problems that we have been talking about also apply. I think it is critical when we start thinking about those issues of substance, application and procedure, that we also need to address the issue of what goes on in tribunals and commissions. What the equal pay case illustrates is that on all three measures the Industrial Relations Commission has just as far to go as the judiciary. There is a problem of contextual understanding.

Now this might just be a process of initiation. Industrial relations is just as much a male dominion as other areas of the law—even if it is a tribunal or commission at the bottom of the 'guano heap'. Perhaps its peculiar status in this respect is because it is about male domination of work. Whatever the reason, we would be foolish in our quest for equality before the law if we ignored the tribunals and commissions. As has been pointed out, they affect more people's lives than almost any court and they are the major forum for women's contact with the law.

Before giving some specific suggestions for change, I will give some details about HREOC: there are six full time Commissioners in HREOC and a part-time President. The President is a male—a retired High Court judge; the CEO position is held by a male Commissioner; and the two Commissioner positions most closely concerned directly with government policy and practice, the Privacy area and the Aboriginal and Torres Strait Islanders and Social Justice portfolios, are held by men. The three caring, sharing Commissioners who deal with complaints of discrimination are women. We have a long way to go. Added to this, our hearing Commissioners who sit on public cases, are all appointed on the classic judicial model, partly because of the problems that both Moira Rayner (in this Conference) and I have alluded to. It takes a lawyer to beat a lawyer, even in HREOC.

Some suggestions follow for your consideration. Yes, let us have judicial education on context, but let us make sure it extends to tribunals and commissions that, arguably, affect more women's lives than do judges in courts. Let us not forget that the issue is not just about individual decision makers. We must also explore other procedures and methods of application of the law that may be better able to address the substantive issues we care about. Let us get our own mechanisms in order. Let us not forget about statutory reform. Issues such as indirect discrimination may require us to rethink basic assumptions about fundamental issues such as the onus of proof.

Finally, let us not forget other mechanisms. The ability to be an *amicus* is one; the right of protest and activism is another. To achieve the changes so patently necessary, I think we need a multiple approach.

14

A letter to the custodians of Australia's legal systems

KATE GILMORE

Dear Sirs,

We write with the intention of setting before you the case for reform of Australia's legal system as it pertains to those crimes that specifically and uniquely affect women.

We understand that the call for reform of the legal system's treatment of women is met more frequently with a demeanour of unease than it is with openness; with dismissal rather than inquisitiveness. In anticipation of such responses we choose to begin by providing the rationale behind our call for reform.

We are familiar with the concerns directed against us by those who are unable to support the reforms we would propose. In anticipation that some of you share these concerns, we wish to assure you that a focus on women and their experience of Australia's various jurisdictions does not introduce a threat to the rights, needs or entitlements of men before the law. To speak of one gender does not, of itself, detract from the other. But to speak of one gender alone is the failing of which we accuse the law.

To make our case for redress of this parlous tradition, we need not assert that the legal system has achieved a perfect outcome for men. Rather we need only assert, as indeed we do, that its imperfection is particular for women. Indeed we would go further and assert that it is more imperfect for women.

However, we are keen that these assertions be tested. We believe that the integrity of the law requires that such assertions are tested. In this regard, we do not shirk the objective testing of our claims. To the contrary we urge a critical analysis of the jurisprudence, substantive and evidentiary regulations, and their attendant administrative procedures that constitute our law: a critical analysis that will reveal the true nature of women's experience before the law.

If, as the defenders of the legal faith and tradition claim, all are indeed equal before the law, equal irrespective of gender, and such an analysis can only substantiate this most basic of legal tenants and thus reveal its critics to be ill informed. If indeed the law acts as its defenders claim, then such an analysis need not be feared, but should rather be all the more welcome for the opportunity to establish the fairness, indeed the justice of that which is ordained to deliver justice.

If, on the other hand, as women suspect, this critical review reveals the law to be acting far beneath the level of its aspirations then we will have before us an opportunity to build a reform agenda, such as can realise a more perfect match between the aspirations of the law and the practice of the law. Again, surely, custodians, this is not a goal to be feared.

Therefore, on our first count we believe that unless there is just cause to shrink from the eye of public scrutiny, there can be no just cause for its rejection. And to date we know of no legitimate public interest in the shrinking from such analysis.

On the second count, we draw your attention to certain facts. Before placing said facts on this public record, we hasten to acknowledge that it is in the interpretation or perceived relevance of these facts that we differ. Nevertheless, we must place before you certain facts about the legal system of which you are the custodians.

It is factual, and in that sense, incontrovertible, that the gender of those who have written the law, taught the law, practised the law, who have developed orthodox critique of the law, and the gender of those most frequently before the law is male. At any moment in the history of the law up until the present day, the majority and more frequently the totality of its custodians, at all levels, have been and are, men.

These are merely the facts. Unless you wish to dispute these facts through a requirement that no such fact may be taken as established, without chromosome testing of said custodians, then we must be in agreement that these custodians are, almost exclusively, men.

Certainly, in recent decades we have witnessed an incursion into the halls of justice by women. This is not in dispute. However, just as one swallow a summer does not make, neither has a recent, (as opposed to a long standing) participation by a few, as opposed to many, women achieved an equal representation or an equivalent participation of women in the ranks of the law's custodians.

Assuming that, on these few rudimentary facts, we are in agreement, we can move to the more controversial issue of establishing through interpretation the relevance of said facts to the question of the efficacy of the law in regard to women.

Here we move to an argument based on precedent. In every sphere of knowledge, in every academic tradition, in each of the respected professional disciplines we now have established evidence and support of the hypothesis that the presence of women (as opposed to the absence of women), is accompanied by significant changes such that qualitative shifts in the outcomes for women as a class are achieved.

As women have slowly been enabled to move into a more diverse range of occupations, so have their incomes slowly increased, gradually advancing towards those of men. As women have moved into the arenas of social science and social policy, so too have we reformed and revised our fields of inquiry and our parameters of policy such that we now consider child care, birthing options, and contraception as issues of some social importance.

As women have moved into the health sciences, we have discovered and uncovered the impact that the choice in gender of medical practitioner has on women's use of the health system. We have developed a greater awareness of the aetiology of diseases that affect women's morbidity and mortality: breast cancer, osteoporosis, anorexia, bulimia.

As women have entered the academic disciplines that are concerned with literature and art, we have uncovered and have been better equipped to refute the traditions that forced Henry Handel Richardson and George Eliot to disguise their gender, that worked to destroy Virginia Woolf and Sylvia Plath, and that imposed neglect and trivialisation upon the genius of Frida Kahlo.

Women have been able to achieve, indeed, have actively struggled for, recognition in the religious traditions. We've witnessed, albeit belatedly, the ordination of women, the redesign of worship through inclusivity of women, the reworking of theology for the de-stereotyping of women.

None of these advances has been secured without effort or met without resistance. However, in each instance we would confidently assert that there has been a positive impact for the whole of the democratic purpose, even for men.

Given the evidence established by these patterns of change and subsequent enrichment in other respected disciplines we can see no good reason why the law should be any less likely to so benefit by the greater participation of women?

After all, is the law a more exact science than medicine? Is the law a more self-conscious discerner of intrinsic worth than is art? Does the law have a more direct path to a higher power than does religion? Would the law place itself above every other human endeavour, to the point where it would stand by the claim that no consequent enhancement or richness would be delivered it through the greater participation of women.

Surely, with the offer of such enhancement in reach, the question becomes not whether women's greater participation in the law is consequential but rather how it might be more swiftly achieved.

Perhaps it then remains for us to establish that there is a need for such enhancement. We would, of course, take issue with this task. We would argue that the onus is on the law to establish that there is no such need.

However, we acknowledge that this onus is not readily accepted by your profession. So we are prepared to establish the case for the need for enhancement and to this end we identify three key indicators.

Our first is a point of principle. It must be taken as given that the law cannot be concerned with men alone or with only their interests. At this juncture we need not argue that this has been the law's singular or even primary preoccupation. We need only argue that the purpose of the law is unmet unless it concerns itself equally with everyone. All classes, all ages, all cultural backgrounds, each gender in the population which it serves. This is a point of principle.

Turning to our second indicator, we examine the question of how women fare before the law which is supposedly concerned with everybody. The answer can only be fully revealed through a thorough analysis of the contemporary legal system. Such an analysis is not available to us to date. However, we can tender that what is known to us provides sufficient grounds on which to assert that women indeed do not fare well. There is evidence of sufficient weight to allow us to say that, on the basis of the law's treatment of women as victims of violence alone, even without regard to the outcomes for women in other respects, we have enough cause to call into question the efficacy of the law, the authenticity of the law and the integrity of the law.

There is evidence in the law's traditions, even in this century, that through statute and in common law our legal system has acted as the regulator, rather than the active condemner, of crimes of violence against women.

As numbers of authors have noted, 'the rule of thumb' originated in English legal deliberation on the acceptable limits to which a man could rightfully and lawfully beat his wife wherein such violence was deemed acceptable (as recently as 1915) so long as the stick used to beat her was not thicker than his thumb. Aside from this judgment clearly advising women that upon considering the possibility of marriage, they should exercise a preference for men without thumbs, it provides an all too recent window into the depth of the legal traditions in different dealings with violence against women.

Of course there are learned members of the legal profession well versed in the relevant contemporary social research, who will be familiar with the evidence, provided in this and other countries, that legal officialdom—the police, clerks of courts, magistrates and judges—brings to cases the most common form of violence against women, which is domestic violence and, at best, variable sets of attitudes and assumptions.

Such research has indicated that a substantial number of these custodians continue to uphold the irrational view that, because the assailant is one's husband or because the venue for the assault is the shared domicile, the crime is rendered less rather than more significant. This degree of irrationality is cause for grave concern regarding the question of how women fare before the law.

You would be aware of recent years' flurry of nationwide reform in those sections of Australia's *Crimes Acts* that deal with sexual offences. This activity constitutes further evidence of a growing recognition among our legislators, that in its letter, traditional law has indeed failed women.

You would be aware, that in each jurisdiction in which such reform processes have been undertaken, there have been raised complex challenges to existing evidentiary procedures to standards of proof, to common law interpretations of consent, and to orthodox assumptions about honest, as opposed to reasonable, belief on the part of the accused.

You would also be aware that because of the nature and the forms of violence against women, the incidence and extent, the implications of these crimes and their subsequent legal management has impacted upon the arenas of family law, property law, labour law, immigration law and anti-discrimination law.

The sum of this activity and the concerns that it has identified goes to support the view that women, in respect of the crimes that most affect their lives, had not fared well before the courts of this land.

But a potent, if not an absolute test of the law's performance in regard to women must also be concerned with the outcomes for women.

This then, is our third element. While we are, once again, not privy to the systematic review necessary to establish without equivocation the mettle of this element, there is enough evidence. Enough evidence to suggest that the law has a case to answer at the level of outcomes for women. Justices Bollen and Bland have themselves provided, in our view, ample evidence of the need for such assessment. While it is tempting to relegate the judgments and sentences for which these judges are now infamous to the status of bad apples in an otherwise healthy barrel, there is in fact no evidence to suggest that these are not typical of, at least, an entrenched and significant faction of judicial opinion about women. There is not evidence to refute with authority the supposition that it is not a case of a few rotten apples in a barrel, but rather a whole rotten barrel of apples.

We are also aware of the custodians' populist and evasive argument that such judicial statements are being taken out of context; that they are exceptional rather than standard. In reply, we would assert that there can be no legitimising context established for such statements and would call for presentation of evidence to support such a claim. Knowing that there is no data to substantiate this defence, we would advise you to name it for what it is: merely self-interested protectionism.

This is an important plank in our raft of claims. Such prejudicial opinion, delivered as it has been from the Benches of our courts, does not merely create a burden on women to prove justification for large scale reform; rather it places a burden of proof on the judiciary to demonstrate that this degree of misogyny does not reside elsewhere than in the well-aged and due-to-be-retired few.

On these elements we base our proposition that there is insufficient evidence to support the oft-promoted claim that the law, even whilst essentially excluding women from its ranks, and particularly its upper echelons, is equally and decently serving women.

We have no good cause to be satisfied that justice is being done, and we must also consider whether justice is being seen to be done.

Again, it must be argued that, in this regard, the law is to be found wanting. When we assert that the public does not perceive that justice is being served, we need look no further than the recent tide of public dissatisfaction with legal processing of crimes of violence against women which, when swept up into the machinations of the political process, has delivered unto us indeterminate sentencing.

Indeed, if the recent conference of local governments across New South Wales serves as a litmus test, it is only a question of time before this crisis of confidence in the legal system turns to the re-introduction of capital punishment in its search for satisfaction that the law is indeed gracious enough to pay due attention to the constituency which it serves.

It is on this latter point that we would reaffirm our assessment that the law has yet to attend to that aspect of public accountability that is concerned with its public image.

We would refer you to the defence against indeterminate sentencing issued by the law's custodians, academics and practitioners. None, bar a few, are prepared to acknowledge the depth of community dissatisfaction. Each has decried as inhumane or barbaric, retrograde or ill advised, the focus on increased sentencing. None, bar a few, have decried with equal passion the crimes which the indeterminate sentencing is targeting. None, bar a few, have cared to move beyond this symptom of deep dissatisfaction to engage in its cause.

No meaningful alternative method to appease through significant structural change has been offered. This ready and self-satisfied dismissal of the secular view of the law is inadequate. It is a shoddy and shameful defence and merely provides further evidence for the urgency for reform.

If, however, the defenders of the law wish to refute this evidence of community dissatisfaction through assertion that it is mere fad or fashion, then we, in turn, cite the evidence of reported crime rates.

Crimes of violence against women are among those which are the most under-reported of crimes. Conservative estimates suggest only one in ten rapes is reported to the legal system. Population-based sampling research demonstrates an incidence of criminal violence against women far outstripping the numbers that are brought before the courts. Therefore it is plausible to pose the view that the community of women who, by virtue of being 51% of Australia's population, are the majority of our community, are voting on this question of whether justice is being seen to be done. They are voting with their feet.

This constitutes thousands and thousands of women choosing, on the basis of an absence of confidence in said legal system, not to present themselves and their experience before it. They do so because they assess that they will not be believed, they will be subjected to sexist, irrational prejudice, that their experience will be systematically trivialised, that they will not receive equivalent attention to that provided to the accused; that, in short, theirs is the greater gamble.

The scale of this lack of confidence, its dimension and its implication constitutes a phenomenon that Weber would have us call a legitimation failure. In Weber's terms, the law retains its efficacy to the extent that people believe in it, respect it and hold its judgments in due regard. In other words, the legitimacy of the law is absolutely correlated to the people's belief in its legitimacy.

Independent of this fact, it has no legitimacy; it has no intrinsic worth in and of itself, other than that which it can engender or elicit in those whom it is designed to serve. In this respect, we submit that a majority of the population, including many sympathetic men, consider the law to have little if any legitimacy in its response to crimes against women. On this basis we assert that the law is in legitimation crisis; legitimation failure.

This then is our case. However, we pause at this time to reassure you that you need not amend your reception of our analysis such that, before you can consider it worthy, you have to develop respect for those who speak from the country's kitchens and laundries, or factories and shop counters. We are not so ambitious.

To ease your path towards genuine consideration of the call for thorough reform and restructure, we refer you to the National Strategy on Violence Against Women which was warmly received by every government across this nation when, in 1992, it was presented to the Prime Minister. The strategy, which was developed by the National Committee on Violence Against Women, identifies as one of five key objectives the achievement of a more just and equitable response by the criminal justice system to crimes of violence affecting women. To this end, the strategy calls on all governments to aggregate, analyse and make public, data on rates of arrest, charge, prosecution and disposal of cases of violence against women.

In addition to urging ongoing reform of substantive law, the National Strategy calls for systematic research into the rates of penalties against perpetrators of violence against women. And, of course, it urges specialist training of all officials including, in particular, the judiciary; the emphasis being that the mutton of judicial ignorance must no longer be tolerated despite being dressed up as the lamb of judicial independence.

As we approach our summation, we make note of the law's cringe at criticism. It is, by its nature, defensive and reactionary against the criticism that we have outlined. In the first instance there is a perception, certainly amongst those of its practitioners who would privately support our contentions, that the law is intolerant of dissension.

Whilst being resistant to holding the likes of its judges to public account, it harbours pretensions of deterrence to those who, from its ranks, would criticise it. Advice without fear or favour, the pursuit of knowledge even where it overturns beliefs long held and firmly cherished, is essential to democratic process. It is beholden upon the law to adopt other than a censorial response to critique from within its ranks.

More importantly, on the occasion of criticism, the pejorative distinction often made between those who are trained in the law and those who are but lay commentators, must be seen to thwart the higher goals of justice in process and justice in outcome. Those of us who play no formal part in the law retain, by definition, the right to assess the law. For the law serves no end in itself. To achieve due process under the technical aspects of the law is a penultimate achievement only. To satisfy its practitioners is not its key objective. The true purpose of the law is functionary; it is the means to a greater end and its success in achieving that end is the point at which evaluation must occur. Ultimately, that evaluation must satisfy the law's constituents, who are the people whom it is designed to serve. On this count, on the basis of the case that we have presented to you, the law must be judged to have failed women.

Our call for reform will not be satisfied by a tinkering at the edges, and not placated by a paternalistic but still tokenistic hearing. Rather, if, on hearing our case, you interpret that we are challenging the very foundation of legal tradition, then you are not mistaken; you are right. The absence of women as agents of the law, the law's failure to deal well with women, its provision of paltry outcomes to women and the depth of public scepticism in respect to the law's efficacy, constitute grounds for a thorough review.

We would recall the dictum that 'better nine guilty men go free than one innocent man be convicted'. This is our final exhibit. On this we are prepared to rest our case: that the law has given priority to the freedom of men over and above justice for women.

As women, in our critique of law we will not be deterred. We have nothing further to lose and we envisage so much that might be gained. To secure your interest and provide incentive for your agreement to and participation in meaningful and fulsome reform, be assured that your satisfaction with the law cannot and will not outlive our dissatisfaction with it. We advise you not to put this to the test.

Sincerely, on behalf of all women who have stood before the law's custodians and have found them to be wanting,

Kate Gilmore

15

When victim/survivors of sexual assault are raped by 'reasonable men', and judged by legal 'reasoning'

THÉRÈSE MCCARTHY

I HAVE STUDIED JURISPRUDENCE, and have many thoughts related to the title of this paper. I wonder, though, whether, as a lay person, a non-lawyer, my critique of the culture and language of law will be taken seriously?

What I offer is an eye-witness and authentic account of how women come to meet the judiciary over sexual assault, their experience of this meeting, and its aftermath. Based on this knowledge, I want to share a vital piece of the justice puzzle: women's experiences—a microcosm of the thousands of voices which echo pain, trauma and fear, throughout Centres Against Sexual Assault, in this country.

The original topic suggested for this paper was 'When women meet the judiciary over sexual assault'. It clearly displayed a notion that is, at best, problematic; at worst an example of unreasonable thinking. Women do not meet the judiciary over sexual assault. The term 'meeting' implies a level of equality absent from most women's interaction with the judiciary at law. Moreover, as most women do not report sexual assault to the police, indeed, most women never speak of the sexual violence perpetrated by men against them, I am sceptical that the majority of women victims meet the judiciary over sexual assault at all.

However, many of these women do meet at Centres Against Sexual Assault, and so I would like to introduce you to these Centres. It is due to these services that more victim/survivors of sexual assault encounter the judiciary, and it is as a direct consequence of the women who have the courage to seek out these Centres that this paper addresses these encounters.

It is the relationship between Centres Against Sexual Assault and the criminal justice system that I wish to promote. It is this relationship's impact which has the potential to fundamentally enhance access to justice for all in the future. Most women attending these Centres report that justice is rarely done for those who do report sexual assault. Fundamental change of this state will only be achieved when the experiences of women have a legitimate place within the processes of the law, not reduced in its significance by current tenets of legal reasoning.

In the spirit of promoting a new relationship, I wish to describe some of our history of how Centres Against Sexual Assault have experienced the judiciary, and of how women have come to know the law. For the purposes of developing this new relationship, let me assume the status of an acquaintanceship. At the moment, this acquaintanceship between advocates for justice for women and the judiciary is not characterised by equality, but in fact is characterised by distance, some cynicism, but good intentions. It is due, in part at least, to the establishment of these Centres State-wide and nationally that we can begin a dialogue between these two systems, both charged with the responsibility to discuss justice within the community.

There is now a network of fifteen Centres Against Sexual Assault (or CASAs) in Victoria, and 73 CASAs throughout Australia. These Centres have a legitimate charter to promote justice for women surviving violence at the hands of men.

The first CASA in Victoria was established in 1978 at the Queen Victoria Medical Centre, at Carlton in Melbourne. Until this Centre was established, according to Dr Peter Bush (the police surgeon at that time), victims of sexual assault were examined on the desks of police stations. Statistics gathered at Centres Against Sexual Assault show a higher incidence of unreported sexual assaults prior to 1978. Times have changed, although we still cannot guarantee the option of a woman doctor to examine recent victims of sexual assault.

In 1987, when the Queen Victoria Medical Centre moved to the suburb of Clayton, a number of other CASAs were established. One Centre alone provides counselling, support, advocacy, information about legal and medical rights to over 2500 women each year. In addition to these women, a range of other health, legal and other professionals contact the Centre to seek expert advice regarding women and children currently at risk of violence, or disclosing sexual violence that occurred at some point in the past. These professionals are provided with therapeutic advice and legal information, in an effort to promote the criminality of violence against women and children, and appropriate responses to the victims.

What is unique about these Centres is their attempt to develop a model which recognises the social context in which sexual assault occurs. One consequence of this standpoint is that Centres are frequently located off-campus from hospitals and are not within the control of the police, medical or legal systems. By locating these Centres in a less institutional setting, they have been able to communicate to women an understanding of the multiplicity of consequences for victims/survivors of sexual assault. A response located solely within the legal and medical systems would necessarily be inadequate.

The consequences of sexual assault are chronic and on-going; they are emotional and psychological, yet they are political, economic and social as well. They affect women's access to public space, human rights and equal opportunity.

The goal of these Centres is to eliminate violence against women and children. The task at hand is to advocate a process which brings justice to women who have experienced male violence. To this end I wish to negotiate a new and just relationship with the law. I wish to colonise law in the interests of creating a new inclusive knowledge.

Because rape is a gendered crime, the consequences of rape also affect women's relationships to men. They affect how women experience a judiciary that is staffed by men, and characterised by notions of 'reasonable' men and man's law. It is this system that women look to for justice, and are rebuffed by it. This represents a crisis of confidence in a system which fails just over half of the population.

CASAs, as organisations, have developed an expertise, a useful knowledge. From this knowledge I will draw on the experiences of women and children who confront this system. These professional workhorses of the community play a role in hearing the voices of the women, of distilling the courage from their experiences and amplifying it for the community to hear. For it is not just the single voices of women we must examine today, it is the deafening commonality of women's experience.

The experiences of these women have implications for all other women. In effect, this sample represents the different categories of women who are tried for their reasonableness in the Australian courts of law. They tell a story, a gendered story. They are treated as a member of one or more categories. Their reasonableness is judged accordingly in view of their race and ethnicity, their socio-economic backgrounds, occupations and ultimately, for being a woman.

Women as a category have a number of archetypes. I suggest that the judge's role in legal reasoning is to determine which archetype applies to the woman on trial. Once appraised, these archetypes are transposed on to a hierarchy of deserving and undeserving women, real and false rapes. These women are unreasonable until proven reasonable. These women are incredible until proven credible. They are unbelievable until proven believable.

I introduce the notion of the 'unreasonable woman'. Before I introduce her, let me digress and pay her homage. For it is she who has the courage to stand by her own truth about her experience. It is she who has the faith to hope that there is a justice she is pursuing, and it is she who, in acting in the best interests of this community, steps forth into the court room in the belief that she has been wronged and will be treated with the dignity and integrity which befits a victim of crime. I want to introduce you to two of these women. The first woman is called Alice. She has asked me to read her story to you, in the interests of helping you understand legal reasoning. Alice's story is one of the stories of women who do not meet the judiciary over sexual assault. Here is Alice's story:

> I had been in Australia for about four months when I applied for the job at the carpet cleaning company.
>
> I heard about it from a friend who came from the same country as myself. She told me that I would be paid in cash. This work was irregular but at least the pay was enough to contribute to the small pool of funds I was saving to sponsor my sister and her child to Australia. When I say sponsor, I mean that I was working towards my own permanency in order to be useful to her in sponsoring her to Australia.
>
> The first day at the carpet cleaning company, my boss communicated to me through a friend (who spoke marginally more English than I), that he wanted me to go to some other building and clean the carpets. He said he would take me and I had no reason to believe that he would not.
>
> That evening was the first time he forced me. He forced me to do many acts, sexual ones, and I was so confused. I was unsure as to what I should do. He was my boss, I was scared he would sack me.
>
> I could not tell my friends. I knew I would lose my job. I was so confused. I knew that when my sister came, she would be ashamed of me. I was ashamed of myself. At night I would read the dictionary to learn the words to explain to him that I did not wish to do this—that it is not part of my culture.
>
> Each time I tried to stop him. Each time he forced me. I felt more afraid and unable to stop him. I thought he could just kill me and no one would even miss me. I have no family here nor any real friends.
>
> After five weeks, he called me into his office and gave me an envelope with some cash in it. He told me to go away and not to come back. I did not understand. I had worked very hard and I had to put up with the worst kind of humiliation and I'd still lost my job. I started to feel sick. I did not know whether it was because of the worry and pain or because something was wrong with my body. I could not face going to a doctor. I thought that I might have some disease or something that would show what had happened to me. I was worried because I thought this information would reach the immigration authorities and that they would deport me. I was so ashamed.
>
> That day, as I was leaving, my friend told me that she knew that this had happened to the woman before me. She suggested that I go to the doctor. The doctor referred me to the Centre Against Sexual Assault. The police

came to the Centre, and after seven hours an interpreter arrived and I told
the police what had happened. I told them that the interpreter did not
speak the same dialect as me. The police said it was that or nothing. I did
not understand.

The police investigated, but said there was insufficient evidence to proceed
with charges. An interview with Alice's employer, according to the police,
revealed that Alice had failed to say 'No' in English, and thus, in legal
reasoning was deemed to have meant yes. Thus, according to the police, the
case was 'dodgy', and wouldn't get anywhere.
    Alice continues:

> The counsellor told me that the police thought I had said 'yes'. She said
> that it didn't mean that I had not been raped. She said that the system
> doesn't seem to understand and that there is nothing wrong with what I
> have done. How can I believe this?

I put to you, my learned friends: What is reasonable about such a system? Is
she incredible because she does not speak English? With all its internal
complexities, I find it remarkable that the legal system could not accommodate
this cultural diversity.
    Alice, in attempting to understand the legal system in Australia, was
concerned that she had reported to the police and thought that this meant that a
judge and jury would decide whether this man was guilty. This assumption was
rendered unreasonable. She was rendered unreasonable.
    Now I want to introduce you to Amanda. Amanda also wanted her story
told. She wanted it told because she too reported rape in the mistaken belief that
she would participate in a process for justice. Here is Amanda's story.

> I reported rape to the police. I had been at a Christmas party for work. At
> that time I was working as a nurse in a residential home for the elderly.
> On the night I was raped, I had a few drinks. I was not drunk, but at
> about 1.00 am. I approached two of my male colleagues and asked their
> assistance to get a taxi home, as the party was in a community hall,
> remote from any thoroughfare. They agreed. However, when we left,
> they took me by the arm and forcibly guided me to a motel a block away.
> They said I could call a taxi from their room. I was a bit scared, but
> thought it was safe because I knew them. When we got back to their
> room, they threw me on the bed and raped me over a period of four
> hours, orally, anally and vaginally. I kept saying stop. I wanted to go
> home. Finally, they let me call a taxi, and I went home. When I arrived, I
> called work and said I wouldn't be coming in. Some hours later, I rang a
> friend and told her I had been raped. She took me to the Centre, and I
> had an examination, and spoke to the police.

I interrupted Amanda to ask whether it was reasonable to expect that she would be safe with two of her colleagues? I ventured to question why Amanda failed to notify the police immediately following the rape? What would the reasonable man do? Back to Amanda.

> One year later, I went to the committal hearing. At this hearing, I was so nervous. There were people I knew who were waiting outside the court room. My workplace knew a version of what had happened. I had taken a lot of time off work because I couldn't stand the way the male patients looked at me, and every time they would talk to me in a sexual way, as is often the case with older men, I became upset and afraid.
>
> In the court room, I gave evidence for four hours. They asked me why I did not fight back, why I had so many drinks, why I had asked them to help me find a taxi and not someone else. They said I had consented. Apart from the counsellor from the Centre, I was the only woman in the room.
>
> When their barrister asked me whether I am a vegetarian, I was confused and upset. I said 'No'. He then asked me why I did not bite off their penises, I became distressed and looked around the court room. At that moment, I realised that this was not their trial. The Magistrate, like all the others, looked at me, waiting for my response. I don't remember the rest of my evidence. The lawyers for the Department of Public Prosecutors, said nothing. They were angry with me because after this, the two men were not committed to stand trial. The DPP said my evidence didn't stand up, that my story didn't hold, that I was a bad witness. What finally got me, was I never got to tell my story. It was as if what had happened to me did not matter, they were so preoccupied with the words I chose to express it. I felt like a player in a game that I had never played before, and was treated as if I was cheating in some way.

Amanda felt that she had failed as a 'good witness'. She was found to have a testimony that could not be understood in a court of law. She had behaved 'unreasonably'. Amanda left the court room believing that she had been found guilty. Her humiliation was complete.

One is forced to ponder: in the interests of justice, what professional codes guide the behaviour of such lines of questioning? What training and education would guarantee that a magistrate or a judge would ensure that such behaviour was not only disallowed, but that the perpetrator of such behaviour would face disciplinary action before the Bar Council? I put to you that no 'reasonable man' in the witness box would ever be asked the questions put to Amanda that day.

The words of Catherine MacKinnon have sinister application in Amanda's case. She argues that women do not want to go to court with cases of sexual harassment or rape precisely because 'in flesh, in the court' women come to embody the standard fantasy of the pleasure of abuse and sexual power. It is not just that they must repeat the violation in words, nor that they may be judged to be lying, but that a woman's story gives some kind of pleasure, in the same way that pornography is construed to give some kind of pleasure. Her account, distorted by the cross-examining techniques of the defence counsel, does not only sexualise her but it becomes a pornographic vignette[122]. Unfortunately, for Amanda, she differs from the vignette, because she is there in the flesh to feel her humiliation. The judge, the lawyers, and the public, can gaze on her body and re-enact the violation in their imaginations.

Like Amanda, and unlike Alice, some women do find themselves in a court of law as victim/survivors of sexual assault. I introduce them all. As I introduce them, I introduce the salient features of the meeting. These reflections are representative of the aftermath; women's analysis of the meeting.

The first feature we must acknowledge is that they are unrepresented. Though many would cry that it is in the interests of the public prosecutor to protect their star witness, there is a conflict of roles for this person at law. They must also attempt to obtain a conviction, and the preservation of the integrity of this star witness may not always be central to the outcome of the case. Indeed, it has been said that a distressed victim does conform to a notion which a jury can identify as consistent with a stereotype of innocent and wronged. Look at Amanda.

Secondly, let me acknowledge the inequality of the victim and the judge. It is heresy to suggest that such equality is appropriate or possible, yet, as a member of the community who has committed no crime, she should be treated as a guest of the court room. Consistent with this treatment, she should be shown hospitality and recognition of her status. Instead, she is equal to none in the court room. Her place is terrifying, unenviable. She has no right to a fair trial, although this is a right guaranteed to the accused. She has no right to an unsworn statement, she has no right to privacy in exposing the most gruesome and frightening aspects of her violation. In essence, she is not just unequal, she is right-less.

Thirdly, let us acknowledge that she is in the court because she is a woman, and her biology and gendered experience places her in a particular position. Rape is a crime committed in the main by men against women and children. She is representative of 52% of the population, yet she is unrepresented in the ranks of those who judge. Further, she is a member of a group, albeit a majority, whose situation, as Catherine McKinnon describes, combines unequal pay with allocation to disrespected work; targeting for rape; spousal assault; sexual abuse as a child; demeaned and objectified physical characteristics; exploitation through denigrating entertainment; deprivation of reproductive control and forced prostitution[123]. These women are part of a group, called women nationally and internationally, who fear the possibility, and frequently the reality, of violence in the home, and at work. They have, due to this fear, less access to public space.

To be treated like a woman is to be disadvantaged in these ways. To be deprived equal access to justice because one is a woman is deprivation of the equal protection of the laws on the basis of sex.

Having met these women and the context of their meeting at law, I introduce the 'reasonable man.' You have met him before, with Alice and with Amanda. These men have detected that the law has a greater understanding of the 'reasonable man.' These men have identified that it is the 'reasonable man' who can rape his employees with impunity. Likewise, 'reasonable men' may systematically violate the unreasonable woman, who unreasonably wants to go home. The 'reasonable man' will escape prosecution because he has no compunction to account for his actions from the witness box, unless he wishes to do so, without cross-examination.

As I utter these words I can hear the voices of the lawyers defending the rights of the accused. (I have already heard them filtering Amanda and Alice's stories through their processes of legal reasoning, justifying the way in which they were treated, on the grounds of evidence, or the search for truth.)

My response is this: case law reveals that we already have one law for men and one law for women; we already have one law for blacks and one for whites; we already have one law for white English speakers, and one for those who are defined out of this category by their race or ethnicity. My response is this: let us demonstrate the integrity and the intelligence required to devise strategies to redress this.

The concept of the 'reasonable man' remains inextricably linked to the Westminster system. In Australian courts, the judiciary endorses and promotes the notion of the 'reasonable man'. This same 'reasonable man' has been known to understand 'yes' when he hears 'no', even where he pleads guilty. According to judges of recent times, the 'reasonable man' has been known to use 'rougher than usual handling' to coerce women into sexual intercourse[124]. Similarly, it has been said by a learned judge that women who are unconscious do not feel pain because of their rape. Their agony is confined to the consequences of having their throats cut from ear to ear[125]. These 'reasonable men', although found guilty of rape by legal reasoning (as if legal reasoning has a life of its own), have, by way of acceptance of extenuating circumstances, had their status firmly restored as 'reasonable rapists'.

It is to the reasonable men in judgment who have the privilege of defining what is just, that reasonable women in this community look for a fair trial. Justice is not forthcoming.

Conversely, the reasonable woman is tried for believing in a reasonable system of redress. Tried, convicted and punished for expecting to be understood when they say no, or feel pain, are roughed up, or even, as in a recent New South Wales case, left alone without transport or money outside a nightclub;[126] from the bizarre to the mundane. It is clear that such words of legal reasoning, recently posited by the judiciary, have the distinguishing feature of attracting media and community comment. Yet how widespread such misogynist and sexist views are remains unclear, given the lack of systematic accountability of the judiciary to the community. Take, for example, the lack of consistent monitoring of judicial sentencing comments, directions to juries, and interventions in the sexist behaviour of barristers in cross-examination. The considerable body of women's experiences tells us that comments such as we have just heard are not aberrant, but form part of the continuum of judicial reasoning. The deafening silence from the 'brethren' in decrying this behaviour as unprofessional and unrepresentative, also contributes to the view that such attitudes are endemic. Due to the prevalence of these opinions, women considering reporting rape to the police require a guarantee that it is not they who will be on trial, it is the construction of the reasonable man.

Women reporting rape deserve to be heard, in a humane system, free from sexual harassment and insult by the defence witnessed by the presiding judge who is thus complicit in it,. It is time for a demonstration of progressive attitudes, consistent with the notions of a fair trial, and equality before the law.

These are not unreasonable claims, but claims made in the context of a despairing community of women and men: women and men who think it reasonable that the experiences of 52% of the population deserve to be heard without retribution, and with the dignity that should be accorded a victim of a violent crime.

There is now a nationally and internationally developed body of reasoning. Centres Against Sexual Assault are at the forefront of the development of this reasoning. This reasoning reflects an understanding of the aetiology of sexual assault, and other forms of violence against women. Such reasoning would only enhance the body of legal knowledge which fails to deliver justice to women. Equally, feminist jurisprudence holds out the promise of a fully integrated theoretical framework. But the struggle goes far beyond the law. Tackling rape law involves concerning ourselves with masculinity and the ruses of power. Family law involves us tackling fatherhood, conceptions of careers, authority, and economic power.

The current exclusion of this body of reasoning from court proceedings and judgment has meant that women's experiences are currently denied credibility in a court of law. This is perhaps because women's stories rock the foundations of the court's well entrenched legend of the reasonable man.

There are sufficient case-law examples to support a call for an examination of the role of the criminal justice system in preventing violence against women and children—for there is no neutrality in these matters. It is time to act upon the considerable amount of evidence before the governments and the community, and to institute processes which ensure that the courts do not hold trials for women who have committed no crime, have no advocate, and no right of redress.

I put to you that the reality of Amanda and Alice is a reality shared by many other women; black, white, English speaking, and non-English speaking. Their stories are never told. The crisis of confidence in the law is of such proportions that it is time to act upon this vast body of unreported case law, and institute changes which are concerned with justice for all women.

16

Judicial appointments

CHIEF JUSTICE ALASTAIR NICHOLSON

S OME YEARS AGO (it seems a long time ago), when I was first appointed to the Supreme Court of Victoria, in my response to the welcoming addresses of the Bar, I said that I expected that within the next few years I would be joined by the first woman appointment to that court. It seems to me that it is taking rather a long time.[127]

It is an unfortunate fact that there are too few women in the Australian judiciary. It is a fact that, of course, is partly historical. It is partly due to the pool from which judges are normally selected, which, at the superior court level, is normally the Bar. And of course, it is partly due to the fact that it is only in recent years that women in large numbers have been practicing in the Bars of the eastern States. Nevertheless, it is obviously due to more than time that there are not more female appointments on the Bench. I agree with the views expressed by Sally Brown about the desirability of that happening, and the effect that such appointments have on other male members of the court.

In the Family Court we are not often given credit for the fact that we do have a number of female judges. The proportion is too low. We have seven. I exclude Western Australia, which has its own State court, but we have seven out of 48. Two of the last six appointments have been women.[128] So I do not think that the picture of appointments to the Family Court, either historically or at present, matches the stereotype of appointments and I think the court has received great benefit from the width of the pool from which appointments have been taken.

Having said that, I also agree with Sally Brown in that the Bar nevertheless does provide a very useful training for judicial appointment. It will be found in the future, because of the number of women at the Bar, that there will be plenty of suitable people from that pool who can be appointed, as well as from elsewhere.

I thought it might also, perhaps, be of interest to touch briefly on the method by which appointments are made, which is a matter that is not often discussed. I think it has to be said that it is entirely informal. It certainly is not an appointment that's made by the Chief Justice of the day. It is an appointment that is very much an appointment of the Attorney-General and he is, I suspect, influenced politically in appointments that are made. I do not mean that the Attorney-General is necessarily making overt political appointments but rather there are differing political pressures that impact on the making of such appointments. My experience, which is confined to appointments at the Commonwealth level, is that there is no resistance and I encountered no resistance to the appointment of women from government. My experience has been that each Attorney-General with whom I have dealt in relation to judicial appointments has been most anxious to extend the gender balance of the courts and I think that is a process that will continue. Certainly, the Attorney-General consults far more widely than simply with the judges or with the Chief Justice. I am not sure how far and how widely the consultation goes, but it does extend throughout the usual professional bodies and associations and there is no doubt that pressure is offered by various groups who do make representations to the Attorney as to who should be appointed.

I think one of the things that we should be careful about if we are going to get rid of that informal process of selection, is that we do not replace it with something worse. It seems to me that some of the American precedents in this area are not very encouraging; for example, the system of election of judges which is widespread there. I invited an American judge to attend a conference in Australia. That judge has been introducing quite rigorous and unpopular case management guideline techniques into his Domestic Relations Court with a view to getting cases dealt with rapidly. He was opposed by the Bar Association of his State. He had to run for election, was very nearly defeated and was not able to accept the invitation until he had won the election. That seemed to me to be an unfortunate sort of a precedent and not one that we ought to follow.

It might be of interest to quote from a judge who is prepared to look much more widely than normal—Justice Michael Kirby—in a speech he made where he said that there would be some who would have all judges appointed to their offices like any other public servant. Advertisements, appointment committees and bureaucrats, jobs only on application, candidates scrutinised for conformity to the current philosophical and social orthodoxy. His Honour continued:

> But the strength of our judiciary has been in the past the fierce independ-
> ence of its members. This has been nurtured in their training in the
> independent legal profession where they grow up without a devotion
> either to political allegiance or to safe pedestrian ways of thinking. In a
> sense it has been this independence of background that has underwritten
> the independence of thought of our judiciary. That mode of thought has
> been essential to the assurance to our inherited and developed liberties.

> While I support changes including greater participation by women and
> people from a variety of ethnic backgrounds on our bench, I would
> caution most earnestly against reducing our judges to simply another
> group of highly paid public servants.

It is not my function to stand and defend the judges but I simply echo the remarks that Sally Brown has made, that when we are making changes let us be careful about how we make them, because we may finish up with something much worse than we already have.

I would also like to briefly touch upon a couple of issues of direct interest from my perspective, that is, from the perspective of the Family Court of Australia. One of the problems of the Family Court is that the allegations of gender bias in the main come from men. If one reads the submissions to the Parliamentary Select Committee, which numbered more than 1000, the vast majority of those submissions were allegations by men against (largely) male judges. The allegations of gender bias were on the basis that those male judges were said to be favouring females in proceedings before them. I think what that probably tells us is the importance of avoiding gender bias, whatever the sex of the judicial officer. It is just not good enough to have to go before any judge who is likely to show gender bias one way or the other. I actually reject the criticisms of gender bias from largely the farthest groups in the community. I do not think they stand up on examination. But nevertheless I think it makes it extremely important that judges of the Family Court, as well as any other judges, carefully examine issues of gender bias, do have judicial education in relation to matters of that sort and so far as possible avoid them.

We have regular judicial education seminars in the Family Court. We have regular national seminars involving not just judges, but counsellors who are, I suppose, two-thirds female and come from a different professional stream, and we have people who are responsible for court administration. So we endeavour to keep a very wide range of people looking at the performance of the court overall.

I think that family law does, nevertheless, need re-examination and particularly from the point of view of women. Most particularly from the point of view of women who have separated and are in the position of supporting dependent children, whether or not the Child Support Scheme extends to them. Some of the studies—and they are all one way—suggest an enormous gap in opportunity between women who have separated and their former husbands in terms of their economic success. The importance of that is not only the deprivation of the women that are involved but also the deprivation of the children. The recent studies by the Institute of Family Studies, published in 1993, made it clear that, whereas prior to marriage break-ups some 10% of the sample women were below the poverty line, after 3 years some 40% were below the poverty line. After six years there were still of the order of 35% below the poverty line, and these were women with dependent children. So that is the sort of area that I believe we should be looking at in reform of family law.

A final matter that I simply want to touch on relates to areas such as mediation. Both the Family Court and I myself have been very concerned about aspects relating to mediation and counselling in cases involving family violence.

We have defined family violence quite widely, as being conduct by an immediate or extended family member which causes harm to another family member to an extent which creates apprehension or fear for that member's personal wellbeing or safety. The conduct may be threatened, it may be physical or emotional, or a combination of both. Now we have given detailed directions that where these situations arise, the important thing is that the person is in fear: not the counsellor's judgment that they are in fear, but the fact that they are in fear. We do make arrangements that they are not forced to attend counselling sessions together with the person they are afraid of. They are not forced to attend mediation sessions at all. Overall, we endeavour to, so far as possible, protect people in that category.

17

Legal representation of victims

Statutory discrimination and gender-biased interpretation of the law

PATMALAR AMBIKAPATHY

I N THE MID-EIGHTIES I discovered crime in my family law practice. I had heard a little bit about it, but I was not looking for it. I imagine, given this approach, I overlooked little coded messages from clients, as did many fellow practitioners of the time. After this discovery, I began to represent victims of criminal and sexual assault in the home.

The criminal justice system denies victims the right to a lawyer for the criminal trial, but I devised a strategy based on the concept of a 'watching brief' to do just that—represent victims of crime in the family.[129]

It followed then that it was necessary to explore every avenue of the law that could help such victims. I discovered the Crimes Compensation Tribunal and started to make claims for women and children. They were clearly victims of crime, even though they had little visibility. They had little visibility because our legal system denied, dismissed or silenced the voices of women and children in this jurisdiction. It simply reflected only one gender's views and it was that same gender that had dominance in the family system. These were, of course, not the views of women and children.

Initially, the law actually bestowed rights of compensation for crimes to all categories of victims, except the ones at home. This was not an accident, caused by gender blindness; it was not even gender bias—it was plain discrimination.

You may find this hard to believe, because I found it hard to accept that this had actually occurred and sadly still does, so allow me to describe how it all began.

The *Criminal Injuries Compensation Acts 1972* to *1988* serve as good examples of legislation that intentionally discriminated against victims of physical and sexual assault at home. In 1972, prevailing community perceptions allowed an Act to be passed in Victoria that denied this class of victims (mostly women and children) compensation.[130] This benefit was reserved for criminal acts outside the home and the main beneficiaries were men: police, prison-warders, bank employees, teachers and men involved in brawls.

It was not until the 1980s that the law was modified to include victims of crimes at home.[131] However, they were still denied equity with the victims of more public crimes, as they were burdened with requirements with which the others were not.[132] They were required to prove that their assailants had been convicted, had admitted guilt or pleaded guilty or had been unable to plead to the charge against them on grounds of insanity.

In 1972, before the law was first modified to include such victims, it was stated that the law reflected ambivalent attitudes towards domestic violence still existing in the community, police and courts.[133] Unfortunately, twenty two years later we are still faced with the same difficulties.

Interestingly, in 1984, legislation again attempted to provide redress to women and children, but predictably it gave with one hand and took with the other.[134] It allowed victims who lived with their offender to make claims if they did not impede police in prosecuting the offender. This apparently well-meaning reform assumed that such victims had the initiative to bring such offenders to justice. All lawyers know that the police can initiate prosecution against domestic criminals and make their victims compellable witnesses. Yet it was also a reality that victims did not often receive the sympathy and support necessary for such a drastic course of action against family members.[135] Thus the reality of victims' lives was such that they were yet again denied the right to claim compensation by this requirement embodied in the law.

In 1988, legislation became even more receptive to the experiences of women and children.[136] They were at last able to make claims equally with other victims and were only barred if they had colluded with their offenders. This is another myth, as I am unaware of many claims that have been denied on the grounds of collusion. For a period of two years this underclass was treated with justice, as legislation was more or less sanitised of gender and age bias.

In 1990, the Tribunal was effectively abolished, in all but name, by a transfer of its jurisdiction to the Magistrates' Court. This was done without any significant discussion with the community and the profession. In fact it even bypassed the Parliament of Victoria and the democratic process. The decision was made and implemented apparently by the Attorney-General's decree. All cases were removed from the Tribunal and placed in Magistrates' Courts all over Victoria. Magistrates began to hear all cases. Some were trained former members of the Tribunal, but many had little experience of the *Criminal Injuries Compensation Acts*.

Two new impediments developed as a result of the Tribunal sitting in Magistrates' Courts, to defeat the legitimate claims of victims injured as a result of crimes at home. First, by introducing a more strict interpretation of the Acts. The Acts, for example, allow magistrates discretion to waive the requirement to make applications within one year of the injury, and this is also meant to make police compile their reports speedily, and by taking into account 'all the circumstances of the case'. Unfortunately judicial interpretation in effect recreated the bias that had been excluded under the Act. This judicially-made law was created by precedent, and was also, obviously, implemented without an Act of Parliament. It swept aside the remedial nature of the Act and interpretations that properly follow from such a classification, and required much more strict compliance with the Acts. Legislation that is remedial in nature, sets out to redress wrongs that the community no longer wishes to tolerate.

The more strict interpretation of the Acts is in contravention of long established legal principles that ensure that Parliament's intention is not defeated by narrow legalistic arguments to deny relief from the wrongs Parliament sought to remedy. *Arnold's Case* set the scene for what I viewed as a denial of justice to this underclass. (See the unreported decision of the Supreme Court of Victoria, 10/12/92, and see further in the postscript below.) In that case compensation was denied because the Applicant had not complied with time limitations imposed by the Act. In the home, children are unwaged and unrepresented, women are unpaid and non-unionised, so who advises them straight after their assaults to report to the police and to make an application? Initial priorities are more about treatment, prevention and protection than claiming monetary relief.

From my experience and the experience of fellow practitioners in this field, it is very rarely the police, the courts or the lawyers that victims consult for matters peripheral to the assaults, or who advise them about this legal compensation they can claim. In fairness to my colleagues, many victims feel unable to divulge their shameful secret. We know, after numerous surveys and research from the 1980s, that many such victims never ever disclose such crimes, let alone report to the police. [137] When they make a claim for compensation, this delay is held against them. If they had no knowledge of this right, it is no longer an excuse in itself, as it was before. If the court decides that a victim *should* have known, this can bar a legitimate claim.

I grant that there are public policy considerations of possible fabrication and the need that police be given a chance to investigate, but delay in the making of police reports is too often held against these victims. Yes, it does make investigative and administrative procedures more difficult, but is there not a balancing public policy consideration for assistance to such victims? How do you report a crime against you when you are living with the offender or have to deal with him regularly at court ordered contact? How far can you get away from him to ensure your safety with an Intervention Order that police cannot guarantee? Police lack resources to mount effective protection of such victims once investigations or prosecutions are in progress. By refusing to acknowledge the real experiences of women and children, judicial interpretation too often effectively denies them access to criminal compensation.

The second tool of interpretation of the law that may deny victims justice, is the requirement of making a claim within one year of the injury. However, the Acts can assist adults who have made applications late. The anguish they suffer is known as post traumatic stress, which comes within the definition of 'mental disorder' under the Act. However, even if a victim suffers from this injury, it can be ignored as it was in one of my cases. The victim's claim failed, on appeal, on the grounds that the woman was capable of making a claim within the time limit set. Her application for compensation failed, although two psychologists reported she still suffered from post traumatic stress. She made the decision to remarry, and according to judicial interpretation, a decision to marry, apparently, indicates that a woman can make other decisions that require her to be mindful of her rights. It could actually be argued that to marry again, after a disastrous and violent first marriage does not override evidence of a mental disorder but actually demonstrates one! Her ignorance of her rights was also not excused.

The theory of equality before the law, as embodied in the 1988 amendment of the present Act, at last allowed this underclass of victims to make claims. However, it is this same enthusiasm now, to treat such victims *equally* with victims of more public crimes (who have the benefit of access to information, advice and representation, and who do not have to go back home and live with the criminal), that denies them the remedy that Parliament and the people of Victoria granted them. We do not need another Act of Parliament to remedy this. Rather, giving credibility and proper weight to the evidence of women and children and expert testimony (from other women in the field; for example, counsellors and others who work with victims) would right what the law still fails to do, namely acknowledge the full import of what has happened to these women and children.

Tribunal and court members must not allow their personal views and prejudices to prevail over women's and children's experiences. This complaint of mine is corroborated by research and expert evidence all of us have access to.[138] Courts are being funded to do a job by taxpayers (who are also women), and many do that well. Those who do not do the job well need to be brought into line by education or allowed to pursue their beliefs in ways that do not deny justice or bring the law into disrepute.

The transfer of cases from the Tribunal to the courts allowed the courts to use their legal experience and view about how a victim *should* behave or be *reasonably* expected to behave to defeat an Applicant's legitimate claim. It is no accident that, when specially trained Tribunals, both men and women, stopped hearing such cases, the *same* law began to be interpreted so differently. At a time when we are more aware of the problems of victims of family crime than ever before, gender-based assumptions in the law again dismiss, deny and silence women and children. We cannot tolerate such a situation.

Madam Attorney-General, bring back the specially trained Tribunals, or give the courts more money for training on how to interpret the law to help victims and not abuse them over again.

Postscript

In *Arnold's Case,* mentioned above, the Victorian Government Solicitor agreed in an appeal to the High Court, that the Victorian Supreme Court was wrong in not allowing a childhood survivor of sexual assault an extension of time to make the application. In another recent case, *In Re H, B & E* (1994) the highest rate of compensation was allowed for childhood surviv ors, as their full disorder did not appear until after 1988 when compensation for pain and suffering was set at $20 000. See also *Dix & Dix v. CCT* [1993] 1 VR 297 where the Supreme Court held that ignorance of the law was an excuse. Lastly, the Tribunal's decision in *In Re J* (1993) is a case where each charge against an offender was separately compensated, in a case where the adult offender had an extended sexual relationship with a child. However, this may not continue to be allowed, as Tribunal members are not bound by cases heard at the Appeals Tribunal. Nevertheless, these more recent cases finally come to terms with the reality of the consequences of criminal assault at home against children.

However, we cannot be complacent in such a difficult economic climate. It is quite possible that budgetary constraints and reforms driven by disquiet at the sums being awarded to women and children, will be introduced into Parliament. Superior courts too may use financial policy arguments, to erode the principles set out in the recent decisions mentioned.

The position of adult women who do not have a repressed memory of the crime done to them, but who do repress dealing with legal or other issues that concern the violence they suffered at the hands of their partners, still remains problematic. Courts are unwilling to accept that such women dissociate from dealing with the assaults, simply to survive, put it behind them, and attempt to get on with their lives. Many have to do this to demonstrate to the Family Court and professionals that they are 'all right' and can take care of their children. If not, there is the ever present danger of being labelled 'unfit' to have the care of their children. When they do eventually make a claim, and are safe enough to face the issues of the crimes against them, these victims are blamed for not having made a speedy application in accordance with the standard of behaviour expected under the Act. Such discrimination still persists.

July 1997 Addendum

In my postscript I drew attention to the latest cases that I stated had: 'finally come to terms with the reality of the consequences of criminal assault at home …'. The present Parliament and politicians have now swept away that reality by abolishing the *Criminal Injuries Compensation Act*, and from 1st July 1997, women and children have been deprived of the small sums of monies that they have had to fight for so strenuously over all these years. All they will be entitled to by right are five counselling sessions IF they can prove they are victims of crime. Once they have exhausted this, they have to prove their need for more! All the old impediments (and some new ones) against them have been preserved in the new *Victims of Crime Assistance Act*.

The new legislation allows a claim for loss of earnings. Once again parliament has legislated a form of discrimination in an Act against victims of domestic crime. Women and children do not usually have wages for their labour at home. Their status deprives them from this remedy. Furthermore, in a jurisdiction where costs are not usually awarded, costs are being threatened in all cases by the Victorian Government Solicitor and endorsed by some Tribunals. This is proving to be an effective way of discouraging victims to appeal. I have described just the tip of an iceberg of strategies employed to defeat claims by women and children. Our Appeals Tribunal, too, seems to have developed an ethos of denying the perceptions of the new but old underclass.

18

Issues with victim impact statements

MAGISTRATE JENNIFER COATE

O THERS DELIVERING PAPERS at this conference have identified how society and the edifice of the law seem to intersect briefly and then endeavour to separate themselves, or at least attempt to maintain a semblance of doing so. So too have discussions on the topic of victim impact statements.

The idea of victim impact statements has been around for some time and some states in Australia have already legislated to introduce them into the criminal justice system and others are intending to do so. So far the discussions in relation to their introduction in Australia have centred around their admission into evidence at the stage of sentencing of a convicted person only. In rape trials in some states in America by contrast, evidence of the victim's trauma has been admitted into the trial process itself as corroborative evidence of the victim's assertion of a lack of consent. This is not how victim impact statements are being used currently in Australia, or as I understand it, are intended to be used.

Those in favour of the introduction of victim impact statements maintain that their introduction will do two things. Firstly, it will allow the victim the opportunity to be heard. The victim will have a say inside the criminal justice system that traditionally focuses on the actions and intentions of the defendant and not the victim. It is stated that the victim, by the introduction of the process of victim impact statements, will no longer feel left out, ignored, silenced and devalued. The second basis on which those in favour of victim impact statements maintain the rights of victims will be advanced, is that it will provide information to the sentencer to ensure that the punishment fits the crime.

Let us examine these two stated purposes: first, that the introduction of victim impact statements will afford the victim an opportunity to have her views, concerns and experiences presented to the court (I use the term 'her' intentionally to focus this discussion on how victim impact statements affect women as victims of crime). Well, is this so? That is, will the introduction of victim impact statements give victims the opportunity to be heard?

In South Australia, a State that has introduced victim impact statements, these statements are largely prepared by the investigating police officers who, as I understand it, tick boxes on a multiple choice format. One can only briefly allow oneself to imagine the format. For example, I was (a) a bit scared, (b) very scared, (c) terrified. Perhaps the police are not the answer for the purposes of the preparation of victim impact statements.

So where do we look? To the experts? Then we are presented with our next perennial problem: who are they? Is an expert in the preparation of a victim impact statement a doctor, a counsellor, a sexual assault worker, a psychiatrist, a psychologist, a man, a woman? Think about it. If and when we decide that we are going to use an expert and who that expert might be, is our criminal justice system going to allow the evidence? Evidence of either the expert or the victim? Once the court has decided this question, the evidence if admissible will be subject to challenge and cross-examination, and therein lies one of the serious problems associated with the introduction of victim impact statements. Will a woman's experience of the criminal justice system really be enhanced by being subjected yet again to cross-examination or listening to the preparer of her report being cross-examined? Surely the public questioning of her experience and her reaction to the crime, the harm she has suffered in this continuing and potentially hostile adversarial context that we have read so much about, will not enhance her experience at all. Will it be empowering for her to be compelled to tell, either personally or via a third party, that her self esteem has been destroyed, that she is no longer able to socialise or work, or sleep, or that she has contracted genital warts?

Some may suggest that the remedy is for each woman to submit the material voluntarily and control what she wants to present. This will still not avoid the adversarial context in which material comes before the court, and one hastens to add that it also sounds slightly fanciful.

Further, it leads, I would predict, to cross-examination that will be directed towards minimising the impact of the crime on the particular woman in order to individualise the crime; to show the victim was unusually frail, or vulnerable, or promiscuous, or old or young and therefore not appropriate to be taken into account, because her individual experience has no relevance to the general deterrence principles of criminal sentencing. There is every likelihood that this process will feel no different for women who have had crimes of violence perpetrated against them and have been poked, prodded and cross-examined for hours through the trial process.

The second stated purpose behind the introduction of victim impact statements is reported to be their use as an aid to the sentencer in deciding what is an appropriate sentence; that is, to look at the harm caused to the victim to decide the level of criminality of the defendant in a particular matter. On the surface this looks sensible, even satisfying to those members of our community who advocate the 'lock 'em up and throw away the key' approach. But on closer examination, firstly in South Australia after the introduction of victim impact statements, the statistics showed that there was little or no discernible change to sentences being imposed. Perhaps one can explain this in the context of the criminal sentencing process which focuses on what the defendant thought and did, not what the outcome of his actions were. In a context which contains a lack of awareness about women's experience of violent crime, it is predictable that nothing will change. The focus of sentencing on principles such as specific and general deterrence will not be affected by the introduction of victim impact statements.

However, what do we do with our victims? How do we give those women who want the opportunity to have their say, to purge themselves of their horror and pain, to have their experiences validated, a time and a place to do so?

David Ford of Croydon wrote in today's Access Age in the *Age* that the term used by the series of the *Age* reports entitled 'The war against women', was misleading. 'A great problem exists', wrote Mr Ford, 'but there is no war'. I say to David Ford of Croydon; spend three months as the sitting member at the Criminal Injuries Compensation Tribunal from Monday to Friday, hearing ten to twelve applications per day, and then tell me there is no war. Know that what you are hearing for only three months is neither the beginning nor the end of the war. Know that what you are hearing only represents an unknown but undoubtedly small proportion of what is really happening to women and children out there, and then conclude there is no war.

After my own three months of sitting on the Criminal Injuries Compensation Tribunal, I felt overwhelmed, even paralysed. I felt the need to make some connection between what I was hearing there and what was happening inside the criminal trial process. I felt strongly that victims needed a forum for expressing their pain and validating what they had experienced. I concluded that the criminal trial process is not that place. It is the Criminal Injuries Compensation Tribunal that can and should serve that purpose. A forum that is non adversarial and not bound by the rules of evidence and focused on the victim.

I ask again, what is the purpose of providing a victim impact statement to the sentencer? Is it really to assist the sentencer? Given the number of judges in our superior courts and the variety of jurisdictions they are required to cover, it is clear that each judge would only hear a limited number of criminal trials that relate to crimes of violence against women and of those, a certain number of those would be pleas of guilty where the victim would not be involved at all.

The opportunity, in this context, for judges to move away from the particular harm and gain an insight into the general harm of crimes of violence against women is minimal.

It is my conclusion that there is great value in requiring judges at all levels of the criminal justice system to sit for three months on the Criminal Injuries Compensation Tribunal. Few people, including the judges of our superior courts, could come away from that jurisdiction unchallenged.

It is also to be noted that because of the different standards of proof required in the Criminal Injuries Tribunal (that is, the balance of probabilities rather than the criminal standard of beyond reasonable doubt) a number of dismissals and acquittals in the criminal justice system in fact present themselves for scrutiny in a different way at the Criminal Injuries Compensation Tribunal. It is my view that, by being so exposed to the overwhelming number of women surviving violent crime, the cause of educating the judiciary would be advanced. By comparison, the victim impact statement model of hearing individualised and isolated experiences of women in an adversarial atmosphere provides only a minimum exposure to learning. At the Criminal Injuries Compensation Tribunal, through exposure to so many individual cases in a concentrated period, judges may be able to observe the general harm of violence against women. Further, judges will be able to hear, and women will be able to say directly to those responsible for the conduct of criminal trials, how the adversarial criminal trial process affected them. This is the process that would allow women victims to have their say to those who sentence.

Postscript

Victorian Legislation regarding victim impact statements was introduced in May 1994.

In 1997 the Victorian State Government made significant legislative changes to the *Criminal Injuries Compensation Act*, reducing the capacity of victims to appear at the tribunal.

19

Gender bias and industrial relations law

MELANIE YOUNG

Tₕᵢₛ...

THIS PAPER FOCUSES ON the attitudes of decision makers to which I have been exposed in my practice as a solicitor in the area of industrial and employment law.

The very same sexist attitudes detailed elsewhere at this conference, permeate the legal decision making process in relation to women in employment. As in the other areas of law we have heard about, employment cases generally involve the exercise of wide discretions and the making of value judgments.

In making Federal Awards setting rates of pay and conditions for working people, the Australian Industrial Relations Commission is to have regard to the interests of the parties and to the interests of the Australian community as a whole.[139] State tribunals, and in some cases the Federal Court, determine unfair dismissal applications by reference to the reasonableness of the parties' behaviour, and whether the employee got 'a fair go' all round.[140] The Anti-Discrimination and Equal Opportunity Tribunals must decide whether conduct is less favourable, whether it is reasonable, and whether certain persons are subject to a detriment.

Marcia Neave has mentioned that some of the decisions in relation to the position of women in employment have displayed sex bias in a subtle way, but I have to say that my experience is quite different. There is no mystery to me at all about the sex bias in legal decisions in relation to women in employment. The views expressed by tribunal and court members are those that we could hear in the Australian stereotypical environment out in the street, at lunch time or even at the football. They are just dressed up in different words with more syllables.

Let us pretend that we are at a barbecue. We are in John and Betty's back yard. It is a nice day and we're all drinking beer. You overhear John talking to Bob. They appear to have met for the first time. Bob says to John, 'So what does your wife do?' John says, 'She doesn't go to work, she just looks after the kids. I wouldn't have her working, it is just not right.'

One of the (hopefully) more outdated Australian beliefs was that women should not engage in paid employment at all. It would also have you believe that paid work actually belonged to men and that women who sought to perform it were encroaching upon territory belonging to men. Women were described in the Industrial Court in the 1920s as being the 'gentle invaders' in the area of paid employment.

Also deeply entrenched has been the notion that men were generally married and were breadwinners. Women were generally married and supported by their husbands, and if they weren't, they should have been. And so from the early 1900s, we had powerful industrial tribunals setting wage rates for large numbers of Australian workers, by reference to John-and-Bob-like reasoning.

Here's an example.

> I found that girls were also employed in the manufacture of the smaller types of attaché cases when made of fibre. It has been the practice in the industry for the girls to make the children's lunch cases and similar small fibre cases up to, and including, cases of 13 inches. But all cases above 13 inches have been made by male labour. Of course, a girl could comfortably make a case much larger than 13 inches, but she ought not to be employed on the making of the very large cases. The making of certain sizes of cases is recognised as men's work. The line has to be drawn somewhere and I am informed that in this industry it is drawn at 13 inches.[141]

Now, why am I telling you about such old cases? Those of you who have actually left the barbecue have thought of that question. The answer is that they remain highly relevant. The effects of these cases have not been redressed. Despite equal pay submissions from women's groups in wage cases since the 1920s, the Australian Industrial Court, superseded by the Conciliation and Arbitration Commission, now the Australian Industrial Relations Commission, whose determinations are generally followed by State Industrial Tribunals have simply refused and/or failed to address the question or the problem of unequal pay.

Whilst the gap is closing, women still do not earn what male workers earn. The latest figures are that women who work in full-time, paid employment earn on average about 83% of the male wage. This figure does not take into account the fact that women predominate in the area of part-time work, because they shoulder the responsibility of caring for the family. It also doesn't take into account that, again due to family responsibilities, women are unable to undertake overtime work at higher rates to the same extent as men.

The problem of unequal pay is obviously due to a large number of factors but it includes the failure of the industrial tribunals to do anything at all about the problem. Wage rates in industries are still founded on rates set many years ago. What has the Commission done about this and what opportunities has it had? We go right back to the famous Fruit Pickers case in 1911 when the Industrial Court set, for the first time, a basic wage, not by reference to the employers capacity to pay or the productivity of the employee, but by reference to the needs of the average employee in the community. This was a very progressive move for working people.

The court fixed higher rates for work which was men's work because it was considered that men have different needs from those of women. The normal needs of men were to support a wife and children whilst the needs of women were to find their own food, shelter and clothing. It was a principle of wage fixation that the tribunal's first task was to determine whether the work under consideration was men's or women's. Higher or lower rates would be set accordingly.

The one feature of the Australian work force which has remained constant is that it is segregated along sex lines. Men predominate in the metal and trade industries, women predominate in the service and clerical industries. In 1926 the Liquor Trades Union claimed that there should be equal pay for equal work for barmaids and barmen. The claim was rejected by the court because:

> … from time immemorial, men have been employed on a man's wage and women have been employed on a woman's wage. And it is one of several in which a similar state of affairs exist and must exist. I call to mind all kinds of domestic service, clerical work, work in shops and so on, where men are employed on a man's wage and women are employed on a woman's wage. And where, in my opinion, they must continue to be so employed.
>
> I can understand an equal wage being awarded in an industry where it is designed to push women out of employment. In other words, if the employer had to pay men and women at the same rate, they would choose the male candidate. But that object is disclaimed in this industry. There has been observed for a long time a tendency to substitute women for men in industries, even in occupations that are more suited for men, and in such occupations it is often the results of women being paid lower wages than men. Fortunately for society, however, the greater number of breadwinners are still men. The women are not all dragged from their homes to work while the men loaf at home.[142]

In the depression years in the 1930s all wage rates were reduced by 10% and this was particularly bad for women who were already only earning 50–60% of the male wage. In the war years, in the 1940s, women performed the men's work, whilst the men fought the war. A Women's Employment Board was established to set the pay rates for women doing men's work and women actually fared well under this system. Pay rates rose sometimes to 80–100% of the male rate. That is not to say that the members of the Women's Employment Board did not hold the traditional sexist views held by others in the Australian community. Some pay rates were reduced because females absent themselves from work much more frequently than males, much to the very great embarrassment of the managers and the industry.

> There is much need to emphasise what a disastrous effect absenteeism has upon production, particularly upon mass production where each process depends upon the one immediately before it, and controls the one immediately succeeding it. The loss of productivity over all the departments of the applicant in this case, is due to the excess of female absenteeism.[143]

In 1969 the Australian Industrial Relations Commission (the Federal Commission) adopted the principle of equal pay for equal work. However, it was only prepared to accept the unions equal pay claim to the extent that it applied to women who performed work of precisely the same character as men. This is no good for Australian women, because the majority of them were, and still are, employed across a few women's industries.

In the 1972 Equal Pay Case, the Federal Commission came to the view that the concept of equal pay for equal work is too narrow in today's world and the time had come to enlarge the concept to equal pay for work of equal value. This meant that award rates for all work should be considered without regard to the sex of the employee. This was really no advance at all for women who had to show that they did the same work as men under the same award to get the same pay. Again, it failed to take account of the fact that few women work in men's industries.

It took until 1974, which is not all that long ago, for the Federal Commission to formally renounce the principle that male wages should be set at a higher rate than female wages, on the basis that the man had a family to support.

In 1983 the Women's Electoral Lobby submitted to the Federal Commission that it should undertake 'proper work value' exercises, comparing work across industries. To this it was said, by the Commission:

> ... we consider that such large scale work value enquiries would clearly provide an opportunity for the development of additional tiers of wage increases which would be inconsistent with the centralised system which we propose for the next two years, and would also be inappropriate in the current state of unemployment especially amongst women.

In 1986 the Nurses Union had another go and submitted that the Federal Commission should adopt the concept of comparable worth which compared job duties and responsibilities between and across different occupations and industries. The Federal Commission again refused the submission, and said that such an approach would (if you can understand this) 'strike at the heart of long accepted methods of wage fixation in this country and would be particularly destructive of the present wage fixing principles'.

In each of the 1990/1991/1992 Wage Cases, and this year, in the Family Court Counsellors Case, a group called the Australian Federation of Business and Professional Women made equal pay submissions to the Federal Commission. Its principal submission was that the Commission should undertake a complete work skills value inquiry as a matter of urgency. Well, what about work value? Let us go back to the barbecue.

Bob replies to John, 'I think it was best for everybody, including Betty, that she didn't go to work. Women just can't work all that well'. John says, 'She does do a little bit of part-time work now that the kids are at school. But it is just cleaning work.'

In the Federal Commission the very same attitudes have influenced the setting of wage rates and conditions for women. It is just dressed up with fancy words. Early on, the Industrial Court considered the evidence established that

> unmarried as well as married women are subject to the physical limita-
> tions of their sex and each suffers a lot from those incidents of industrial
> work, most detrimental to the female reproductive system. Such as
> overstrain from the excessive speed, complexity, prolonged standing and
> the absence of monthly days of rest.[144]

So not only do women have an inherent incapacity, but their work has always been undervalued, and this continues today.

Another difficulty for women is that women's work tends to be very difficult to value, whereas usually men's work is not. The Federal Commission finds it easy to assess the productivity of vehicle production at the GMH factory who produce four cars a day, but they find it more difficult to assess the productivity of say Family Court counsellors who are predominantly women. How do you measure their productivity? Is it the number of hours they work? The number of couples they see? The number of couples with children they see? The number of couples who stay together? The number who divorce? The number who don't cry? There's no doubt it is a difficult task, but the Commission really has just failed to take it on board at all.

It is obvious that industrial tribunals are of fundamental importance to women. The Australian Industrial Relations Commission potentially has tremendous power, because on one view it holds one of the keys to advancing the position of women in the community generally. It is fairly difficult to argue with the proposition that women need economic independence to achieve equality. The Federal Commission doesn't just deal with individual disputes coming before it. It sets rates of pay and conditions across whole industries, and at times, it makes decisions that affect the entire work force covered by Federal Awards.[145]

A relevant development in the last decade is the attempt by the Australian State Parliaments to advance the position of women in employment, by enacting anti-discrimination and equal opportunity legislation which is more progressive than some community values. Most equal opportunity cases at the State and Federal level are in relation to employment, whether it be refusal to employ a person, to afford them benefits during the employment, or dismissing them.

In addition to the points already raised by Rosemary Hunter and Moira Rayner about the undesirability of the high level of legal formality in the discrimination complaint process, I would like to make a few more points. It goes without saying that the reasoning of the Anti-Discrimination and Equal Opportunity Boards and Tribunals is usually light years ahead of the Industrial Relations Commission. But we must not forget that occasionally members of the Tribunals and Boards are not immune from sexist community values and may fall into bad ways.

The other point I would like to make is that Anti-Discrimination Tribunals, and here I speak particularly of the Federal Human Rights and Equal Opportunity Commission, have been absolutely hopeless in assessing the level of harm suffered by complainants. Awards of $7000 and $8000 are awarded to women who are sexually harassed and sometimes raped in employment. These women would get greater sums of damages from a County Court judge if they had lost their finger in an industrial accident case.

There are already enormous disincentives for women who have been sexually harassed and assaulted at work to proceed with legal action. However, the pitiful awards of compensation often mean that an action may not even be economically viable because the complainant may not recover enough to pay her own legal costs.

The other significant area in which industrial tribunals have failed to understand the reality of women's position in relation to employment is the need for child care in order to be able to work. For years women's groups have been submitting to the Federal Commission that the Commission ought to recognise child care as an industrial issue and provide for it in awards. The response, or rather the non-response, of the Commission in 1983 was:

> ... many of the problems which the Women's Electoral Lobby has raised
> are a matter for management, union and governments rather than for
> award provisions.

I know you are dying to get back to the barbecue.
You see Betty. She has getting a beer for John. She does not look very well.

Little wonder. You ask her what she's been doing lately. Each day she prepares three meals for five people, irons 40 shirts, washes clothes and cleans, attends part-time paid work, collects her pay at 70% of the wages of her male colleagues, has to look at the pictures of naked women on the calendars on the walls at work, picks up the kids from school and organises this barbecue.

Does she have any choice in this situation? No, because it is a vicious circle. My principal message to you is that whilst the problem of violence against women in the home, in employment and elsewhere is justifiably immediate and urgent, we must not underestimate the importance of women's economic independence, often only available through paid employment.

We must not forget this when developing a strategy of action and we must not continue to let the industrial tribunals off the hook.

20

Department of Social Security prosecutions and sentencing of women offenders

ANNE THACKER

I HAVE A FAIRLY SHORT point to make, and we have all heard it before: 'The punishment must fit the crime'. It is not only the famous Gilbert and Sullivan who make that comment. Legal texts on sentencing all say the same. However, the application of what purports to be gender neutral criminal law may amount to something else when applied to women 'social security offenders', especially those who live in poverty.

I use the description 'women' because it is mostly women who come before the courts charged with having illegally obtained Department of Social Security benefits and/or pensions. I say 'women living in poverty' because it is well documented that 60% of people living in poverty in Australia today are women.

My observation, from six year's experience of court appearance work on behalf of defendants, including women charged under the criminal provisions of the *Social Security Act* and/or the *Commonwealth Crimes Act*, is that magistrates and judges have difficulty with the task of sentencing women and the sentence is not, in my opinion, always right.

The issue focuses on attitude. Attitude is dependent on understanding the lives of the defendants before the court. In Department of Social Security prosecutions, too often, wider community attitude intrudes. The sentencer succumbs and aligns with wider community views rather than keeping a rational and fair perspective on the offending behaviour.

It is not a new observation that 'ripping off the Tax Office' (principally a male activity) is considered socially acceptable by comparison with Social Security fraud. This phenomenon is apparent in the court room and is evidenced in the disparity in sentencing between these two types of offences.

The fact is, the government loses (directly and indirectly) more money through taxation fraud than it does via Department of Social Security fraud. It might also be said that the money obtained illegally from Department of Social Security fraud is put to a comparatively essential community service, namely child-rearing, when no one else is likely to do the job. Nevertheless, there is a harsh, (and often emotional) response to 'social security offending' even where the expenditure of the money obtained is not for the offender herself. Nothing is ever said about the failure/refusal of the children's father to provide; that is not relevant to the charge against her.

It might be the case that we agree that Department of Social Security criminal activity is dealt with harshly and that we part company with the justification for doing so. Sentencers often remark on the need to protect the public purse, the fact that there is not a bottomless purse to be drawn from, and the overriding terrors of the floodgates being opened.

However, I say there must be something terribly wrong with a community which tolerates tax evasion, Medicare fraud and other types of frauds—God forbid anybody suggesting that any fraud of the Veteran Affairs Department, for example, would ever be criminally prosecuted—but which becomes enraged by the actions of people who act so often out of need to fulfil the basic requirements of living.

There is no doubt about it; there has always been dilemma when sentencing those described as 'needy offenders' as compared to the 'greedy offenders'. I am directing my comments to the situation of the 'needy offender' and the imperative that she be recognised and dealt with as such. (We could also debate what amounts to 'needy' in the context of Australian society today.)

Inappropriate sentences include:
• heavy fines; for example, some magistrates in particular, consistently fine all offenders an amount equal to the amount illegally obtained, without reference to actual ability to pay;
• imprisonment where sentencers see 'no other alternative', because fining exacerbates the poverty of the household, or a community based order is not practical; for example, because childcare is unavailable; and
• ordering full restitution to the Department of Social Security without exception.

Let me use one example: in 1991 the criminal prosecution of Ms Simmonds was heard which may be compared with the criminal prosecution of two barristers for tax evasion in the same year.

The case against Simmonds charged that she had obtained approximately $47 000 illegally from the Department of Social Security. She had commenced receiving a benefit in 1964. However, in 1978 she commenced a part-time job under a false name and continued in that job until 1990. During the twelve-year period she falsely stated to the Department, six times, that she was not in employment. Simmonds had three children and by 1991 they were aged 27, 21 and 15, and she was still supporting the youngest. Simmonds pleaded guilty to one charge of imposition on the Commonwealth and one charge of fraud. Her motivation was put simply: she needed the money to exist and to assist with the education of her children. She had received no financial support from any of the three men who had fathered her children. She had always resided in Ministry of Housing accommodation. She had never owned a car. She had never owned any personal possessions of any value. When you worked it out, the overpayment was about $80–90 per week and her average wage/income over the period was $200 a week.

She was sentenced to 18 months imprisonment, suspended on her entry into a three-year bond to be of good behaviour with a recognisance in the sum of $2000 attached.

Further, a restitution order was made for the full amount of $47 000. I have been unable to discover whether or not the restitution order was attached to the suspension of imprisonment conditions. I can say that, in my experience, it is the case that restitution is often attached so that for the three-year period she must repay the $47 000 or face the court again to be dealt with for breach of the good behaviour bond. The imprisonment sentence, or some part of it, could then be activated. The point I am making is that for a further three years, Simmonds was subject to the scrutiny of the criminal justice system.

The tax evaders, by comparison, had both underestimated their incomes by about $100 000 over three-year periods. They each evaded the payment of some $50 000 of tax. Neither of them had any prior convictions (I do not believe Simmonds had any prior convictions). The first one was sentenced to six months imprisonment, suspended for 12 months. The second was sentenced to three months imprisonment, suspended for 12 months.

Comparison of the maximum penalties provided for the offences under the Tax Act and under the *Commonwealth Crimes Act* (used for Department of Social Security frauds), reveals that the maximum penalties are almost double with respect to *Tax Act* frauds: under section 86A of the *Tax Act* the maximum penalty is twenty years or $200 000 fine or both. Under section 29D of the *Commonwealth Crimes Act* the penalty is ten years or $100 000 fine or both.

This leads me to the matter of what sentencers may do when sentencing offenders. There are, undoubtedly, limitations on what is available. Sentencers must operate within the relevant Act following the maximum penalties provided. As you can see they have some considerable leeway—something up to twenty years imprisonment or ten years imprisonment, depending on whether it is Tax Department or Department of Social Security fraud.

There are some things that can be done by a judiciary that is well informed, has studied and come to an awareness and understanding of the position of women who defraud the Department when, in every other aspect of their lives, they are exemplary citizens. Almost without exception, these women plead guilty at the earliest opportunity and they are able to say to the court, 'I am X years old, I have never been in trouble before'. It is the classic opening plea in mitigation for one of these matters.

What I am saying is that the concept of justice is a much broader concept than the single issue of legality. Once need is established, the sentencers could take the broader view of justice and sentence in a way that fully recognises the context of these women's lives, and fully appreciates that creative sentencing is called for to overcome the additional burden caused to these women by fitting them into categories of sentences not designed directly to accommodate the type of offence for which they are before the court. Ultimately, the legislation requires review to create more viable options.

The discussions in court often centre upon the fact that there is no viable option: imprisonment or suspension of a term of imprisonment become two extremes. Women, who in every other aspect of their lives are exemplary and model citizens, remain subject to the criminal justice system for far longer than many other offenders in more heinous categories of offence. It works like this—imprisonment is ordered and then suspended with conditions attached in circumstances where it is not intended that the imprisonment would ever actually be activated. The general assumption is that 'she won't get into trouble again, she's a first offender at her age.' Unfortunately, the conditions are breached for reasons never contemplated by the sentencer—for example:

- lack of any affordable, or often any, childcare facilities which means an inability to attend the Office of Corrections to perform the community based order;
- isolation and fear for safety as the only woman completing community work with a gang of male offenders, so she does not go back; or
- inability to make restitution as ordered.

The community endorses (to say the least) women's dependency on men, with the consequence that women have fewer choices about their independence. The history and explanation of this matter and how it impacts with the law, is well documented—see, for example, *The Hidden Gender of the Law* by Jenny Morgan and Regina Graycar, and Jocelynne Scutt's *Women and the Law*. One example is related to the change to Department of Social Security pensions and benefits. Historically, the Department sought to assist families in need. It no longer professes to do that. The Department will now assist only particular categories of 'needy applicants'. 'Needy applicants' live with (what I call) the demise of the basic wage. The basic wage was introduced in the 1920s, designed to keep a man and wife and children. The concept of a basic wage no longer has that purpose. What we have witnessed to replace it is the development of the Family Allowance. Unfortunately, both the systems lock women dependent upon them, into a cycle of poverty. Employment restrictions for women (who are still clustered in the lower paid sections of the workforce) exacerbates the problem. You are never going to get a promotion with Family Allowance, regardless of need. In fact we have, recently, seen the reduction of Family Allowance payments. It has been the institutionalisation of gender roles, including the division of labour according to sex, which has shaped women's domestic responsibilities and their patterns of employment and which confines women generally to an income with a low ceiling.

So far as development of the law is concerned, we face another problem, in my view: Department of Social Security fraud charges are dealt with by the Magistrates Courts in the main, with more serious charges (in terms of the amount obtained) heard by the County Court. An appeal process is available. It is only via the appeal process that the Supreme Court will hear one of these types of cases. A consequence that flows from this is a limitation on/restriction to the development of ideas and understanding of the offences and/or offending behaviour. Some of the matters I have raised today are not appropriate for discussion in a plea in mitigation in the Magistrates Court. One reason is that there is no time in the busy Magistrates Court list. It is in the superior courts that development of principle takes place and rules are made which must be followed by the lower courts. We have the benefit of a long history of criminal law refined in detailed examination over many cases scrutinised by the superior courts. However, this is not happening in Department of Social Security fraud cases because these cases rarely reach the superior courts.

The sentencing principle of deterrence is used in relation to Department of Social Security cases as a justification for sentences in a way in which it is not used in other cases. It has only been recently that the Victorian Supreme Court had the opportunity to hear an appeal in a Department of Social Security case and therefore the opportunity to consider this issue: *DPP v. Cory Jones* (30.10.92), an unreported (and I emphasise that fact) judgment of the Full Court, comprising Phillips CJ and Crockett J, Nathan J dissenting.

Nathan J's decision is often referred to by some magistrates, even though he was dissenting! He confirmed the view that there is justification for treating Department of Social Security fraud offenders harshly to protect the public purse, which is 'not a limitless font but the product of the work and enterprise of fellow citizens'. He states:

> Social Security frauds are in the nature of stealing from friends and neighbours. General deterrence as a sentencing factor is likely to be effective with regard to crimes of this sort.

By contrast the majority rejected this narrow focus of attention on general deterrence which is a significant shift of judicial attitude. However, the majority judgment also and most unfortunately, reveals an apparent inability by the judges to articulate why they agreed with Mrs Cory's counsel that no actual term of imprisonment should properly be imposed, as it does not detail specific factors that led to their decision.

Developments in the law are needed to take account of the wide variety of circumstances that come before the courts. Such development would make for fair application of the law, which so often appears gender neutral but which, when applied equally to offenders in unequal circumstances, is not so.

21

Judicial attitudes and women's credibility
Barriers to equality in law

KATHY MACK

> Listening to women and believing their stories is central to feminist method.[146]
>
> Feminist method starts with the very radical act of taking women seriously.[147]
>
> Believing women is a radical step because the world generally and the law in particular regard women as less worthy of belief than men, specifically because they are women.[148]

I will first describe the general credibility gap between men and women, then expand on ways that judicial attitudes reflect and reinforce the lessened credibility for women. Two particular areas I will address are:
- judicial treatment of reform legislation which attempts to restore some credibility to women's evidence when testifying to sexual assault; and
- the impact on women when there is a strong judicial policy in favour of out of court settlement, especially the move to mediation in family law.

I will then point out why changing judicial attitudes, and hence judicial education, is essential to remedy the credibility gap facing women in law.

The refusal to hear women, to take us and what we say seriously, to accord women the same respect and credibility men automatically receive is one of the major barriers to achieving equality. Some say that judges should reflect community attitudes. Denial of belief in women is a community attitude I do not want reflected in judges' attitudes and decisions. I want judges to recognise that this refusal to listen to women, seriously and with respect, is a form of gender bias.[149] I want judges to act to remedy this bias and offer women the equality the law promises and that judges promise to deliver when they take their oaths of office: to 'do equal justice'.

The central responsibility of the legal system is justice. It is '… unthinkable that the courts could be content merely to mirror social bias, rather than aspiring to higher ideals of fairness …'[150] I believe that judges want to be fair. If they understand the ways that even apparently natural conduct is biased and damaging, I hope they will want to avoid behaviour that will bring themselves and the system they seek to serve into disrepute.

Some examples of the credibility gap between men and women I will describe can be seen in non-legal settings. Frequently replicated studies have shown that when matched groups of teachers are asked to evaluate identical sets of essays, those essays attributed to men receive higher marks than identical essays attributed to women. The supposedly male-authored essays receive praise as being better written or more persuasive.[151] Similar research has been done with evaluation of formal articles, although the devaluation of women's work was much more marked among male groups than among female groups discussing the articles.[152]

Another study examined over 16 000 teacher evaluation forms which students at the University of California are required to submit in each subject. Women teachers were rated superior in the categories of being better prepared, having mastery of the material, and being more responsive to students. However, male teachers were evaluated as more credible, more authoritative, and more persuasive, and this difference was much more dramatically marked for male students, showing a dramatic prejudice in favour of male teachers.[153]

Another aspect of this gender credibility gap is shown by general social expectations about how a credible speaker is supposed to sound: like a man. Studies have identified a number of language features associated with powerlessness. Examples include: superlatives, intensifiers ('so' 'such'), fillers ('um' 'you know'), empty adjectives, tag questions with rising intonation (even with an accurate assertion), hedges ('sort of'), and politeness markers.[154] It appears that these features are used more often by women than by men, though class, education and the particular power relationship between the speakers are also significant factors.[155] Other qualities more likely to occur when women speak are high pitched voices and frequent smiling.[156] These are also associated with powerlessness (or fear) and hence lack of credibility. Women use less numerical specificity, less often, where men use more specificity with less accuracy.[157] Women are more likely to speak in hesitant language even if they are sure, where men are more likely to speak with assurance, even if unsure or wrong.[158] However, with eye-witnesses at least, a confident manner does not necessarily indicate accuracy.[159] Other studies have shown that good looks help men, but cause women to be devalued as they are believed to have succeeded for reasons other than talent.[160]

The cumulative effect of these qualities is to cause women to be perceived as less credible, even when accurate and honest. '… Both women and men perceive women as being less credible than men in all the senses of the term, and the recent years have by no means eliminated these attitudes'.[161]

How does this gender gap in credibility, this denial of credibility to women, operate in the legal system? The North American gender bias task force reports, which have been previously described, have documented in great and specific detail many ways in which women lawyers, litigants, and witnesses experience discriminatory treatment from male lawyers, courtroom personnel and sometimes judges. Examples include asking a woman who has just won a trial if she is sleeping with the judge, or a court clerk saying to a pregnant lawyer as she entered the courtroom 'What do you think this is, a delivery room?'[162] This biased conduct includes inappropriate forms of address, suggestive comments, and even verbal and physical harassment. This undermines credibility and puts additional unwarranted burdens on female advocates, parties and witnesses which is inconsistent with stated ideals of neutrality and equality in law.[163]

We all have stories of our experiences with this sort of direct and subtle bias. I will tell one of my own. My first full-time job after law school was in a prosecutor's office in California. On the first day, the phone rang on my desk. I answered with my name. Brief pause on the other end. Male voice: 'Well this is Joe Bloggs, I wanted to talk to the lawyer handling the Jones case, but I guess you'll do.' Not terrible as such stories go, but it has stayed with me. I shall now return to the two areas which I indicated at the outset that I want to particularly address:

• judicial treatment of reform legislation which attempts to restore some credibility to women's evidence when testifying to sexual assault; and
• the impact on women when there is a strong judicial policy in favour of out of court settlement, especially the move to mediation in family law.

The first issue, the ways in which the law, formally and informally, denigrates women and devalues their testimony when they speak of being sexually assaulted has been thoroughly described in other papers. I would only add a couple of points. The disadvantages of using a less powerful speech style in a legal context may go beyond simply damaged credibility. One recent study suggests that listeners, including judges, are more likely to treat the powerless speaker as being to blame in a dispute.[164]

Many of the formal barriers in law, the special rules diminishing women's credibility when testifying about rape, such as the expectation of recent complaint, the use of sexual history, or requirements of warning of a need for corroboration, have been re-examined and changed by statute.[165] Unfortunately, an examination of the treatment courts have given these legislative changes shows the limited impact of law reform in this area, the tenacity of the legal system's distrust of women and a continuing acceptance of false beliefs about women and rape throughout the judiciary.

In Canada, the United Kingdom, and some states in the United States and Australia, there has been clear evidence of the failure of the courts to properly implement laws which attempt to control the use of sexual history of women who accuse men of rape.[166] In both Canada and South Australia, the legislature has had a second try at preventing this particular mistreatment of women as witnesses in courts.[167]

An examination of Australian appellate cases shows that trial judges have continued to warn juries that it is unsafe to convict without corroboration, after legislation has removed the requirement for such a warning or even forbidden such an instruction.[168] In cases where judges have not warned juries to be careful of women testifying about sexual assault, apparently in accord with the legislative directions, convictions have been overturned on the basis that warnings attacking the woman's credibility were needed in the particular circumstances of the case, as a matter of the court's discretion, thereby undoing the impact of the remedial legislation. [169] [170]

I have described some problems of gender bias with judicial application of reform legislation in the area of rape law. A similar problem exists with divorce reform legislation: '… judicial attitudes impede the implementation of the law on the books, and help explain the disastrous financial status of many women and children following divorce.'[171] Again, this is a problem that has been fully canvassed elsewhere in the conference. The particular point I want to address is the impact of the denial of credibility experienced by women in light of the increasing push for mediation and other forms of informal dispute resolution in family law.

In the Australian legal system, marriage is, by definition, a relationship between one man and one woman.[172] This means that divorce is necessarily a dispute between one man and one woman. Although the interests of any children of the marriage are critical and there may be other family or financial interests to be considered, the core dispute remains one between a man and a woman. Because of this gendered pattern of divorce, issues of gender bias in the dispute resolution process and in disparate outcomes are more significant and, paradoxically, both more and less apparent, than in other areas of dispute.

Gender bias is more apparent because, in so many disputes between a woman and a man, any systemic bias will eventually occur often enough to be noticed. Even though a particular divorce dispute is treated individually, with emphasis on factors specific to that family, when the overall picture of family law disputes is examined, patterns of bias emerge. At the same time, gender bias is less apparent because the structure of gender roles and the male–female relations within the family are so deeply embedded in our society and have been so thoroughly constructed as private and natural that actually seeing the gender bias within the structure is difficult.

In recent years there has been much attention paid to concerns that women (and the children who live with them) are considerably worse off financially than men after divorce.[173] Concern about this issue has led scholars to look closely at dispute resolution processes in family law for explanations and possible solutions to this disparity in outcome.[174] One proposal to improve dispute resolution in family law is to emphasise mediation.[175] In some ways, it has been suggested that mediation could help offset the disadvantages imposed on women by the lack of credibility accorded them, disadvantages which may be aggravated by the adversarial legal system. Women's voices may be able to be heard in a mediation process which emphasises good communication and cooperation. Among the ground rules a family mediator usually lays down are requirements that participants do not interrupt each other, that they listen to each other, that each speaks for himself or herself and avoids putting words into the other person's mouth. These will all help women who are attempting to speak in a world where men are much more likely to interrupt women or to monopolise conversation time.[176] Training for mediators in recognising gender bias and developing strategies for minimising its impact may also be helpful, and this is becoming a more usual part of mediator training in Australia. Where the mediator is skilled at structuring and reframing disputes and helping parties to understand feelings, it may have the effect of defusing the impact of some power imbalances.[177]

The biggest problem with mediation for women is that fair mediation assumes equal bargaining power. The reality is that husbands, at the point of divorce, are likely to have more bargaining power than their wives. Women are likely to have little money readily available, and certainly less than their husbands.[178] Thus, women may not be able to hire a lawyer or an accountant and legal aid may not be available. In most marital households, men are likely to have greater information, especially about family finances. If, as is usual, the man's income is the major cash resource for the household,[179] he will know its amount, its disposition, other related entitlements such as superannuation and the status of assets purchased with family funds, all of which may be wholly or partly concealed from his wife. Men's greater physical power can lead to intimidation. Women report pressure from their husbands, both during and outside mediation to settle on terms favourable to their husbands.[180] There is widespread agreement that mediation is inappropriate if physical violence is involved, as it too often is in family breakdown.[181]

The credibility gap is also a major factor in making mediation inappropriate for women. In litigation, a woman has a trained advocate acting for her, whose professional voice will be heard. In mediation, a woman has to assert her own needs and interests in her own voice. In part because of their experiences of not being heard or taken seriously, women generally expect fewer entitlements and are less experienced at asserting their own entitlements.[182] It is often harder for a woman to identify and claim her own needs; she may be readier to assert another's interests (for example children).[183] She may also feel the need to clothe her own claims in the form of another's needs. Instead of asking for what she needs for herself, a woman may ask for money on the basis that the children need it.

In spite of the ideal of mediator neutrality, the informality of mediation may permit greater scope for bias.[184] Even a well-trained, experienced mediator is socialised into gendered views,[185] which we all are to a greater or lesser extent. Thus the mediator may suppress women's legitimate expressions of anger, expect women to be less assertive and more cooperative and may penalise them if they fail to conform. [186] [187] The mediator may defer to the more assertive, 'powerful' male,[188] for example by accepting male work obligations as of more importance than those of women,[189] or by pressuring a more compliant woman, who speaks less powerfully, to settle.[190]

This analysis may appear to perpetuate the stereotype of women as victims, dependents, or even worse, blaming women for their own disadvantages in bargaining. This is not so.[191] To the extent that women are more vulnerable in bargaining situations, it is the 'hostile world in which women live, not women's inherent weaknesses [which] creates each of the tangible and intangible differences I describe'.[192]

What can be done about this credibility gap, one among many of the ways women lack power and are disadvantaged in the world at large and in the legal system? The full remedy for gender inequality lies in broad social change so that the context in which women speak enables them to be heard and believed. Better education on the nature of gender bias and its impact, for judges as well as other members of the legal profession, is an essential step in this change. Why focus on judges and courts, when gender bias is clearly part of a larger social problem of gender inequality?

As I said before, one reason is the special place of the legal system, whose central responsibility is justice. It is 'unthinkable that the courts could be content merely to mirror social bias, rather than aspiring to higher ideals of fairness.'[193] A second reason is to recognise the special role of judges within the legal system. Judges as a group may be no better and no worse than others of their age and class and educational background. Some are quite aware of issues of bias and are concerned; but many more are not. However, judges promise to be better in this regard. They take an oath to be fair and impartial, and to apply laws in a legal system that promises equality. So judges, who determine what the law will actually deliver, cannot demonstrate bias or prejudice on the basis of gender, or class or race, even if such biases are present in the community.

Again, I believe that judges want to be fair. A judge's personal commitment to fairness and justice and to the ideal of equality under the law will be a powerful motivation to understand and act to end gender bias when it is shown to exist. The power of the judiciary within the legal system gives judges a particular opportunity to act positively to counteract bias. A judge's standards of fairness (or bias, however unconscious) set the legal rules and professional standards to which all others conform.

Judges apply the laws, and, as is shown by an examination of law reform in rape, have enormous impact on whether such remedial legislation actually has the positive impact Parliament intended. A judge's behaviour, in open court, in chambers, at public and private functions, sets the standards for lawyers, litigants, witnesses, jurors and other court personnel. Judges can indicate directly and by example what is appropriate treatment for women, as lawyers, as litigants, as witnesses, in court and in chambers; and what is not acceptable. Where divorce disputes are mediated, judges have the duties of overseeing the referral to mediation from the courts, determining the training needed for mediators and approving or rejecting mediated settlements.

There are two main objections which have been made to general judicial education as well as education specifically about bias. First is the claim that a few lectures won't make any difference, and second is the assertion that such educational programs amount to indoctrination into some 'politically correct' view and are a threat to essential judicial independence. Both objections assume judges are incompetent. The essence of the judicial role/task is to listen to evidence, or presentations by lawyers, to weigh the information and arguments and use it for what it is worth. The first objection assumes judges are so closed-minded and unwilling to listen that nothing said will make a difference. The second objection assumes the opposite: that judges are so weak-minded that any presentation which effectively challenges their views will lead to their instant intellectual collapse.

I also want to challenge the label 'politically correct' when it is attached to information about the social reality of gender bias. When one side of a debate sinks to name-calling, you can be sure that side is in trouble. There have always been rules about what views are acceptable or 'correct', what should be thought and said, and what should not. For many years these rules, in society generally and in law, were rules that denigrated women. It was politically correct to deny the value of women's work, to pay women less when they were paid at all, to deny women reproductive freedom, and to subject them to violence. These 'politically correct' views were backed up by a dominant ideology that upheld male power, class power and race power for whites. Those who fear losing the undeserved power given by these criteria (which do not reflect merit in any form, but only accidents of birth) are unable to answer the challenge with facts or logic or reason, so they sneer and call names, like 'hairy armpit old tart' if they are vulgar or which are 'politically correct' if they wish to appear sophisticated. No person of good will, in these changing times, should fear the opportunity for information, new ideas, and frank discussion.

Experience in North America with integrating attention to gender issues into regular programs of judicial education has been positive, according to feedback from the judges and from the community.[194] Because the legal system both structures and reflects wider social values, it is essential that the legal system recognise its own gender bias and implement needed changes. An essential reform which can be immediately implemented is to provide information about gender bias to judges, lawyers, court personnel and other professionals in the legal system. Of these, the most important is judicial education.

22

The criminal trial in the County Court

CHIEF JUDGE WALDRON

I WILL FOCUS ON the County Court and particularly that part of the County Court operation which relates or impacts most significantly on women; namely, the trials of serious sexual offences—indictable offences as they are called—in which, ordinarily, the female complainant is the most important witness in the trial.

In this context I will review the nature of the criminal trial, the role that the judge plays in a criminal trial, and also the sentencing role of the judge. I will then go on to consider the question of judicial education and the judges' attitude to it. Finally, I will review how the judges are generally portrayed and have you understand how I, at least, really see them to be.

In a criminal trial the Crown must prove each element of the offence or offences charged on the criminal standard of proof: beyond reasonable doubt. Therefore, in a case where a sexual offence is alleged, the victim, usually a female complainant, must give evidence. In turn, in order to allow the accused an opportunity to defend himself or herself, the victim, the complainant, is invariably cross-examined. Inevitably and unavoidably, I suggest, a criminal trial is a stressful experience for all involved. The more serious the offence, the more severe the criminal sanction if guilt is proved, the more tense or stressful the proceedings are likely to be.

Well, what then is generally required of a trial judge? A trial judge is required to exhibit a number of qualities. First and foremost he or she must be true to his or her oath of office, to impartially apply the law without fear or favour. Therefore he or she must be fair, must be unprejudiced, must be objective in applying the law, whatever his or her personal views may be as to the merits of the particular law.

What then, particularly, is required of the trial judge in a criminal trial for an indictable offence such as an offence involving a serious sexual offence? What must be emphasised is that the role of the trial judge is strictly circumscribed. He or she must control the trial so as to ensure that it is conducted fairly to both the Crown representing the community (including the complainant), and the accused. He or she must apply the law of evidence (much of which has been amended by a statute in recent years concerning sexual offence); must see that Counsel act properly; must direct the jury on the law and give the jury some assistance concerning the evidence, particularly linking the evidence to the elements of the offences charged. But they must not, and I emphasise, must not, intrude on the jury's function as the judges of the facts, and the actual deciders of the case.

The judge is entitled to make comments concerning the evidence, but such comments, if made at all, must be qualified by a warning to the jury that if such comments do not appeal to them it is both their prerogative and their duty to ignore them. If a judge intrudes into the jury's function, or indeed intrudes to the extent of actively entering the conduct of the trial, that intrusion constitutes a valid ground of appeal. I state all of that to emphasise that the trial judge is required to be an aloof, dispassionate umpire in the trial process, applying the rules as laid down by others, that is, either by the legislature in the form of statute law, or by the appeal of court.

Now I accept that judges should be sensitive to the situation of the female complainant. Indeed I believe that they are. However the trial judge must be fair. Professor Kathleen Mahoney's paper, 'Gender bias in judicial decisions', presented at the Perth Supreme Court (1992), essentially emphasises the need for the judicial process to be truly fair, for it to understand and take account of the differences between men and women, to recognise and understand the unique situation of a woman as a woman. I readily accept that. However, in achieving that, the law must not permit unfairness to the accused man or woman who is on trial. It must be understood that there is no room for affirmative action in the courtroom itself. Redressing old rules is one thing, denying a fair trial to an accused is another.

Personally, I believe that we are about to enter an era where the trial judge will be more interventionist. The *Criminal Trial Act 1993* will encourage it, and indeed the need to control the lengths of trials will simply require it. In the process I believe that the judge will have a greater opportunity to see that trials are conducted fairly, that is, to be better able to exclude unnecessarily lengthy and irrelevant cross-examination.

Let me now look at the role of the sentencing judge. Here again the judge must follow well defined legal principles; sentencing principles as they are called. Additionally, if the statute law lays down particular principles or guidelines, the sentencing judge must apply them. I think that we are all aware of those guidelines having been changed recently with the amendments to the *Sentencing Act*. Therefore, although the judge has a discretion as to the appropriate sentence to be imposed, it must be exercised judicially.

Stating it generally, the judge must take account of the nature of the crime, the effect on the victim, the criminality of the offender and any aggravating or mitigating features which apply to the offender. It is a complex and difficult task. The community interest must be borne in mind, but so must the rights of the offender.

Considerations of punishment and deterrence must be weighed against those of reformation and rehabilitation of the offender, and a just result must be striven for. Inevitably, judges do not achieve the correct result all the time; however the following statistics from the 1991/1992 financial year may give an indication of the performance of the County Court judges on sentencing. For that year, of 1443 sentences which were delivered by County Court judges, 111 appeals against severity of sentence were brought by prisoners, of which 41 succeeded and the sentence was reduced, and 21 appeals against alleged inadequacy of sentence were brought by the DPP, of which 8 succeeded and the sentence was increased.

Having said all that, the judge should be sensitive to community attitudes and values. Therefore I am of the view, and indeed the strong view, that ongoing voluntary judicial education concerning all matters which pertain to the administration of justice and the judicial function including gender equality is desirable. The law itself, and the structure of society and its values, are all constantly changing. Therefore, ongoing judicial education, both additional to and within a judge's duties is, I believe, a necessary attribute of judicial life.

What is the type and scope of judicial education experienced by the County Court judges? First of all, they are obliged to keep up with the law both in regard to changes in the statute law and in regard to judicial decisions of appellate courts. Second, it is desirable that there be in-service education on a variety of other issues, and the judges do have that education. The County Court judges have taken positive steps, in more recent times, to prosper the cause of ongoing judicial education. We have now conducted six annual live-in seminars, each of two days duration.

To give you some examples of topics covered at the seminars, each year sentencing problems form part of the seminar program. Last year, the law and the history of the crime of rape were considered in the context of changes to the *Crimes Act* relating to the crime of rape. This year, judges had the advantage of the paper given by Dr Edward Ogden of the Department of Forensic Medicine, on the impact of crime on its victims as post-traumatic stress disorder. In addition to those seminars, certain individual judges have, over recent years prior to its disabandonment, been honorary consultants to the Victorian Law Reform Commission, concerning particular references including its rape references. At the moment I am a member of the Attorney General's Law Reform Council.

Finally, I do want to say something in regard to judicial education in respect of the imminent initiative of the Australian Institute of Judicial Administration (AIJA). I should say that the County Court judges are strong supporters of the activities of the AIJA. Over the years, many of them have attended AIJA educational seminars, and in doing so they reflected what I have perceived to be the attitude of the various levels of courts throughout Australia. To my observation, the concept of judicial education is well supported amongst the Australian judiciary. In that context it is pertinent to observe that the AIJA is in the course of developing appropriate forms of assistance to Australian judges and magistrates on matters of gender. I expect, knowing that the institute is scrupulous in its determination to respect the independence of the judiciary and to preserve the necessary voluntariness of judicial education, that the AIJA program will be positively received.

I readily accept the proposition that the position of women relative to the law should be included in ongoing judicial education. It is important to emphasise, nevertheless, that ongoing judicial education must be both comprehensive and voluntary. The judges must be willing participants. As I have already said, I believe that the County Court judges have shown themselves to be so.

Professor Mahoney has very rightly emphasised the need to avoid stereotyping of women. I wholeheartedly agree, and want to assure you that speaking in respect of the County Court, it is equally wrong to stereotype judges. Unhappily, over recent years, really over a course of years as I have observed it, certain elements of the media have endeavoured to stereotype judges, and have endeavoured to give the impression that judges are simply out of touch, come from a favoured part of society, and are simply not appreciative of those who come to the courts.

I happen to come from what is very much a working court. The judges are there to apply the law and to administer the law in the most basic fashion at the trial level, where people are coming as witnesses, and as accused. I simply want to assure you that these judges come from a variety of sections of the community. It will be readily said that there are no women judges, but that is not the judges' responsibility, let me say first of all. The judges are appointed and they do their job as well as they can. It is for others to make the decisions in regard to who should be appointed. All that I want to give you assurance about is that, although you are rightly concerned about gender matters, the judges of the County Court are in fact doing their job in a responsible manner concerning the female complainants coming to the court in regard to serious sexual offences.

23

Women and the law
Judicial attitudes and their impact on women

JUSTICE JANE MATTHEWS

THERE IS A CONSIDERABLE history to the issue of gender bias and gender awareness in our legal history. Chief Justice Malcolm mentioned it elsewhere in this conference and I want to touch on it very briefly because it is something from which we must learn.

Back in the 1970s, a number of feminists, particularly in the United States, were complaining that, notwithstanding the apparent gender neutrality of the laws, in fact they were operating unfairly to women. They were voices in the wilderness then. In 1979 the United States National Association of Women Judges was formed and this gave credibility and weight to the views of these women. A National Judicial Educational Program was commenced and in 1982 the first of the Task Forces was established in New Jersey. By 1988, the Conference of the United States Chief Justices urged that positive action be taken by every Chief Justice to address gender bias concerns in the State courts. By now the vast majority of states in the United States have established Task Forces. Their findings have been remarkably uniform as to the existence and effect of gender bias, which is pervasive throughout the whole of the court system.

In 1987 Canada took off its shackles and has moved very fast in the area, obviously taking advantage of the great deal of work that had been done in the United States. In Australia we are later again in recognising the problem, but I am confident that we shall be more rapid still. Apart from anything else, we now have the joint experience of the United States and Canada to assist us. One thing I should also mention here is that on St Patrick's Day 1992, (although the day itself wasn't significant), a group of us banded together and started the Australian Association of Women Judges. It is in the process of combining with a similar New Zealand association and is affiliated with an international association. It includes magistrates, and now numbers some 45 members, which is a very high proportion of those who are eligible to join, showing a high degree of female judicial solidarity in this country. Gender bias was always to be our first plank. As it happens we have been overtaken by events, something about which we are all very glad indeed.

Gender bias was a subject of which, until recently, most male judges had never heard. Now it is very much a part of the public domain. Everyone has their own views on it. This brings me to a note of caution. This conference displays unanimous acceptance of the fact that gender bias exists in our legal system, and that urgent steps must be taken to address it. This is clearly the right approach and is appropriate as a starting point, but we must recognise that we are the converted on these issues. The real problem is that those who are most in need of education in this area, those who are most likely to perpetuate the problems of gender bias in the system, are those who are most resistant to the message. In the short term I think that one of the greatest challenges is going to be to present this message in a manner which is strong enough to be persuasive and to get across the fact that gender bias is alive and well in our system, while at the same time being sufficiently non-confrontationist that it does not further alienate those who already find the idea very threatening. For those are the people whom we need to reach if we are to succeed at all.

Kathleen Mahoney, in my view, has been invaluable in this respect. Her talks to judicial officers in the various States have introduced a note of rationality and objectivity into what was fast becoming a media-fest of blind attacks on less than sensitive judicial comments made in sexual assault cases. It would hardly surprise you to learn that there has been something of a judicial backlash about this. For whatever else judges may or may not be, they are extremely hard working people, with an extraordinarily difficult job to do, which they take very seriously indeed. It is not an easy burden, believe me, to know that other people's lives might well be broken as a result of your determinations. There is not a single judicial officer that I know who does not strive very hard indeed, sometimes at considerable personal sacrifice, to perform his or her job conscientiously and well. You cannot blame them for their backgrounds; you cannot blame them for the fact that most of them, by dint of the system which has brought them to the top of their profession, come from a fairly select and privileged group. Nor should we stereotype male judges because of their backgrounds, as Judge Waldron says. We women who have been victims of centuries of stereotyping must be very careful to avoid it ourselves. The fact is that judges in Australia, as Kathleen Mahoney found with judges in Canada, and indeed as you would expect, cover the whole spectrum. You get those who have always appreciated that gender bias does exist, those who are quite incapable of accepting the possibility of it, and the majority of them somewhere in between. It is the ones in the middle that I think we should be aiming for, and hopefully then we can gradually move the ones at the edge, or if the worst comes to the worst, isolate them.

A lot has been said about getting more women judges on to the Bench. That is obviously a high priority. There were a number of chords, particularly in Sally Brown's paper, which struck home with me. I still get, after thirteen years on the Bench, senior barristers coming to my court, looking straight at me and saying to the witness 'Now please tell his Honour exactly what happened'. Only six months ago, I was at the swearing in of a new Supreme Court Judge, a very gentlemanly person. The representative of the Bar who was welcoming him said this; 'One of the primary attributes for a good judge is to be gentlemanly'.

How do we get more women on to the Bench? I really think it is another problem, but the fact is that at the moment women comprise 50% or more of graduates coming out of the law schools in New South Wales but only 15% go to the Bar. If we continue to draw on the Bar as our pool for judges, we are simply not going to get women into judicial positions.

But I see no difficulty in going beyond the Bar for judicial appointments, provided that we supplement or accompany this with a system of induction training for judges, designed to fill what ever gaps there may be in their background or in their personal experience. In the case of non-barristers this will probably include education in courtroom trial experience.

It is assumed these days that barristers are going to be instant judges. What happens is, they close up shop at 5 o'clock on a Friday afternoon as a barrister. They are sworn in as a judge at 9.30 on the Monday morning. At 11.30 they do their first case. It is assumed that overnight they have instantly acquired all the qualities which are going to make them good judges. I do not think that we can make that assumption. There are a number of areas which we should be looking at to educate judges as they come to the Bench. If we were to introduce such a system, it would make it much easier to widen the pool from which they come. And at the same time, we can introduce them to gender awareness programs.

So there are strong arguments for having judicial education right from the very beginning. I believe that this would have the positive effect of widening the pool for judges and better qualifying our judges for what, believe me, is the very onerous task they have.

I come then to what I think is probably the most significant area we have explored in this conference: the ways laws themselves can operate to disadvantage women within the system. I would like to adopt Elizabeth Evatt's characterisation of the problem; namely that women are disadvantaged either through the substance of the law or its applications or its procedures. These days there are very few laws, if any, that are gender biased on their face. This does not necessarily mean that they are gender neutral, but that the bias is much more difficult to identify. Often, and indeed I think in almost all cases, it is not the law which is the problem, but the context of societal inequality in which the law operates. So that an apparently impartial application of the law serves only to perpetuate and validate pre-existing inequalities.

In some cases, we need to be looking at changing the laws. The norm which places little or no value on work done in the home is an obvious candidate for this. A number of others have been identified throughout this conference. But I think that, in the end, it must be that the greatest areas of entrenched inequality, and thus the areas where we really need to be concentrating our attentions arise in the application of the laws—Elizabeth Evatt's second category.

Wherever a judicial discretion exists, there is a danger that it will be exercised by judges who have not been educated about the gender issues involved, and who therefore have no regard to those issues. Time and time again in this conference, we have heard about discretionary laws being interpreted so as to further disadvantage women or indeed, other disadvantaged groups. Family law, anti-discrimination law, industrial law—it would be impossible to categorise them, and indeed one should not try to do so. The greater the area of discretion, the greater the potential for disadvantage and the more important it is that the judges who are applying these laws, and exercising their discretion, are made aware of the gender issues involved.

Kathy Mack referred to the time, back in the late 1970s and early 1980s, when the States were abolishing the right to cross-examine complainants in sexual assault cases, about their prior sexual history. Some States, particularly South Australia, left it open for judicial discretion as to when this cross-examination should be allowed. After a very short time the embargo on cross-examination was reduced to such an extent that it barely existed any more. And so, as Kathy said, they had to have another go at amending the legislation.

I repeat, it is often not the laws which are directly to blame for this. More often than not there is pre-existing societal injustice, so that an impartial application of the law will be bound to perpetuate inequality.

So what do we do about it? In some cases, maybe we do have to change the laws in order to remove or restrict the area of discretion, but there are often difficulties with this. There are often very good reasons why there should be a judicial discretion in these areas. In this situation, what we must do is alert the decision makers, the judges, about the gender issues involved. This can be done on a two-pronged basis.

First, and most importantly, by educating the judiciary generally about how to be aware of gender bias against women and aware of bias against other disadvantaged groups. It is here that the AIJA program and the Western Australian Task Force are of massive importance. I would hope that, before long, the Chief Justices in all the other States will follow Chief Justice Malcolm, and indeed their North American counterparts, and establish similar initiatives.

The second thing we must do is enlarge our rules on standing before the courts. As we have heard before, LEAF has made a major difference in Canada; it has given concerned groups, feminist groups and others, an opportunity to come before the courts where gender-sensitive cases are involved, and to make submissions and sometimes call evidence as to the gender issues involved in that particular case. The fact is that we simply cannot do this here because of our laws on standing. A group such as LEAF would have no impact at all under our system. I think that priority should be given to considering changing those laws on standing, enabling interest groups to appear before courts, make submissions, and be able to call evidence in particular cases as to the sensitive issues involved.

This two-pronged approach—judicial education, bolstered by submissions in particular cases, has led to the situation which Kathleen Mahoney told us about, where the Canadian Supreme Court has reached a stage of genuine gender sensitivity. It has, in effect, rewritten the laws on self defence so as to accommodate the problems of women who kill their violent partners. If we can achieve a similar level of sensitivity in our courts then we will have achieved a great deal.

Finally, I must say something about the problems of women in sexual assault cases. Frankly, I do not know whether these reflect defects in the substance of the law, or the application of the laws, or procedure. I suspect it is all three. But we simply cannot ignore the criticisms of the system made by Kate Gilmore; and perhaps the most moving part of this conference was Thérèse McCarthy's exposition of Alice's and Amanda's stories. This is not merely a gender issue any more. It is an issue of the law failing to achieve its supposed objects of fairness and impartiality. I take into account what Chief Justice Malcolm writes regarding the amendments which have been introduced, and other initiatives in Western Australia. Nevertheless, both of these stories, Alice's and Amanda's, unfolded within the context of our existing system, and as David Malcolm himself said, we have all heard many stories like them; it is not as if they are isolated tragedies.

We must learn from them. The response has to be multi-faceted, but I think one thing we can do now—and it does not even involve money—is to put women Crown Prosecutors into sexual assault cases. I was a Crown Prosecutor for a couple of years before going on the Bench. It was only towards the end of my time there that I started dealing with sexual assault cases. In each case, the victim, the complainant, almost literally fell upon me with relief at the fact that there was a woman, as she perceived it, representing her in court. In fact, of course, the Crown Prosecutor does not represent a complainant in court. But the Prosecutor is the closest thing that the complainant has to a representative, and it is important that the complainant feels some degree of empathy with that person. So strong was this reaction from women complainants, that I saw it as a real contribution that I as a woman could make. At the time I was the only female Crown Prosecutor, so I wrote to the 'powers that be' in the Crown Prosecuting Department and asked if I could be briefed in more sexual assault cases. Their response was to take me away altogether and put me on to the Bench, where I have presided now over innumerable sexual assault cases, and have seen the relief on the face of the complainants at having a female judge. But I really think it is much more important to have a female Crown Prosecutor.

It is clear that we have simply failed to appreciate the damage done to victims of sexual assault. In Helena Kennedy's wonderful book, *Eve was Framed*, she tells the story of a man who received brain damage in a motor vehicle accident as a result of which he suffered a personality change which sometimes caused him to manifest serious violence. On two separate occasions he committed terrible atrocities against women: degrading, humiliating, sexual acts, in one case in the presence of her child; in the other case accompanied by stabbing. As a result he was imprisoned for life. His victims sued for criminal compensation, and initially received £1000 and £3600 respectively. This was later increased on appeal to £7000 and £10 500 respectively. The offender, in the meantime, sued for compensation for his injuries in the motor vehicle accident and received over £45 000.

Alice's story, which we heard this morning, is the story of a woman who suffered multiple disadvantages in our society. She was a migrant, she had little English, she was culturally isolated. Kathleen Mahoney tells us that, in Canada, they initially made the mistake of dealing with problems of judicial awareness only in relation to gender. Then they realised that this was a mistake, and that there were some people, such as migrant women, whose problems were falling through the cracks and not being met. So they then had to go back and widen their areas of concern.

Now we have the benefit of being able to learn from the experiences and the mistakes of others. I think it is most important that we do so. I am very glad to see that the base has been widened to include race and problems of other underprivileged groups in society.

There are many criteria by which you can judge the success or otherwise of a social debate. The most important, no doubt, is whether it leads to constructive change. In the case of this conference, I am confident that the mere ventilation of the issues, as we have done here, will continue to reverberate in a very constructive way for a long time: indeed, I would hope, indefinitely.

Whatever the direct outcomes, I know that all of us involved have learnt a great deal; we have had our horizons widened. It has been a fascinating and exciting venture. The contents of this volume, reproducing the papers given at the 'Women and the law' conference in 1993, are provocative, exciting and I am sure, also constructive.

24

Strategies for increasing awareness within the law concerning sex bias

DR JOCELYNNE SCUTT

RECOMMENDATIONS FROM THE Strategy Group, Women and the Law: Judicial Attitudes as they Impact on Women Conference, Melbourne 10–11 June 1993 at the Women's Research Centre, Deakin University.

Preamble

Recognising that sexist, racist and ethnophobic biases are entrenched within the legal system, there is a need to address these issues in the context of the whole of the legal system, and in terms of the place of the legal system within the broader society.

1 Access

Access to the law is impeded by lack of money, lack of information, procedures and practices which do not recognise various forms of disadvantage and which do not provide resources or sufficient resources to eliminate against disadvantage—for example, only English is the recognised language.

Recommendation A

All courts and tribunals—including the High Court, Federal Court, Supreme Courts, County/Districts Courts, Magistrates Courts; Administrative Appeals Tribunals, Social Security Appeals Tribunal, Commercial/Credit Tribunals, Equal Opportunity Boards/Tribunals, Human Rights and Equal Opportunity Commission, etc.—should use identical forms for the conduct of cases, the 'identifier' indicating the jurisdiction being the title of the relevant court or tribunal.

Reason

Currently forms used in the various courts and tribunals have different headings and formats depending on the jurisdiction. This is confusing as well as a waste of lawyers' and litigants' money. It adds unnecessary expense without any advantage.

Recommendation B

A standard fee should apply to the lodging of a claim, as a 'one up' court fee, in whatever jurisdiction the claim is lodged. (Fees for legal representation are separate from this.) Exemption on grounds of hardship should exist and be publicly advertised.

Reason

Some jurisdictions have a 'one up' fee. Others require separate payments at various stages of the process—for example a separate fee for filing each Affidavit, each/any Application, each/any Summons or Notice of Motion etc. A litigant should know in advance the total of the actual court fee relevant to their case.

Recommendation C

Legal aid guidelines must be non-sexist, non-racist and non-ethnophobic.

Reason

(a) The current emphasis on making legal aid available where an applicant's liberty is at risk may militate against women being granted legal aid: decision makers may believe that a woman is less at risk because of a belief in the 'chivalry factor'—the (erroneous) notion that women, including women who are mothers, are less likely to be sentenced to imprisonment for offences of which they are convicted.
(b) The emphasis on grants where an applicant's liberty is at risk ignores the very real risks women face in other areas—for example, a woman who is unable to obtain legal aid for intervention order applications/breach applications is highly likely to be 'at risk'.
(c) The emphasis on grants where an applicant's liberty may be at risk ignores the risk to children and women where an application for custody or defence of custody application relates to physical and/or sexual abuse.
(d) The emphasis on grants where an applicant's liberty may be at risk ignores the economic risk women and children may suffer where applications for maintenance or increased maintenance are an issue.
(e) Many other instances of disadvantage by reason of this guideline may be identified.

Recommendation D

Grant and review processes within Legal Aid Commissions must be non-racist, non-sexist and non-ethnophobic.

Reason

At the review level, discretion operates, which is likely, without specific attention being paid to prevent it, to be exercised differentially in favour of male litigants.

Recommendation E

Interpreters must be readily available where persons of non-English speaking background appear in courts as accused persons, litigants and witnesses.

Reason

Although interpreters are more readily available than in the past, problems remain. This means that cases may be adjourned because an interpreter is not available; a case may go ahead despite an interpreter not being available; a case may be dismissed without being heard or properly heard.

Recommendation F

Costs: a review of the method of dealing with costs in particular cases must be undertaken—for example, in equal opportunity/sex discrimination/anti-discrimination cases.

Reason

Equal Opportunity/Sex Discrimination/Anti-Discrimination Acts contain provisions that the losing party bears their own costs and pays the winning side's costs, except in stipulated exceptional circumstances. These provisions can create real problems: the main problem is the deterrent to taking action in the first place based on inability to pay should the Applicant lose; furthermore, a respondent with 'unlimited' resources can draw out proceedings with little fear of being ordered to pay the other side's costs, so that ultimately the applicant is forced to give up, because of the mounting costs with no prospect of having those costs paid by the respondent.

2 Language

Language is central to the way people think and behave. Legal language has effects outside the statutes, judgments and courts in which it appears and is heard. The language judges use in the courts, whether in the course of procedural matters, during trials, or in their judgments, is influential in the way the courts operate, and in the legal system generally.

Recommendation A

Non-sexist, non-racist and non-ethnophobic language must be used in all court forms, statutes, court proceedings, judgments/decision, and in law school lectures, examination papers etc.

Reason

Sexist, racist and ethnophobic language supports and reinforces sexist, racist and ethnophobic behaviour inside and outside the legal system.

3 Legal education

How lawyers are educated affects not only their own conduct in their work (whether as solicitors or barristers, prosecutors or defence counsel, government lawyers, judicial officers, judges, magistrates, tribunal/board members, etc.). It also affects the way litigants, accused persons and witnesses are perceived and dealt with in the courts and the legal system generally. It is crucial to whether or not lawyers generally, including judicial officers, are able to 'cope' with change, to accept new ideas, to keep their minds open to challenge and to new perspectives on the law and the work they do.

Recommendation A

All qualified lawyers must, in order to retain a practising certificate, whether as solicitor or barrister, be required to complete a specified number of legal education courses, including women and the law, sexism/racism/ ethnophobia and the law, or feminist jurisprudence.

Reason

Initial qualifications in law need to be continually updated, on a regular basis. Continuing attention to non-sexist, non-racist and non-ethnophobic education is essential to ensure that the attitudes and behaviours do not persist, or at least have a possibility of being recognised, acknowledged and countered.

Recommendation B

Legal education in law schools must incorporate women and the law, sexism/ racism/ethnophobia and the law or feminist jurisprudence courses as a compulsory subject in first year. All subjects must incorporate feminist jurisprudence and a non-racist, non-sexist and non-ethnophobic perspective. This must be a requirement for accreditation of any course.

Reason

Continuing complaints from women in law schools indicate that sexism is entrenched in such law teaching. Further, there is little value in educating judges and magistrates in this area, if those appearing before them are not similarly educated.

Recommendation C

Police prosecutors/Director of Public Prosecutions prosecutors must be required to undergo continuing legal education including non-sexist, non-racist, non-ethnophobic education/feminist jurisprudence.

Reason

As above. Further, many of the problems in sexual offences trials may arise from prosecutors being imbued with sexist notions relating to women as victims and survivors—for example:
- women as perennial liars and not to be trusted in 'sex' cases;
- it didn't happen, and if it did it is not really serious/didn't really hurt her;
- no long-term damage; or
- 'no' means 'yes'—or pretty often, anyway.

Recommendation D

All court personnel—registrars, masters, associates, clerks, court attendants, court recorders—must undergo regular non-sexist, non-racist, non-ethnophobic training.

Reason

All persons holding any position in the legal structure influence the way the courts operate and the way litigants, witnesses and others experience the process. For example:
- a court attendant comes into direct contact with witnesses, litigants, jurors and others who may be positively affected by non-sexist/racist/ethnophobic attitudes/behaviour and negatively affected if treated in a sexist/racist/ ethnophobic way; and
- associates have regular and ongoing contact with judges and court personnel—they may influence judges and court personnel through their behaviour and attitudes.

Recommendation E

For judges/magistrates/other decision makers:
(1) A compulsory orientation or induction course must be established for all persons appointed to the judiciary/magistracy, and other decision maker positions.
(2) No person may be appointed to the judiciary/magistracy without having completed, in the course of their legal careers, a stipulated number of continuing education credits each year.
(3) Ongoing or continuing legal education courses must be established for all judges and magistrates and
    (A) all judges and magistrates should be encouraged to attend;
        OR
    (B) all judges and magistrates should be required to complete a stipulated number of credits each year.
    Note
    (i) judges/magistrates include acting judges and magistrates and retired judges and magistrates who are 'on call';
    (ii) a compulsory component of the courses must be non-sexist, non-racist, non-ethnophobic training/ feminist jurisprudence.

Reason

No person in any trade or profession is qualified without training, or appropriate training.

No person in any position of authority and public service is entitled to perform the functions of the office without education in non-sexism/non-racism/and non-ethnophobia.

Recommendation F

Jurors—Orientation courses must be established for all persons who are called up for jury, to alert them to sexist, racist and ethnophobic biases.

Reason

It is important to ensure that all members of the community who may play a part in the legal process have an opportunity to fulfil their role without bias, or with less bias.

Recommendation G

Journalists/media—All journalists/media who engage in court reporting must attend an orientation and continuing education course re non-sexism, non-racism and non-ethnophobia.

Reason

Processes and outcomes of court proceedings come to the attention of the public through (in the main) the media. It is essential that the reporting be done in a way that recognises and is alert to sexism, racism and ethnophobia.

Recommendation H

Expert witnesses—persons who are to appear as expert witnesses in courts and tribunals must undergo an orientation and continuing non-racist, non-sexist, non-ethnophobic/feminist jurisprudence training.

Reason

Experts are used frequently in certain types of case, and their evidence and attitudes frequently affect court outcomes.

Recommendation I

Law school moots/mock trials—a compulsory component of all law school education must be participation in moots/mock trials which alert the students to sexism, racism and ethnophobia. These trials should be organised in conjunction with other faculties—for example, social work, medicine—using students from these courses as expert witnesses in particular.

Reason

Women do not often appear as expert witnesses in courts, and infrequently have an opportunity for gaining this experience. This must change: women rarely appear in authoritative roles in the courtroom. Having women in positions of authority as recognised experts can have a positive effect on the whole courtroom atmosphere/environment and procedures.

Further, most law schools concentrate on 'pretend' appeals instead of doing trial work in advocacy courses. Yet trial work is far more useful, as this is where most barristers/litigating solicitors appear, most of the time.

Recommendation J

Funding and associated resources must be provided by the Federal Government to the Australian Women's Research Centre, Deakin University, to establish a pilot program for law schools, in conjunction with interdisciplinary consultants, re non-sexism, non-racism, and non-ethnophobia/feminist jurisprudence. This would be a module that could be adapted into all law courses.

Reason

It is important to determine the course design which works best to achieve the aim. There is a need for monitoring and evaluation to determine which approaches work best.

Recommendation K

Legal education in schools; legal studies courses must be a part of the school curriculum, with a good non-racist, non-sexist, and non-ethnophobic/feminist jurisprudence component.

Reason

Ideas, attitudes and behaviours are shaped from a young age. The law is intrinsic to people's lives, and it is a patriarchal institution. From a young age this fact should be exposed to children and young people, with information about positive efforts made to change it.

Overall reason re legal education

All litigants, witnesses and people coming into the courts and all who are involved in the legal process have a right to appear in/operate in a non-sexist, non-racist and non-ethnophobic system. Legal education is central to the way the law and the courts operate.

4 Standing

It is important that those who have a legitimate interest in the issues raised in the courts and in particular court cases have an accepted avenue for having their concerns heard by the courts. At present, although they have been expanded in recent years, standing rules in Australian courts have been interpreted relatively narrowly. This must be changed.

Recommendation A

Rules of standing, that is, who has a right to appear in a particular case, must be broadened and extended so that groups with an interest in the litigation/subject matter of the litigation have a clear right to appear as *amicus curia* (friend of the court) or interveners.

Reason

Many cases that involve individual litigants have an impact that goes way beyond that individual. It is appropriate that groups with an interest have a right to appear to run arguments and give assistance to the court or tribunal, which will/may be of assistance to the individual litigant and to the broader community she represents. Sometimes the opposite may prove to be the case— that is, an opposing argument/opposing evidence needs to be put/brought and there should be latitude within standing rules for this to occur.

Recommendation B

Resourcing of interest groups—resources should be made available by State and Federal Governments for the establishment and ongoing research of advocacy centres which represent women's interests in litigation and take on test cases—for example, the Legal Education Assistance Fund (LEAF) in North America. Women's Legal Resources Centre funding must also be established/ increased by State and Federal Governments.

Reason

Funding and resources must come from somewhere to secure women's rights in litigation.

5 Judicial appointments

It is essential that the legal system change from its current bias towards white middle class men as those who sit as judges and magistrates. In a multicultural, multiracial society comprising 52% women and 48% men, it is clear that bias in the courts will be inevitable so long as the judicial appointments system remains as it is.

Recommendation A

The criteria for judicial appointments must be clearly articulated and made known publicly.

Recommendation B

The criteria must include:
(a) legal competence as necessary but not sufficient;
(b) legal competence to include an awareness of the discriminatory nature and effect of laws and legal processes, and the potential for discrimination in discretionary decision making and legislative/case law interpretation;
(c) demonstrated awareness of women's disadvantage, and racism, sexism and ethnophobia; and
(d) the requirement that the recommendation of the President of the Bar Council or Law Society and their equivalents should carry no greater weight than the recommendation of other relevant and interested/ knowledgeable groups—for example, Women's Legal Resource Groups; Feminist Lawyers Groups; Women Lawyers Associations.

Recommendation C

Appointments should be equally open to be made from:
(a) practising barristers and solicitors;
(b) barristers and solicitors in government service;
(c) academic lawyers; and
(d) legal members of boards and tribunals.

Recommendation D

Positive action must be taken by governments to ensure that women and other disadvantaged groups gain access to experience which can enable them to be considered for appointments to courts and tribunals, or to higher levels of courts and tribunals. For example, there is no good reason why a tribunal or board member, or legally qualified commissioner for equal opportunity, or magistrate should not be appointed to (say) the Supreme Court, Federal Court or District/ County Courts.

Recommendation E

Attorneys-General and Ministers for Justice should immediately convene a meeting to hear submissions and the criteria for judicial, magisterial and tribunal/board appointments, and to produce as an outcome a list of criteria for appointment, that list to be publicly promulgated. Any change to or inclusion in the criteria at any time should be made publicly known together with written reasons for the change/inclusion.

Recommendation F

The law in some States (for example, Victoria) should be changed so that seven years admission to practice in any jurisdiction is an appropriate qualification for appointment, rather than seven years admission in the particular jurisdiction. This is the law in Queensland and there is no good reason for ignoring practice in any Australian jurisdiction as an appropriate qualification.

Reason

Persons (women) who are well qualified in accordance with current criteria are not being appointed or, once appointed are not being appointed to 'higher' levels within the court and tribunal structure. That the courts are dominated by non-women (and non-Aborigines and non-other-than-Anglo-Irish) members is clear and incontrovertible evidence of a bias in selection procedures.

If the courts were dominated by non-males, and non-Anglo-Irish people, there would be an instant recognition on the part of those discriminated against of a deep-seated problem.

6 Court and legal process monitoring

It is essential that there be a process for monitoring court practices, both in terms of procedures and outcomes.

Recommendation A

An independent complaint unit should be established at state and federal levels to receive complaints and support complainants through a complaint adjudication process. The unit should be independent of the courts and legal profession, with membership comprising community members and legal profession members.

Detailed statistics on complaints (frequency, court, tribunal, issues, etc.) should be kept.

Complaints to be received re discriminatory, negligent or unprofessional conduct of solicitors, barristers, judicial registrars, masters, judges, magistrates and other relevant decision makers in the court and tribunal system.

Reason

The appeals system is important but does not deal specifically with the issues that need to be addressed to enable people with complaints to have them dealt with justly. It is obvious that if there are problems within the legal system re sexism, racism and so on, that problems will not suddenly disappear at appeals level.

Recommendation B

A unit should be established in each Attorney-General's department to take a 'roving role' in the courts, with sufficient resources and personnel to attend courts and tribunals, to sit in on any cases they choose, to monitor and keep records of the conduct of the proceeding, and to monitor the courts and tribunals generally.

Recommendation C

The reports/records of these units should be 'fed into' the pilot program for legal education into non-sexism, at the Women's Research Centre, Deakin University, and to any law school course designers who have established non-sexist, non-racist, non-ethnophobic/feminist jurisprudence courses, for use in shaping the course. They should also be 'fed into' courses for the magistracy and judiciary.

Recommendation D

An enquiry should be established into the discrimination inherent in the case law system, with a review of all case law as and where it affects the rights of women, reviewing and analysing the way in which case law is operating so as to continue and further entrench sexism, racism and ethnophobia.

Reason

It is important that there be public accountability of courts and those working within them. Further, there is a need for monitoring to ensure that when the system works positively, this can be built on in the legal education process so that negative acts, etc. will not be repeated.

7 Constitutional reform/equality under the law/international forums

It is important that our own Australian Constitution and also State Constitutions do not perpetuate discrimination. It is further important that international forums that exist for the raising of discriminatory and anti-human rights practices and policies in the law be accessed by Australians.

Recommendation A

A Bill of Rights be incorporated into the Australian Constitution.

Recommendation B

In particular, a provision stipulating that equality under the law is a fundamental requirement should be included.

Recommendation C

A referendum should be undertaken, after a positive educational program and dissemination of information, in relation to this.

Reason

Rights should not be left up to the 'good will' of courts, governments, citizens, etc. They should not be 'discretionary', depending on the perspectives/biases/ prejudices of the party determining whether or not they exist or apply to a person or category of person.

It is recognised that 'equality' and 'rights' can be problematic. But not having a clear statement of fundamental rights is even more so.

Recommendation D

International forums where complaints about the abrogation of women's rights can be made should be accessed by, and be able to be accessed by, women and women's groups. Information and education as to how to make use of and apply to such forums should be made readily available. Law schools should include this in their courses.

8 Ongoing working group

It is important that the impetus of the conference and this ensuing book is not lost and that ongoing activity is assured, along the lines of the issues raised here, and developing awareness of issues pertinent to women and the law, and the legal system.

Recommendation A

An ongoing working group should be established to work on particular areas of concern—for example, problems with victim compensation legislation and processes.

Reason

It is important to recognise the knowledge and expertise amongst participants at the conference and contributors to this book, and it is important to harness it.

Afterword (1997)

A very few of the Recommendations from the Women and Law Conference have been implemented by governments, state and federal. In some areas, the position is far worse now than it was in 1993.

Justice strategy

In 1995 the Federal Labor government in implementing its justice strategy, devised by the Minister for Justice, Duncan Kerr, and the Attorney-General, Michael Lavarch:
- provided funding to the Australian Institute of Judicial Administration to establish a pilot program for 'gender bias and awareness' for judges; and
- provided funding for the setting up or expansion of women's justice or legal centres.

The pilot program has held a number of conferences on 'gender' bias and awareness, with judges attending; a number of judges have gone overseas (primarily to Canada) under this program to enlighten themselves as to what has been done or is being done to eliminate bias in the judiciary and court system. Sadly, these programs have not confronted the essential issue, which is that the system is biased against *women* rather than some 'gender' or other. The notion of 'gender' bias implies that there is equal bias against men and women for 'gender' reasons. This is not the case, for although individual men may be disadvantaged within the legal system, structural and pervasive prejudice and bias against women militate against women as a group (as well as individually) gaining justice. This is so, too, in terms of race: racial and ethnic groups that are in the minority in Australia suffer racism and ethnophobia in the courts and legal system generally, by reason of structural and pervasive prejudice and bias. This affects women and men members of these racial and ethnic groups. Until this is recognised, and the depoliticising nature of the use of the term 'gender bias' is confronted, programs will not eradicate bias and prejudice against women, nor gain women justice in the legal system.

Women's legal or justice centres have been established in Western Australia and South Australia with funding under the justice program, and are engaged in casework as well as policy advice and advocacy. As well, it is understood that, in New South Wales, a legal centre specifically catering for Aboriginal women was funded through this program. Existing centres have used the funding to continue their casework, policy advice and advocacy.

With the change of government federally, changes in policy direction do not augur well for either of these initiatives. The present federal Liberal government (like state Liberal governments) is opposed to the funding of community organisations or groups that engage in advocacy. It seems, therefore, that to maintain funding, women's legal centres will be obliged to renounce their advocacy role. There have also been stringent cuts in Aboriginal and Torres Strait Islander Affairs funding, so it is doubtful whether there will be continuing funding for any legal centre directed toward the needs and concerns of indigenous Australians and, in particular, women. With this in mind, any expansion of funding for legal centres catering for indigenous women is similarly doubtful.

So far as bias and prejudice within the judiciary and the legal system generally is in issue, it may be that initiatives such as that taken by the Chief Justice of the Western Australian Supreme Court, David Malcolm, will continue whatever state or federal governments do in funding. Some judges in other jurisdictions (for example, Michael Black, Chief Judge of the Federal Court) have indicated some readiness to embrace the notion that programs to eradicate bias have a place. Whether this means that they would continue or implement programs without government funding being made available for that specific purpose is yet to be seen. With cutbacks in funding generally, it is a moot question whether courts would earmark any of their 'general' funds for this purpose.

Costs and legal aid

With the change of Federal Government, there has been a massive reduction of legal aid. In 1996 the Attorney-General, Darryl Williams, declared that federal funding would no longer be available for legal aid in state matters; legal aid offices could use federal monies for federal matters only—that is, federal crimes, family law, immigration, etc. There could be seen to be some advantages in this for women, for the problem has been that with the major portion of legal aid going on criminal matters, women have been severely disadvantaged. However, that family law is now an area where federal legal aid funds can 'go' does not mean that it is 'targeted' so that women seeking funding for family law cases will get it. Rather, the policy appears to continue that maintenance applications and the seeking of intervention orders (for example) are not high priority, and indeed there seems to be no change in policy which would mean that these applications receive funding when in the past they have not.

Sex-based and other forms of discrimination

In 1996, the Federal Government determined that matters under the *Sex Discrimination Act, Racial Discrimination Act* and other human rights legislation would no longer be dealt with by hearings or 'enquiries' in the Human Rights and Equal Opportunity Commission. Rather, cases would go to the Federal Court. There are advantages for women in this, in that the Human Rights and Equal Opportunity Commission has had truncated powers, which has meant that an applicant (or 'complainant') can win her case, yet if the discriminating party refuses to 'pay up', she (or he) is required to go to the Federal Court for a re-hearing of the matter. This is, frankly, ridiculous. Further, the Human Rights and Equal Opportunity Commission has had an extraordinarily timid approach to the recognition and protection of the right not to be discriminated against, when they have dealt with cases in hearings. There has been a tendency to 'cave in' to respondents who/which play 'procedural tactics' in an effort to force the applicant/complainant to drop the case or to settle (on terms that the respondent wishes to dictate).

Some decisions of the Commission have been strong and valuable. However, it is in the procedural area where applicants need to see that their right to have their case heard is not impeded. The Federal Court should be much tougher where procedural tactics are used by respondents. As well, it is time that human rights were regarded as being as important and valuable as property rights, or more so. Until courts have to take human rights into account because cases come before them on a regular basis, they will not orientate to this perspective. In New South Wales, where the Court of Appeal has dealt with sex discrimination cases for some twenty years, the standard of judgments has noticeably improved over time. This needs to happen in the federal arena, for even if an applicant/complainant gains a 'good result' from the Human Rights Commission under the system as it has been, they run the risk of having to fight again in the Federal Court, whether because the respondent ignores the decision, or appeals against it. This means that an inability to understand discrimination issues, or to have any sympathy with this, will persist in the Federal Court, without cases regularly coming before the judges.

There is a need, however, to ensure that the issue of costs is addressed in the Federal Court taking over this area, and that there is a regular and proper/ adequate program of education for Federal Court judges, judicial registrars and court personnel generally, into the nature, spirit and terms of the *Sex Discrimination Act* and other discrimination/human rights legislation which will now be within the court's initial jurisdiction. This program must be ongoing.

A number of women's and community groups and individuals made submissions to the Parliamentary Committee on legal and constitutional issues, when it looked at the Human Rights Legislation Bill in mid-1997, including the Women for Workplace Justice Coalition, Feminist Lawyers, Victorian Trades Hall, Women's Electoral Lobby, Rosemary Hunter (of Melbourne University Law School), and others.

Amongst other issues raised was the reduction of court filing fees for human rights/discrimination matters and rules to govern properly the award of costs against a losing party, or for a winning party. The Victorian Trades Hall— Jenny Draddy/Feminist Lawyers—Melanie Young/Jocelynne A. Scutt submission recommendations on costs included the following:

RECOMMENDATION 4

Filing fees should be set in this jurisdiction at levels that are reasonable having regard to the fact that Complainants are generally from economically disadvantaged groups and, even where they may be on a 'good' salary, are not as financially advantaged as the general run of litigants.

RECOMMENDATION 5

Alternatively or simultaneously, there should be clear and fair rules as to dispensing with filing fees for Complainants in human rights/discrimination cases.

RECOMMENDATION 6

The rule that 'each side bears own costs' should be modified in the human rights/discrimination jurisdiction as follows.

Preliminary hearing re costs—Determination as to prima facie case

Before a case goes to a hearing in the Federal Court, a preliminary hearing should be held where it is determined whether or not the Complainant has a *prima facie* case. If it is determined that the Complainant has a *prima facie* case, then it follows:
- if the Complainant goes ahead and *loses*, the rule 'each side bear own costs' applies;

- if the Complainant goes ahead and *wins*, the Respondent should be required to pay the Complainant's costs.

If it is determined that the Complainant does not have a *prima facie* case, then it follows:
- if the Complainant goes ahead and *wins*, the Respondent should be required to pay the Complainant's costs;
- if the Complainant goes ahead and *loses*, then the costs of the Respondent can be ordered to be paid, in the discretion of the Court.

Preliminary hearing re costs—Rules as to procedure

To prevent Respondents from prolonging arguments as to the question of a *prima facie* case, in order to 'wear down' the Complainant etc., the preliminary hearing as to *prima facie* case should be restricted to a maximum of one (1) day only, with each side being required to make their argument within this time. There should be no extensions of time set aside for hearing (that is, no more than one (1) day granted).

Preliminary hearing re costs—Payment of costs of preliminary hearing

If it is determined that the Complainant has a *prima facie* case:
- the costs of the preliminary hearing should be paid by the Respondent;

If it is determined that the Complainant does not have a *prima facie* case:
- each side should bear their own costs.

Standing

The issue of standing in a context vitally relevant to women arose before the High Court in 1996 in *SuperClinics and Ors v. CES and Ors*. There, CES had sued various parties because she had not been advised in a timely manner by her medical practitioner that she was pregnant. She discovered she was pregnant too late to avail herself of abortion had she wished to terminate the pregnancy. She sued for damages, including the financial upkeep of her daughter, born from the pregnancy. Initially, it was held that the Respondents had no liability, because abortion is an 'illegal operation' and CES was not entitled to avail herself of an illegal operation nor to damages because she had not been able to do so.

On appeal, the New South Wales Court of Appeal held that abortion is not, in specified circumstances, an illegal operation, so that CES had a right to sue. When the matter came before the High Court, the Catholic Bishops and Catholic Hospitals sought leave to intervene, which they were granted. The Abortion Providers Association then sought leave to intervene, which they were granted. The Women's Electoral Lobby (WEL) and a number of other groups were preparing to seek leave to intervene, when the case was settled. This illustrates the importance of women's groups and advocacy groups representing women's interests being ready to seek leave to intervene in cases affecting women's interests. With the High Court having granted leave to the forestated organisations, it may well be difficult for it to reject future applications for leave to intervene, by women's groups and others, seeking to put to the court issues relating to women's interests/wellbeing/rights that will not otherwise be before the court. This is a decision that women should use to women's advantage.

Endnotes

1. Comments by members of the judiciary led to the inquiry by the Senate Standing Committee on Legal and Constitutional Affairs on Gender Bias and the Judiciary, May 1994.

2. The Australian Institute of Judicial Administration resolved to set up a Gender Awareness Committee in November 1992 (*Gender Bias and the Judiciary: Report by the Senate Standing Committee on Legal and Constitutional Affairs*, May 1994, Senate Printing Unit, Parliament House, Canberra, para. 5.11, p. 115). It now develops programs incorporating gender issues for member of the judiciary as part of its education program (Olsson, Justice LT, Australian Institute of Judicial Adminstration, 70 ALJ 1996: 374)

3. 'Equality before the Law' (Discussion Paper 54). This reference to the Australian Law Reform Commission was announced on 10 February 1993 as part of the Government's 'New National Agenda for Women'. 'Equality before the law: Women's equality', Report 69 Part I was released in April 1994. Report 69 Part II was released in October 1994.

   The Justice Statement, launched by the Prime Minster, Paul Keating MP, on 18 May 1995, allocated $2.7 million over four years to gender and cultural awareness programs for judges and court staff. (Justice Statement: 'Balancing the scales', press release, Michael Lavarch MP, Attorney-General, 18 May 1995).

   The Australian Institute of Judicial Administration (AIJA) organised a conference as part of its gender awareness program, entitled 'Eureka 1995—Equality and Justice Conference' which was the culmination of extensive research and consultative processes. It was attended by 150 judicial officers (Olsson, Justice LT, Australian Institute of Judicial Adminstration, 70 *ALJ* 1996 at 374).

   In November 1995, the National Alternative Dispute Resolution Advisory Council was established to advise on ways of minimising gender biases and imbalances in ADR services. The Council is chaired by Professor Hilary Astor, from the University of Sydney, who has a particular interest in how alternative dispute resolution processes affect women (press release, Michael Lavarch, Attorney-General, 16 November 1995; press release, Michael Lavarch, Attorney-General, 14 November 1995).

4. The Family Court of Australia in 1994–95 did substantial work for the AIJA by undertaking extensive consultations on women's experiences of the legal system. Gender issues were raised in judges' meetings and a conference of the southern region of the court was attended by a broad cross-section of staff and judges as well as judicial registrars from three States (Family Court of Australia, *Annual Report 1994–95* at 11).

   In 1995–96 gender awareness programs were further developed and were considered to be of great benefit by the Chief Justice, the Honourable Alistair Nicholson AO RFD (Family Court of Australia, *Annual Report 1995–96* at 4).

5. In July 1993, the Chief Justice of Western Australia, the Honourable Justice David Malcolm AC, proposed the appointment of a Task Force on Women and the Law to investigate the extent to which gender bias exists in the law and the administration of justice in Western Australia and to make recommendations for its elimination (The Honourable Justice David Malcolm AC, Chief Justice for Western Australia, 'Women and the law—Proposed judicial education program on gender equality and task force on gender bias in Western Australia', *Australian Feminist Journal,* vol. 1, August 1993 at 139).

   In 1995 the New South Wales Department for Women published its report on research on gender bias and women working in the legal system.

6   In 1994–95 the Office of Status of Women initiated a collection of national data by the Australian Bureau of Statistics (ABS) on violence against women. It commissioned national research into community attitudes, and research into the extent and nature of violence against women (Department of the Prime Minister and Cabinet, *Annual Report 1994–95* at 56)

In May 1995 the Prime Minister launched the National Women's Justice Strategy (press release, Michael Lavarch, 16 November 1995).

The Justice Statement allocated $2.3 million over four years to tackle family violence and to improve coordination between the Family Court and domestic violence orders (Justice Statement: 'Balancing the scales', Michael Lavarch, press release, 18 May 1995).

In August, the Office of the Status of Women released a report on community attitudes to violence against women (Department of the Prime Minister and Cabinet, *Annual Report 1995–96*).

The national network of women's legal services was launched on 16 November 1995 by the Attorney-General, Michael Lavarch. 'Women's legal services not only provide legal advice and support to women but play a vital role lobbying for legal reform and educating the community about women's rights' (press release, Michael Lavarch, 16 November 1995).

The Office of the Status of Women commissioned and promoted the report 'Sexual assault law reform: A national perspective' to encourage community participation in the Model Criminal Code reform process. Support was provided to hold a conference on sexual assault and the law (Department of the Prime Minister and Cabinet, *Annual Report 1995–96*).

In November 1996 a discussion draft of the Model Criminal Code, Chapter 5, 'Sexual offences against the person', was released.

7   In September 1993, the Attorney-General, Michael Lavarch, released a discussion paper entitled 'Judicial appointments: Procedure and criteria'.

The Government, when referring to judicial appointments in the Justice Statement of May 1995, indicated that it would seek to ensure that appointees are of the highest calibre and that a broader field of candidates would be identified for judicial office (Justice Statement, May 1995 at 63).

8   *Gun control*

In response to the Port Arthur massacre, the Howard Government worked towards achieving the May 1996 Nationwide Agreement on Firearms. Under that agreement, each State and Territory has instituted a comprehensive reform of firearms laws banning self-loading rifles and shotguns and pump action shotguns. Approximately 430 000 firearms have been handed to authorities as part of an amnesty and buyback scheme (press release, Attorney-General and Minister for Justice, 22 June 1997).

National criminal code

The Model Criminal Code Officers Committee has released discussion papers on topics including 'Non-fatal offences against the person' and 'Sexual offences against the person'. These papers include proposals for uniform criminal laws relating to sexual acts committed without consent, and threats. Currently, these proposals have not been implemented uniformly in Australia.

9   'Equality before the law: Justice for women' Report 69 Part I was released in April 1994. 'Equality before the law: Women's equality' Report 69 Part II was released in October 1994.

10   'Report by the Joint Select Committee on Certain Aspects of the Operation and Interpretation of the *Family Law Act 1975* (November 1992): Government response—Principles', Canberra, 1994.

The Government supported the Committee's recommendations, which shifted the FLA focus from litigation to mediation and alternative dispute resolution. However, the government recognised that ADR is not appropriate where there is a serious power imbalance, especially in cases where there is domestic violence.

The Government accepted the recommendation for improving the enforcement of access orders. The presumption of equal sharing as the starting point for the allocation of matrimonial property was accepted.

Family Law Reform Act 1995

The Family Law Reform Act 1995 (Cwlth) received royal assent on 16 December 1995 and the majority of its provisions commenced on 11 June 1996. The Act seeks to emphasise parental responsibility, strengthens the role of counselling, mediation and arbitration and brings changes in terminology used in family law disputes: no longer 'custody' and 'access' but the use of 'parenting plans', 'parental agreements', and 'parental responsibility'.

Joint Select Committee on Certain Family Law Issues, 1994, 'The operation and effectiveness of the Child Support Scheme', AGPS, Canberra.

This report acknowledged the success of the Child Support Scheme in improving the welfare of affected children and the changing community attitudes to the ongoing responsibilities of parents in separated families. The final report presented 163 recommendations, covering administration, changes to the child support formula, review processes and community awareness campaigns.

Response [interim] to the report Joint Select Committee on Certain Family Law Issues, Child Support Scheme, Canberra, 1995.

Fifty-three of the recommendations in the initial report related to improving the administration of the Child Support Scheme by the Child Support Agency. The interim Government response supported these improvements. Many of these have been improved by the CSA. No final response addressing the remaining recommendations was released.

Violence against women

Recognition of interstate protection orders occurs under a reciprocal legislative scheme. Orders must be registered to be effective in the new State (*Protection Orders (Reciprocal Arrangements) Act 1992* (ACT); *Crimes Act 1900* (NSW) ss. 562–562U; *Domestic Violence Act 1992* (NT) s. 18; *Domestic Violence (Family Protection) Act 1989* (Qld) ss. 40–46; *Domestic Violence Act 1994* (SA) s.14; *Justices Act 1959* (Tas) s.106GA).

[11] The *Crimes (Child Sex Tourism) Amendment Act 1994* inserted a new part into the *Crimes Act 1914*. The Act created a range of sexual offences involving children committed by Australian citizens or residents while outside Australia, and created a range of offences relating to the organisation or promotion of child sex tourism.

[12] During the celebrations of the tenth anniversary of the *Sex Discrimination Act* in July 1994, the Prime Minister announced six proposals 'to improve the effectiveness of the *Sex Discrimination Act*'. Five of these proposals were given effect in the *Sex Discrimination Amendment Act 1995*. They include prohibition of discrimination on the grounds of potential pregnancy; the insertion of a preamble which sets out the principle of equality; the creation of a new test for indirect discrimination and the narrowing of the defence forces exemption. The Howard Government is proposing further amendments in the Sex Discrimination Amendment Bill 1996. The Bill is currently before the Senate.

[13] As quoted in G. Withers (ed.), *Handbook for Judges*, The American Judicature Society, 1975, at 62.

[14] Ibid.

[15] C.J.B.C. Nemetz, 'The concept of an independent judiciary', 1986, 20 *UBC LR* 290 at 286.

[16] J. Griffith, *The Politics of the Judiciary*, Manchester University Press, 1997.

[17] R. Abella, 'The Evolutionary Nature of Equality', in K. Mahoney and S. Martin (eds), *Equality and Judicial Neutrality,* Carswell, Toronto, 1987, at 4.

[18] Ibid.

19 In 1986, the Faculty of Law at the University of Calgary convened a national interdisciplinary conference entitled, 'The socialization of judges to equality issues', resulting in the first major book on the subject in Canada: Mahoney & Martin (eds), *Equality and Judicial Neutrality*, Carswell, 1987. This was followed by the inclusion of gender, race and class bias issues in judicial continuing education programs throughout the country. Groups such as the Manitoba Association of Women and the Law began to research gender bias in the courts and, in November 1988, published the first provincial report, 'Gender equality in the courts'.

In 1991 the Law Society of British Columbia formed a Gender Bias Committee, which in turn created a task force to thoroughly investigate gender bias in British Columbia courts. They issued a 600-page report in September, 1992 describing endemic gender bias in law as well as legal practice. The Western Judicial Education Centre, through its Western Workshop, has included gender and race bias topics in its last three meetings since 1989, and both the Canadian Judicial Council and the Canadian Judicial Centre have developed written and video course materials dealing with bias issues, making them available to all Canadian judges, and planned three national conferences in 1992–93 for federally appointed (superior court) judges throughout Canada.

The Justice Minister of Canada convened a national conference entitled 'Gender bias in the law and the courts' in June 1991. She stated that ridding the judicial system of gender bias was firmly on the government agenda. The President of the Canadian Bar Association underscored her remarks and stated a similar commitment from the Bar, and two justices of the Supreme Court of Canada, in a recent judgment, identified gender bias as an endemic problem.

20 R. Abella, *Supra*, note 5.

21 Ken Cooper-Stephenson, 'Past inequities and future promise: Judicial neutrality in charter constitutional tort claims', in K. Mahoney and S. Martin (eds), *Equality and Judicial Neutrality,* Carswell, Toronto, 1987, at 226.

22 Ibid.

23 In the American context see Lenore J. Weitzman, *The Divorce Revolution: The Unexpected Social and Economic Consequences for Women and Children in America,* The Free Press, New York, 1985. For the Canadian context, see E. Diane Pask and M.L. McCall, *How Much and Why? Economic Implications of Marriage Breakdown: Spousal and Child Support*, Canadian Research Institute for Law and the Family, 1989.

24 See P. Chesler, *Mothers on Trial*, Seal Press, Seattle, 1986.

25 J.A. Wigmore, *Evidence in Trials at Common Law*, (revd edn), Little, Brown, Boston, 1961–88, 924 at 736. Wigmore's view that women contrive false charges of sexual offences by men and that accusations of sexual assault are to be regarded with deep suspicion, were legalised through judge-made laws which allowed a woman to be extensively questioned about her past sexual history, which required corroboration (or at least a warning of the dangers of convicting on the uncorroborated evidence of a rape complainant) or which required evidence of a recent complaint to support the credibility of the victim. In 1983, L.B. Bienen attacked Wigmore's views as being unscientific, based on manipulated authorities and selectively and untruthfully used. See Bienen, (1983) 'A question of credibility: John Henry Wigmore's use of scientific authority in Section 924a of the Treatise on Evidence', 19 *Cal West LR* 235.

26 Mona G. Brown, Monique Bicknell-Danaker, Caryl Nelson-Fitzpatrick, Jeraldine Bjornson, 'Gender equality in the courts: Criminal law', A study by the Manitoba Association of Women and the Law, 1991, at 3/51.

27 [1979] 1 SCR 183 (1978).

28 C.A. MacKinnon, 'Reflections on sex equality under law', 1991 *Yale Law Journal* 1281 (No.5).

29 *Andrews v. Law Society of British Columbia* [1989] 1 SC 143 at 166.

30 See *R. v. Turpin,* [1989] 1 SCR 1296 at 1331, where the Supreme Court of Canada held that s. 15 was designed to advance the purposes of 'remedying or preventing discrimination against groups suffering social, political and legal disadvantage in our society'.

31 *Brooks v. Safeway*, [1989] 1 SCR 1219.

32 Ibid. at 1235.

33 [1990] 1 SCR 852.

34 Crimes Compensation Board Award dated June 22, 1988, Award No. 1901/88; Crimes Compensation Board (Sask.) Award dated March 15, 1990, Award No. 2511/90.

35 S. 11(a) *Criminal Injuries Compensation Act.*

36 Crimes Compensation Board Award, dated July 31, 1990, Award No. 2511/90.

37 'Women in transition, a Canada works project', Thunder Bay, Ontario (1978) cited in L. Macleod, *supra*, note 3 at 29. See also R.E. Dobash and R. Dobash, *Violence Against Wives: A Case Against Patriarchy*, Free Press, New York, 1979; L. Chalmers and P. Smith, (1988) 'Wife battering: Psychological, social and physical isolation and counteracting strategies' in A.T. McLaren (ed.), *Gender and Society*, Copp Clark Pitman Ltd, Toronto, 1988, at 221; Lisa Freedman, 'Wife assault', in C. Guberman and M. Wolf (eds), *No Safe Place: Violence Against Women and Children*, The Women's Press, Toronto, 1985, at 41; L. A. Hoff, *Battered Women as Survivors,* Routledge, London, 1990.

38 8 November 1988 (Ont. Dist. Ct.) [unreported].

39 National Judicial Education Program, 'Judicial discretion: Does sex make a difference?', New York, NOW Legal Defence and Education Fund, 1981 at 9. See also, K. Mahoney, (1989) '*R. v. McCraw:* Rape fantasies v. Fear of sexual assault', 21 *Ottawa LR*, No. 1 at 207.

40 *Stephen Jospeh McCraw v. Her Majesty the Queen* [1991] 3 SCR 72 at 83. For a more extensive commentary on the case, see K.E. Mahoney, (1989) 'Rape fantasies v. Fear of sexual assault', 21 *Ottawa LR* at 207.

41 Ibid. at 85.

42 Ibid.

43 Norma Wickler, (1991) 'Educating judges about Aboriginal justice and gender equality', The Westerm Workshop Series, 1989, 1990, 1991, Department of Justice, Canada.

44 For example, see K. Mahoney, 'International project to promote fairness in judicial processes: Report on the Geneva workshop on judicial treatment of domestic violence', 5 February 1992, Palais des Nations, Geneva, Switzerland.

45 e.g. education of the profession, increasing participation by women.

46 Justice Deirdre O'Connor will chair the committee developing this program.

47 Attitudes of judiciary: Easteal, commenting on prostitution and light sentences, reports 'Thus, a judge in Victoria recently gave a rapist a less severe sentence since the victim was a prostitute whom, the judge felt, would not be as psychologically affected by rape. *This type of attitude and trial experience have to change in order to both encourage more survivors to report and prosecute and to increase the negative sanctioning of rapists'*(citation of Hakopiani case).

48 *Rape: Reform of Law and Procedure, Supplementary Issues,* 1992, Report No. 46 at 6.

49 Citation of Johns case trial and appeal

50 The Senate, 28 May 1993, motion of Senator Vanstone. The Inquiry is to report on or before the first sitting Tuesday in September 1993.

51 'Despite the general currency of feminine discourse, little political educational or juridical attention has been paid to men as a class in respect of domestic violence, rape or sexual harassment. By ignoring the collective responsibility of men and by always focussing on the individual perpetrator, the law privileges maleness and upholds the collective right of men to dominate women' The term 'domestic violence' has been described as oxymoronic. 'The home and hearth connotations of 'domestic' colour and soften our repugnance towards the concept of violence, thereby reifying the popular stereotype epitomised by the police dismissal of a violent assault in the home as 'just another domestic''. Thornton, 'Feminism and the contradiction of law reform', 1991 19 *International Journal of the Sociology of Law* 453.

52 Foreword to R. Graycar and J. Morgan, *The Hidden Gender of the Law*, Federation Press, 1990.

53 Justice Bertha Wilson, 'Will women judges make a difference?'

54 The Honourable Justice David Malcolm CJ, of WA, 'Feminism and the law', address to the Zonta Club, Perth, 28 September 1991.

55 Justice Bertha Wilson 'Will women judges make a difference?' *Osgoode Hall Law Journal*, 28(3), Fall 1990, pp. 507–522.

56 Justice Bertha Wilson, ibid.

57 Section 15.

58 Mason CJ. The UK has no such guarantees, but is bound by the European Convention on Human Rights.

59 Bill of Rights, 14th amendment.

60 New Zealand *Bill of Rights Act 1990*, s. 19.

61 See 'A Bill of Rights for Australia?', Exposure Report by the Senate Standing Committee on Constitutional and Legal Affairs, 1985.

62 M.J. Mossman, 'Essays on law and poverty: Bail and security', Research report, AGPS, Canberra, p. 47: 'In this respect, there appears to be a power in legal method to 'transform' the perspective of women in law; is there, after all, any potential for 'perspective transforming' of legal method by feminism?'

63 N. Naffine, *Law and the Sexes: Explorations in Feminist Jurisprudence*, Allen & Unwin, Sydney, 1990, p. 145.

64 Kirby, 'The judges; A Bill of Rights for Australia?', exposure report by the Senate Standing Committee on Constitutional and Legal Affairs, 1985 para 1.32: 'The appointment of members of the judiciary is though generally unrestricted executive action. Members of the judiciary are, typically, drawn from a narrow unrepresentative band of Australian society.'

65 C. Gilligan, *In a Different Voice*, Harvard University Press, Massachusetts, 1982, puts forward the thesis that women see themselves as essentially connected to others and as members of the community while men see themselves as essentially autonomous and independent of others.

66 Governments should ensure the appointment of women to the judiciary at all levels in accordance with international targets. Extracts from the Report of the Expert Meeting on increased awareness by women of their rights, including legal literacy, Bratislava, 18–22 May 1992.

67 Geoffrey de Q. Walker, *The Rule of Law*, Melbourne University Press, Melbourne, 1988, at 194. Mr Walker is highly critical of the Family Court, for example, because its members include a substantial proportion of former solicitors, academics and women (at 267–268); Chief Justice Gibbs, on the Family Court.

68 Report of the National Committee on Violence recommendation 90.

69 National Strategy on Violence Against Women, 1992, at 30 and 65.

70 Recommendation 31 para. 5.07.

71 *Australian Capital Television Pty Ltd v. Commonwealth* (1992) 177 CLR 106. Hereafter 'Political Ad Ban case'. References to particular judges without accompanying case citation are to the Political Ad Ban case. Also delivered on the same day was *Nationwide News Pty Ltd v. Wills* (1992) 177 CLR 1. In that case the High Court struck down as beyond power a Federal provision empowering the Industrial Relations Commission to punish for contempt. The reasons relied on by the court did not, unlike the decision which is the subject of this essay, rest solely on a finding of an implied constitutional guarantee of free speech: see for example Mason CJ, at 8 and 11, who relied on the test of reasonable proportionality in *Castlemaine Tooheys Ltd v. South Australia* (1990) 169 CLR 436, and Brennan J, at 27, who found that representative democracy included an implication limiting prohibition of criticism of matters significant to Australia's economic and political life.

Since 1992, other cases have considered the right to speech. See, for example, *Theophanous v. Herald & Weekly Times* (1994) 182 CLR 104, which extended the freedom to State law embodied in common law or statute, and *Stephens v. West Australian Newspspers* (1994) 182 CLR 211, which extended it in relation to discussion of State political matters.

72 Report of Senate Select Committee, op. cit., evidence of Mr P. Adams, 13.

73 Ibid.

74 See M. Carter and Beth Wilson, 'Rape: good and bad women and judges', 1992 *Alt LJ* 6.

75 In November 1993, Sally Brown was appointed a Judge in the Family Court of Australia.

76 'Domestic violence is criminal assault', editorial, 5 June 1993, p. 17.

77 Someone newly interested in the area might commence by reading (in alphabetical order) the recent publications by Regina Graycar and Jenny Morgan, *The Hidden Gender of Law*, The Federation Press, 1990; Rosemary Hunter, *Indirect Discrimination and the Workplace*, The Federation Press, 1992; Margaret Thornton's *The Liberal Promise: Anti-Discrimination Legislation in Australia*, Oxford University Press, 1990; and Jocelynne Scutt, *Women and the Law: Commentary and Materials*, The Law Book Company, 1990.

78 Last year I received a total of 235 formal complaints of sex discrimination; in 11 months this year I have already received 329, up 45%. Last year I received 1758 informal complaints of sex and pregnancy discrimination: so far this year I have received 2236, up 27%. Last year I received 131 formal complaints of sexual harassment, this year so far 148, and last year 803 informal complaints and enquiries, this year 1219, up 52%.

79 '... to give effect to certain provisions of the Convention on the Elimination of all forms of Discrimination against Women ... to eliminate, so far as is possible, discrimination against persons on the ground of sex, marital status or pregnancy ... to eliminate, so far as is possible, discrimination involving sexual harassment ... and to promote recognition and acceptance within the community of the principle of the equality of men and women' (Section 3).

80 Since repealed and re-enacted in 1984.

81 In *Hall v. Sheiban* (1988) EOC 92-227, for example, Einfeld J, then President of the Human Rights and Equal Opportunity Commission, said that a conciliator must provide a 'full, fair and detached assessment of the strengths and weaknesses of both sides and of the possible remedies' (77,142).

82 (1986) EOC 92-173.

83 *Nestlé Australia v. The President and Members of the Equal Opportunity Board* (1990) EOC 92-281.

84 (1992) EOC 92-465.

85 *Flynn v. Pearson; Glastonbury Child and Family Services v. Pearson*, Nos 11476 and 11480 of 1992, J.D. Phillips J, 20 April 1993.

86 *State Electricity Commission of Victoria v. Commissioner for Equal Opportunity and Andrew Rabel*, unreported, No. 10218 of 1992, Ormiston J, 5 May 1993.

87 *City of Moe v. Pulis* (1988) EOC 92-243.

88 *Ross & Ors v. University of Melbourne* (1990) EOC 92-290.

89 (1992) EOC 92-450.

90 This was reported on the same day as the Human Rights and Equal Opportunity Commission rejected Dr Proudfoot's complaint of sex discrimination in the delivery of women's health services because of the differently-worded exception in the Commonwealth *Sex Discrimination Act 1984* (see *Proudfoot & Ors v. Australian Capital Territory Board of Health & Ors* (1992) EOC 92-417).

91 *Department of Health v. Arumugam* [1988] VR 318.

92 *C.P.S. Management Pty Ltd v. Equal Opportunity Board & Ors* (1991) EOC 92-332 at 78,292-78,293.

93 See note 14 above.

94 See Margaret Thornton, *The Liberal Promise: Anti-Discrimination Legislation in Australia*, Oxford, 1990, especially at 198–216.

95 Unreported No. 8224 of 1992, Ormiston J, 12 May 1993.

96 In *Keefe v. McInnes* (1991) EOC 92-331, the complainant, a paraplegic racing car driver, complained that he had been discriminated against by the Confederation of Motor Sports in refusing him a competitor's licence. He won before the Board. The respondent appealed. The Board was found to have erred in law. McInnes paid his own and the other side's costs. The matter was sent back for determination by the Board according to law. He lost. He had to sell his home.

97 Title of Chapter VI in Margaret Thornton op. cit.

98 See Chapter VI, op. cit., and especially 177–178.

99 See Delgado, Dunn, Brown, Lee and Hubbert, 'Fairness and formality: Minimizing the risk of prejudice in alternative dispute resolution', 1985 *Wis L Rev* 1359, cited by Patricia J Williams in 'Alchemical notes: Reconstructing ideals from deconstructed rights', [1987] 22 *Harvard Civil Rights–Civil Liberties Law Review* 401,407.

100 *Sinnapan & Anor v. State of Victoria* (1994) EOC 92-611.

101 In *The Law Institute Journal* (1992) at 907.

102 Ibid. at 908.

103 Ibid. at 908.

104 Oxford University Press, 1990, Chapter VI.

105 For further discussion of this point see Rosemary Hunter, *Indirect Discrimination in the Workplace*, Federation Press, 1992, at 227–230.

106 [1989] ALR 88.

107 See *Pulis and Banfield v. Moe City Council* (1986) EOC 92-170; *Ross v. University of Melbourne* (1990) EOC 92-290; *Proudfoot v. ACT Board of Health* (1992) EOC 92-417. Recent decisions of the Victorian Anti-Discrimination Tribunal are more promising in this respect. See, for example, *Stevens v. Fernwood Fitness Centres Pty Ltd* (1996) EOC 92-782.

108 For example, Australian Federation of Business and Professional Women submissions to the 1990, 1991 and subsequent National Wage Cases.

109 For example, the Comparable Worth test case (1986) IR 108.

110 *Re Australian Journalists Association*; in the matter of an appeal (1988) EOC 92-224; *Re Australian Journalists Association*; application for exemption (1988) EOC 92-236; *Municipal Officers Association of Australia*; approval of submission of amalgamation to ballow (1991) EOC 92-344.

111 For example, *Abi Thompson v. Catholic College, Wodonga* (1989) 4 VIR 227.

112 *Sex Discrimination Act* (Cwlth) s. 50A; *Industrial Relations Act* (Cwlth) ss. 111A (discriminatory awards), 150A (review of awards), 170MD (approval of certified agreements), 170ND (approval of enterprise flexibility agreements), 170BA-BI (equal remuneration for work of equal value), 170DF (unfair dismissal), 93, 93A (performance of functions). See now the *Workplace Relations Act 1996* (Cwlth) ss. 111A, 113 (discriminatory awards), Schedule 4, cl. 49 (review of awards), s. 170LU, (approval of certified agreements), s. 170VG (registration of Australian Workplace Agreements), s. 170BC (equal remuneration for work of equal value), ss. 88B, 93 (performance of functions). A further issue has arisen in relation to perpetrators of sexual harassment, who in some cases have had claims of unfair dismissal upheld, and reinstatement awarded, by industrial tribunals. See, for example, *Andrew v. Linfox Transport (Aust.) Pty Ltd* (1996) EOC 92-807.

113 'Legislation against sex discrimination: Questions from a feminist perspective', *Journal of Law and Society* 14 (1987) 411 at 418.

114 Justice Kirby has now been appointed to the High Court.

115 The Victorian *Equal Opportunity Act* has been repealed and replaced by the *Equal Opportunity Act 1995*. The 1995 Act does have an objectives section (s. 3), and it also includes some specification of factors to be considered in determining whether a respondent's actions are reasonable (s. 9(2)). However, the factors specified are weighted in favour of respondents.

116 Section 22 (2) (b).

117 The first of such programs was implemented in British Columbia in 1989, dealing with topics of sexual assault, sentencing, the treatment of natives and young offenders. The techniques included the re-enactment of a sexual trial with the actual judge and counsel assisted by actors, a television documentary and the exposure of the judges to discussions with the victims of sexual assaults, native elders and other members and representatives of native groups. The re-enactment of the sexual assault trial climaxed with the victim running hysterically from the room screaming 'None of you will ever understand'. While a number of judges did not like the experience to which they were exposed in the program, the general opinion was that it should be repeated. The program was repeated in 1990 in Alberta, with the focus on abuse in relationships involving children, the elderly and mothers, as well as native issues. As of 1990 twenty two States in the United States of America were examining gender bias problems. By 1992 the number had increased to thirty two. Judicial education programs have been instituted in many of these States.

118 Memorial Lecture at Osgoode Hall Law School early in 1990. Copies were distributed to all members of the Society for the Reform of Criminal Law.

119 46 *NYURev* 675.

120 In an adress to the Zonta International District 23 Conference in Perth in September 1991, I stated my views publicaly for the first time and said that I would be keen to conduct a pilot program in the Supreme Court of Western Australia.

121 In the Supreme Court on 14 August 92. The seminar was attended by judges, masters and registrars of the Supreme Court, judges of the District Court and the Family Court, the President and Commissioners of the Industrial Relations Commission, magistrates, the Equal Opportunity Commissioner, the Director of the Office of Women's Interests, the President of the Women's Advisory Council, a large number of lawyers of both sexes, including representatives of the Womens Lawyers' Association, and many women from the various groups which I have mentioned.

122 *Feminism Unmodified: Discourses on Life and Law*, London, Harvard University Press, 1987.

123 C. MacKinnon, 'Feminism, Marxism, method and the state: Towards feminist jurisprudence', *Signs*, 1982, Vol. 7, No. 3, 515–544.

[124] Comments attributed to Justice Bollen, the *Age*, 13 May 1993.

[125] Comments attributed to Justice O'Bryan, the *Age,* 13 May 1993.

[126] The *Herald-Sun,* 22 May 1993.

[127] Justice Rosemary Balmford has since been appointed to the Bench of the Supreme Court of Victoria.

[128] The Family Court now (1997) has 12 women judges, the last appointee being Justice Christine Dawe in Adelaide. Two of the last women appointees have come from the Bar, two were previously magistrates and one was formerly a Children's Court judge.

[129] P. Ambikapathy, 'Representation of victims of crime', *Law Institute Journal of Victoria,* 1987.

[130] *Criminal Injuries Compensation Act 1972.*

[131] *Criminal Injuries Compensation (Amendment) Act 1980.*

[132] *Criminal Injuries Compensation (Amendment) Act 1980.*

[133] J. Willis, in Dr J. Scutt (ed.), *Violence in the Home*, Australian Institute of Criminology, Canberra, 1980.

[134] *Criminal Injuries Compensation Act 1983.*

[135] 'Criminal assault in the home', Department of Premier and Cabinet, Victoria, 1985.

[136] *Criminal Injuries Compensation (Amendment) Act 1988.*

[137] (a) D.E. Stewart, 'Violence in the family', Discussion Paper No. 7, Institute of Family Studies, Melbourne, 1982.

(b) R. Baker, 'Domestic violence: Police powers', Domestic Violence Conference, 27–28 July, 1982, Human Resources Centre, La Trobe University, Victoria.

(c) P. Grabosky, 'How violent is Australia?', *Australian Society*, Vol. 2, No. 6, 1983, 38–41.

(d) J.A. Scutt (ed.), 'Violence in the family: A collection of conference papers', Australian Institute of Criminology, Canberra, 1980.

(e) Scutt J.A., 'Domestic violence: The police response', in C. O'Donnel, and J. Craney, (eds), *Family Violence in Australia*, Longman Cheshire, Melbourne, 1982.

[138] Saulwick Poll, the *Age*, 4 June 1993.

[139] This was the case before the introduction of the *Workplace Relations Act* (Cwlth) in 1996 which significantly reduced the award making and dispute settling powers of the AIRC and made much greater provision for the setting of wages and conditions by agreement between the parties in the employment relationship. This has separate disadvantages for women which are not the subject of this paper.

[140] After the introduction of amendments to the former *Industrial Relations Act* (Cwlth) in 1994, many such applications were determined by the Industrial Relations Court of Australia and the AIRC and, after the introduction of the *Workplace Relations Act* (Cwlth) in 1994, mainly by the AIRC with a few being determined by the Federal Court.

[141] *Australian Saddlery, Leather, Sail, Canvas, Tanning, Leather-dressing and Allied Workers Trades Employees Federation v. Carter Patterson and Company & Ors* (1925) CAR 892 at 895.

[142] *Federated Liquor and Allied Trades Employees' Union of Australia v. W Ashton & Ors* (1926) 24 CAR 309 at 313.

[143] *In the Matter of an Application by Ministry of Munitions* 47 CAR Appendix 182 at 187.

[144] *Federated Clothing Trades v. J.A. Archer* (1919) 13 CAR 647 at 707.

[145] *Federated Liquor and Allied Trades Employees' Union of Australia v. W Ashton & Ors* (1926) 24 CAR 309 at 313.

[146] Cain, 'Feminist jurisprudence: Grounding the theories' (1989) 4 *Berkeley Women's LJ* 191.

[147] Littleton, 'Feminist jurisprudence: The difference method makes' (1989) 41 *Stanford Law Review* 751.

[148] L.H. Schafran, 'Gender bias in the courts: Time is not the cure' (1989) 22 *Creighton LR* 413, 415–6; L.H. Schafran, 'Eve, Mary, Superwoman: How stereotypes about women influence judges', *The Judges' Journal,* Winter 1985, reprinted as Appendix A in Schafran and Wikler, 'Operating a task force on gender bias in the courts: A manual for action', Women Judges Fund For Justice. Literature reflects this disability as well '... [W]omen are rarely believed when they testify as victims' and '... no account is available to us [in traditional stories] of a woman who is both good and in control of her story'. Heilbrun, 'The Thomas confirmation hearings, or how being a humanist prepares you for right wing politics', in 'Sexual harassment: Myths, literature and law' (1992) 65 *Southern Cal LR* 1279, 1569.

[149] In this paper, I am using bias in the sense developed by the various North American Supreme Court Task Forces which have enquired into the existence of gender bias in the legal system and the judiciary. Gender bias occurs when decisions are made or actions are taken based on preconceived or stereotypical beliefs about the 'true' nature, roles or capacities of men and women ('Final report of the Massachusetts Gender Bias Study: Gender bias in courthouse interactions' (1989) 74 *Mass LR* 50, 51; New Jersey Supreme Court Task Force on Women in the Courts, Report of the First Year, June 1984, 1). These preconceptions result from lack of knowledge (L.H. Schafran, *Promoting Gender Fairness Through Judicial Education: A Guide to the Issues and Resources,* Women Judges' Fund For Justice, 1989, 1) and often seem natural so that the element of bias is not readily understood or identified (New Jersey Report 1).

Gender bias does not require intent (*Promoting Gender Fairness* 1). As has been said in another context: small boys throw stones at frogs in jest, but the frogs die in earnest. Any distinction, whether intentional or not, which has the systematic effect of imposing burdens, obligations or disadvantages on one group over another reflects bias (Law Society of British Columbia, 'Gender equality in the justice system: A report of the Law Society of British Columbia Gender Bias Committee' C 1-2).

The impact of gender bias often occurs as a consequence of (apparently) less serious incidents, committed unknowingly, which, when taken on an individual basis, seem to have a minimal impact or to be trivial. In developing remedies, it is important to recognise that the cumulative effect of these apparently minor or isolated events is considerable, because impact occurs beyond the immediate event and becomes part of a pattern which injures women and the credibility of the system itself.

[150] 'Vermont Task Force report on gender bias in legal system' (1990) 15 *Vt L Rev* 395, 400

[151] 'New York Task Force on Women in the Courts', at 183, citing Paludi & Strayer, 'What's in an author's name? Differential evaluations of performance as a function of author's name' (1985) 12 *Sex Roles* 353.

[152] Penelope Bryan, 'Killing us softly: Divorce mediation and the politics of power' (1992) 40 *Buffalo LR* 441, 474 fn 133.

[153] Schafran, L.H., 'The less credible sex', *The Judges' Journal*, Winter 1985.

[154] Ross, 'Proving sexual harassment: The hurdles' (1992) 65 *Southern California LR* 1451, 1455, citing Conley, O'Barr and Lind, 'The power of language: Presentational styles in the courtroom' (1978) *Duke LJ* 375, 1380–81, 1386; Morrill and Facciola, 'The power of language in adjudication and mediation'.

[155] Morrill and Facciola, above, 196; Epstein, *Deceptive Distinctions: Sex, Gender and the Social Order,* Yale University Press, New Haven, London, 1988, Ch. 10.

[156] Estrich, *Real Rape,* Harvard University Press, Cambridge, Mass., 1987, 218.

[157] Veach, 'Linguistics and women attorneys in the courtroom', National Conference on Women and the Law, San Francisco, 1980.

[158] Kinport, 'Evidence engendered', (1991) *U of Illinois LR* 413, 446.

[159] Loftus, *Eyewitness testimony*, Harvard University Press, Cambridge Mass., 1979, 100–101.

160 Heilman and Stopeck, 'Attractiveness and corporate success: Different causal attributions for males and females' (1985) 70 *J of App Psychology* 379, cited in fn 289; New York Task Force on Women in the Courts, Final Report (1986).

161 New York Task Force on Women in the Courts, Final Report, quoting L.H. Schafran, 'Eve, Mary, Superwoman: How stereotypes about women influence judges' (1985) 24 *Judges J* 12, 16.

162 Massachusetts Report 57–58.

163 Massachusetts Report 53.

164 Morrill and Facciola, above, 204.

165 For a summary of reforms in this area see: Scutt, *Women and the Law: Commentary and Materials,* The Law Book Company, Sydney, 1990; Graycar and Morgan, *The Hidden Gender of Law*, Federation Press, Annandale, NSW, Australia, 1990; Law Society of British Columbia Gender Bias Committee, *Gender Equality in the Justice System,* Volume Two, Law Society of British Columbia, 1992; *R. v. Seaboyer* (1991) 83 DLR 193, 221, (dissent) (Canada); Estrich, *Real Rape: How the Legal System Victimises Women Who Say No*, Harvard University Press, Cambridge Massachusetts, USA, 1987; Temkin, *Rape and the Legal Processs*, Sweet and Maxwell, London, 1987.

166 *R. v. Seaboyer* (1991) 83 DLR 193, 221, (dissent) pointing to *R v. Forsythe* (1980) 53 CCC(3d) 225; Birch, 'Corroboration in criminal trials: A review of the proposals of the Law Commission' (1990) *Crim LR* 667 fn 81; Adler, 'Rape—The intention of parliament and the practice of the courts' (1982) 45 *Modern Law Review* 664, 672; Report of the New York Task Force on Women in the Courts (1986), 67–70, 75–6; Estrich, 'Palm Beach stories' (1992) 11 *Law and Philosophy* 5, fn 31; SA Parl. Debates, 17 October, 1984 at 1184.

167 *Seaboyer*, 248 (dissent); SA Parl. Debates, 17 October 1984 at 1184. Indeed, the Canadian legislature has now embarked on a third try, Bill C-49, passed by the House of Commons, June 15, 1992.

168 Case stated by the Director of Public Prosecutors (no. 1 of 1993) (1993); *B. v. R.* (1992) 110 ALR 432; Mack, 'Continuing barriers to women's credibility: A feminist perspective on the proof process' (1993) 4 *Crim L Forum* 327; 'Gender bias and the judiciary', report by the Senate Standing Committee on Legal and Constitutional Affairs, May 1994, 51–55.

169 *Longman* (1989) 168 CLR 79; *B. v. R.* above; Westerman (1991) 55 ACR 353; *M. v. R.* (1994) 181 CLR 487.

170 In criticizing the courts for these decisions, I am not insisting that all women always tell all the truth in claims of sexual assault. What I am pointing out is that the law has, historically, explicitly made the contrary assumption: that women are inherently untruthful and more likely to lie about sexual matters than all other witnesses. (For example, why is there no warning that victims of theft are likely to lie about the number and value of items stolen, because of a motive to gain additional insurance compensation?) What is being sought is a fair balance which gives women a real opportunity to be heard, without unwarranted and unjustified burdens on their credibility.

171 Minow, 'Consider the consequences' (1986) 84 Mich LR 900, 907.

172 Henry Finlay & Rebecca Bailey-Harris, *Family Law in Australia* (4th edn), Butterworths, Sydney, 1989, pp. 62, 131

173 Lenore Weitzman, *The Divorce Revolution: The Unexpected Social and Economic Consequences for Women and Children in America*, New York, The Free Press, 1985. Living standards improve for two thirds of men in Australia after divorce; for two thirds of women, living standards decline. Peter McDonald (ed.), *Settling Up: Property and Income Distribution on Divorce in Australia,* Australian Institute of Family Studies, Prentice Hall of Australia, 1986, at 100, 103–104, 114 (hereafter, *Settling Up*).

[174] Tina Grillo, 'The mediation alternative: Process dangers for women' (1991) 100 *Yale Law Journal* 1545–610; Eve Hill, 'Alternative dispute resolution in a feminist voice' (1990) 5 *Ohio State Journal on Dispute Resolution* 337; Janet Rifkin, 'Mediation from a feminist perspective' (1984) 2 *Law & Inequality* 21.

[175] *Courts (Mediation and Arbitration) Act 1991* (Cwlth). The literature on mediation generally, and family mediation specifically, has expanded enormously since this paper was given. See, for example, Boulle, *Mediation: Principles, Process, Practice,* Butterworths, 1996.

[176] Bryan, above.

[177] Astor and Chinkin, *Dispute Resolution in Australia*, Butterworths, Sydney, 1992, at 107–8; Gay Clark and Lyla Davies, 'Mediation: When it is not an appropriate process' (1992) 3 *ADR* J70; Davis and Salem, 'Dealing with power imbalances in the mediation of interpersonal disputes' (1984) 6 *Mediation Quarterly* 17.

[178] Lenore Weitzman, 'Gender differences in custody bargaining in the United States', in Lenore Weitzman and Mavis Maclean (eds), *Economic Consequences of Divorce: The International Perspective*, Clarendon Press, Oxford, 1992, 402–403; Penelope Bryan, 'Killing us softly: Divorce mediation and the politics of reflections on promoting equal empowerment and entitlements for women' (1985) 8 *J of Divorce* 49–52. In Australia in 1984, at the end of a marriage, 59% of women had incomes of less than $10 000 per year; 78% of men had incomes over $17 000 (*Settling Up,* 136).

[179] Milton C. Regan, 'Divorce reform and the legacy of gender', a review of 'The illusion of equality: The rhetoric and reality of divorce reform' (1992) 90 *Mich LR* 1453–1467; Bryan, above, 449–50.

[180] Pearson and Thoenness, 'Divorce mediation: An American picture', in Robert Dingwall and John Eekelaar (eds), *Divorce Mediation and the Legal Process,* Clarendon Press, Oxford, 1988, at 79.

[181] Gribben, 'Mediation of family disputes' (1992) 5-6 *Aus J of Family Law* 126, 133; Schaffer, 'Divorce mediation: A feminist perspective' (1988) *U Tor Fac LR* 162, 182–3; Astor and Chinkin, above, 26, 57–60; Bagshaw, 'Gender issues in family mediation', FIRM National Conference, June 1990 5–8; Family Court Rules of Court Order 25a, Rule 5(c).

[182] Bagshaw; Weitzman (1992) 401–2; Bryan 474–7; Ricci, 'Mediator's notebook: Reflections on promoting equal empowerment and entitlements for women' (1985) 8 *Journal of Divorce* 49.

[183] Astor and Chinkin 110

[184] Delgado, Dunn, Brown, Lee, and Hubbert, 'Fairness and formality: Minimizing the risk of prejudice in alternative dispute resolution' [1985] *Wisconsin LR* 1359; Astor and Chinkin, 102–105.

[185] Grillo 1587 et seq.; Shaffer 184–5; Bagshaw 3.

[186] Grillo 1574–5.

[187] Rose, 'Women and property: Gaining and losing ground' (1992) 78 *Virginia LR* 421; Grillo, 1601-4; Bagshaw 5.

[188] Bryan 460–463.

[189] Grillo.

[190] Astor and Chinkin 111; Ricci 52.1570-1

[191] Weitzman 402; Astor and Chinkin 109.

[192] Bryan 448.

[193] 'Vermont Task Force Report on gender bias in the legal system' (1990) 15 *Vt L Rev* 395, 400.

[194] Winkler, 'Indentifying and correcting gender bias', and Schafran, 'The success of the American program', in Mahoney and Martin (eds) *Equality and Judicial Neutrality*, Carswell, Toronto, 1987.